WILD DISTORTION

TINA SAXON

ISBN Digital: 978-1-7353272-0-4
ISBN Print: 978-1-7353272-1-1

Cover design by: Hang Le
Photographer: Wander Aguiar
Models: Wayne Skivington & Ivenize
Editing and Proofreading by:
My Brother's Editor

PROLOGUE

RYKER

"You had ONE job."

Coach throws the magazine down on his beat-up wooden desk. One that has traveled with him throughout his career. I try to hide my disdain for the stupid comment. My smiling face flashes back at me from the cover with the words *Suspended for Three Games* stamped across it.

"And that wasn't it!" His voice booms in the compact room as he stabs his finger on my picture.

"That's bullshit," I snap, pointing at the magazine. "I passed my drug test."

Hands on his desk, his mouth twists with anger as he leans forward. "Ryker, you were arrested because you had marijuana on you." I open my mouth to argue that they set us up, but he growls for me to shut it. "In a fucking state where it's illegal. And we both know; it wasn't yours to begin with."

True. We both know. But I'm not admitting shit. I've taken it this far, I'm not backing down now. At least it was a state that doesn't sentence first-time users to jail time and my attorney got it reduced to a misdemeanor.

"I can't believe you're risking your career for that tool."

I glance over at Bree, my PR rep, who has been silent the whole time. The tool that Coach is referring to is also a client of Bree's. And a teammate.

She shrugs in agreement. He has potential. He just needs someone to guide him in the right direction.

That is my job. I'm the leader of this team and I made a snap decision in the moment to help him out. Do I regret it? Hell yeah, in hindsight. I never imagined they would suspend me for three games.

I had a terrible feeling when we left the bar that night. A bar in a town where we had just decimated their team. Emotions were running high and a few of our guys had just gotten into a fight with some local guys. I needed to get them out of there before the cops came.

I'm the dad of the group. The sensible one.

And now... the suspended one.

I'd bet a million dollars one of those guys called their local cop buddies because when they pulled us over, they weren't doing a normal traffic stop. They already suspected we had drugs on us. Probably because Jarod had just bought some.

I didn't know any of that until it was too late. I had already offered to hide it in my pocket because he was freaking out, thinking we were getting stopped for speeding.

The only thing that went through my head when getting cuffed was how disappointed my mom would be. And Coach's berating is a walk in the park compared to the talking-to I received from Mom. When she started crying, might as well have stabbed stakes in my heart. It felt the same.

I glance over at Bree. "Anything you'd like to add?" She's not only here to witness Coach rip me a new asshole. There's a reason.

"We both agree it's best to send you away for a few weeks."

I sit up in my chair, straightening my spine, wondering where they want to send me. "What the hell does that mean?"

"We need you to stay out of the public eye while this dies down. You're on every entertainment avenue there is. You are the hot topic. *Good boy turns bad.*" She air quotes the last part. I roll my eyes.

"Okay, so I'll rent a cabin for a couple weeks and disappear."

She shakes her head. "They'll find you, Ryker. These people are vultures. We need you out of the country."

"That's extreme."

"Maybe. But it's a done deal. You're going to Tahiti for fifteen days. Leaving tomorrow at six a.m."

"You're seriously banishing me to a small island in the Pacific? Holy shit." I jerk my head to Coach, waiting for him to agree with me that this is asinine. Way overboard.

"Think of it as a reset button. You can come back and finish the season strong." Not exactly what I expected him to say.

"So, I don't have any say in this?"

They both shake their heads and I sigh in resignation. I guess it could be worse. They could've shipped me to Alaska. Pushing up to my feet, I put my ball cap back on. I was trying to be respectful while getting my ass handed to me.

"Guess I'll see you guys in a few weeks."

"Ryker." I stop with my hand gripping the doorknob and look over my shoulder at Coach. "Three rules. Train. Stay focused. And for fuck's sake, no women."

I give a sharp nod.

Thank god he didn't say no whiskey.

CHAPTER ONE

ASPEN

"Girls just wanna have fun," I sing out loud into the handle of my duster, terribly off tune to the eighties hit from Cyndi Lauper. Perks of the job. No one is around to hear me butcher songs. Swinging my hips to the beat, I round the corner to start on the bedroom.

Oh my!

Tall, tan, and toned is passed out cold on the bed. Did I mention, naked? *Very naked.* My gaze travels from his closed eyes down his muscular tanned stomach, ripple after ripple, to his... *Wow!* I mean, my island experience is limited, but I didn't know they came in *that* size. It rests, long and hard, against his thigh. My cheeks heat at the sight and a tingle buzzes in my lower belly.

I whip around, yanking the earbuds out of my ears and fan myself as the wall holds me up. My gaze darts around the room. Empty whiskey bottles top the coffee table. Clothes thrown haphazardly on the couch. The sliding glass doors are wide open and salty sea air fills the room, but that's normal. People that come to the island like the humid air.

"No. I'll lose my job," I whisper to my subconscious telling me to take another peek. "That, or the ancestral spirits are planning my punishment already." I shake my head, fighting with myself.

What if he's dead?

He's obviously had a lot to drink and I have a responsibility to make sure he's all right. Put the customer first. *Always.* My singing didn't wake him up, he might very well need my help.

Pushing off the wall, I peek my head through the door and zone in to his torso. See, I'm making sure he's alive. In the corner of my eye, his dick pulses, and I jerk my head up to see his face and our eyes meet.

"Whiskey, there's enough room for you to join me."

I gasp at the rough, sexy voice, not hearing a word he said, rather focusing on the fact that he was talking.

To me.

This is not good. Men that come here are usually arrogant assholes, and I was just caught watching one sleep naked. He could ruin me and I just handed him the power to do it.

"Orana." The word flies out of my mouth, over my shoulder, as I rush toward the door. The word we're trained to say whenever we interact with a guest. For a quick beat, I squeeze my eyes shut. Why did I just say *hello?*

Dashing out of the last bungalow, I speed walk, pushing my cart down the walkway, until I spot Mama Doe's cart outside bungalow four.

Flustered and irritated with myself, I dash into the hut. Her singsong voice carries through the place from the back bedroom. I stand in the living room, shake out my hands while I gather my thoughts.

"Aspen, girl, what are you doing? You should be working." I jump at the strong Tahitian voice coming from behind me. Spinning on my heel, I decide lying would be the best.

"I'm not feeling so well."

"Girl, you look flushed." She places the back of her hand

against my forehead, her eyes filling with concern. "You're sweating." She would be too if she saw what I did and then got caught. "You need to go to Dr. Blaise. Maybe you caught the same sickness as the others." The person's shift I'm covering is out sick.

I shake my head. That won't be necessary. "It's not that serious." Dr. Blaise creeps me out. He's an old man that stares at me like I'm a buffet, waiting to be devoured. I'd like to tell him I'm rotten meat so he'll stop. That is the last place I want to go. "Actually, I must have needed a break. I'm already better."

She eyes me, crossing her arms over her chest. This was a stupid idea. One thing about Mama Doe, she can smell a lie. That's one of the prime reasons she's referred to as Mama Doe. She sees all and hears all.

"What has you rattled, girl?"

A man, built like a god.

"Your face is turning red." Her howling laugh ripples out. "Did you walk in on something?"

It happens. I've learned while working at a hotel, there are some guests who like being caught in the act. Some things you can't ever unsee. Except, we're supposed to exit with a hushed sorry and act like nothing ever happened.

Not take a second peek.

Mama Doe goes back to her cart, grabs the window cleaner, all while chuckling and shaking her head. "Girl, you've been here long enough to see everything. Go back to work."

I drop my chin and nod. Forget what happened and treat this like any other incident. All I need to do is make a note on the room order that the guest was busy and tonight's staff will return to his room later. Crisis averted. Except, hopefully, he won't remember waking to the peeping cleaning lady.

CHAPTER TWO

ASPEN

"Manu, please help." Dante gets down on one knee on the beach, his smile reaching his brown eyes. I push his tattooed shoulder, and he falls back into a roll, hopping up to a standing position, arms out wide. A few hotel guests clap in the distance as if we're putting on a show. It doesn't help that he takes a bow.

"Would you stop? And stop calling me that. We're not kids anymore. I have a name."

"If I call you by your actual name, will you help? Ari's sick and I can't take out ten people by myself." *Is everyone sick on this island?* He follows me as I make my morning delivery to one of the many hotels on my list.

I let out an exasperated sigh, knowing he won't give up. "What time?" If I didn't need money, it'd be easier to say no.

THE BOAT GLIDES to the dock at the upscale resort. Dante hops out to grab the list of passengers from the excursion desk and round them up. Rather than help him, I use the time to mentally prepare for the foreigners by pulling out masks and snorkel gear, throwing them in a pile to hand out. Most people are nice, but there's those that ask too many questions, or end up getting seasick, or worse, hit on me.

Why did I agree to help Dante? Money. Just remember it's about the money.

As I bend over, the breeze whips my wild hair, right into my mouth. "Merde," I sputter as I fish out a lone strand of hair on my tongue.

"Is that Tahitian?" A deep voice comes from behind me.

Glancing over my shoulder, my heart stops beating as I stare into the eyes of the naked man from yesterday. Except he's not naked now. He's wearing turquoise board shorts and a white t-shirt that fits him like a glove, especially around his biceps.

I jerk around, redistributing the gear from one spot to another to make it seem like I still had a job to do. Without turning, I reply, "French."

As he talks to Dante, I grip the edge of the boat and take a few calming breaths.

This is not good. Not good at all.

The boat drifts from the dock. I push up on my feet and spin in place, swallowing the panic lodged in my throat before speaking. "Where is everyone else?" Our only guest stretches out on the rear bench of the empty boat, his long muscular legs out in front of him and arms across the back. Dante steps to the boat controls, starts the engine, ignoring the fact I'm about to implode.

"I didn't want to be with a bunch of people," the guy answers as a matter-of-fact, completely uninterested in us as he stares out to the water. Can he do that? Dante is a charter boat for excursions, not a private rental.

I glance at Dante and he shrugs. "Simple day for us."

No. No, it's not.

I slink down the seat in front of the captain's chair, wrapping my hair up in a bun, saltwater misting me as we glide over waves. My mind replays yesterday morning and I try to erase the thoughts from my brain. Who am I kidding? It's been on repeat since I ran out of there, and that was before he was a mere three feet from me. Now, I'm stuck with him on a boat for five hours.

"Manu."

I shift and glare at Dante as the boat slows. At what age will he stop calling me by my childhood nickname?

He tilts his head to the guy. "Offer him some water."

"Why don't you?" The words fall out of my mouth and Dante's eyes widen in surprise. I even surprised myself. This goes against everything they taught us. Mama Doe would be disappointed.

I blow out an irritated breath and grab water from the ice chest. "Would you like some water?" I hold it out and he angles his face to me. I can't see his eyes from behind his sunglasses, but I can sense them dragging up my body, leaving a tingling sensation in their wake.

I'm used to men staring at my body. A long time ago, I learned that foreigners see the body as a sexual tool, one that got me a lot of things. Except the one thing I wanted most; a way to escape the island. Tools are meant to be used when needed. Men didn't need me once they left. I was part of the experience. But not anymore. That's the old me.

"Thanks," he says, taking the bottle from me. I ignore the spark inside my belly when his warm fingers touch mine.

Don't go down that path again, Aspen. He's off-limits.

I swore men like him off years ago.

Dante gives me a quizzical look when I wrap a pareo around me. The colorful cloth hides my bikini-clad body, which is strange since we'll be in the water shortly. And I'm not shy. I shrug a shoulder. "The wind is chilly today."

"Eaha te tumu?" he asks, lowering his sunglasses on his nose, dipping his head. Dante has been my best friend since we were little. And we've lived together in the past. Sometimes I hate that he can read me like a book. Like right now. Covering my body usually means I feel guilty for something.

"Nothing is wrong," I answer quietly. Even though I grew up here and speak fluent Tahitian, my father forbids it. He allows only French or English. But the French only comes out when I'm excited or mad. Dante's eyes narrow, not believing it for a second. "Fine. I used salt instead of sugar in one batch of cookies last night," I fib. "You know I hate when they come out bad."

His laugh carries above the wind, causing the man to turn his attention to us. "Manu, please tell me you gave them out." I gasp that he finds my lie amusing. The guys would love for me to give foreigners messed-up cookies. That'd give them a story to tell for decades.

"Of course not. But what if I had? That could've ruined my business." I'm getting worked up over something I know would never happen.

I send him a sour expression and whip around, stretching my legs on the white padded bench, not wanting to hear any more about my make-believe incident.

The point to anchor approaches, and my nerves buzz again. *He won't remember.* He had just woken up and by the amount of empty liquor bottles, had a hell of a hangover. And saw me for no longer than a minute.

We pull up to a couple other charter boats anchored and Dante yells back and forth in Tahitian about where they've spotted sea animals. I grab a pair of masks and snorkel gear.

"Be careful where you step, the coral is rough," I say to the man. He stands and takes off his shirt. *Don't react.* He eyes me for a moment. *Don't react.* Rich men with abs like when women gawk. He assumes he's the first attractive guy to come around. He's not. I've seen it all. Well... maybe not as *big* as him, but I recognize his type. I just wish I hadn't given in to temptation.

I don't linger for him to take the gear. Rather, I drop it on the seat and get ready myself. My pareo slides off me and I step up to the side of the boat to jump in.

"Manu," the man calls and I twist my body, shocked he called me that. "Is that your name?"

Dante burst out laughing, and I scowl at him before pasting on a smile for the stranger. "No. You can call me A."

"A? Like A, B, C?"

Dante doubles over and if I could kick him, I would. "Yes. Like A, B, C. Without the B and C."

"Nice to meet you A. I'm Ryker. Would you mind putting sunscreen on my back? I can't reach and I'd rather not burn."

I reluctantly nod and drop my mask, taking the two steps down into the boat. He places the spray into my stretched out hand. "Thank you, A." I can't help but laugh with him about how ridiculous it sounds. Couldn't I have thought of an actual name rather than a letter?

I twirl my finger in the air, motioning for him to turn. At least, it's spray. It's bad enough I have to look at his broad, powerful shoulders. How his back narrows down to his waist and his board shorts hit right above his butt. I shake myself out of my fixed stare at his heavily sprayed back. "Done," I say.

"You were very thorough," he jests with a knowing grin.

Despite the heat on my cheeks, I shrug. "Better than getting burned out here. You're on your stomach the whole time when snorkeling."

Without waiting for him or Dante, I dive into the warm water, my second home engulfs me. I'm in the ocean almost as much as on land. My spirit is free when I'm swimming with sea life.

When I surface, the sound of excited voices means only one thing. There's something below us. Diving to check it out, a giant manta ray glides a couple feet beneath me. This one is a female.

She flies through the ocean, but not without boats chasing her so their passengers can get a better look.

Swimming to the top, I notice our passenger watching me just below the surface. We both come up for air and he smiles. His smile is crooked, in a sexy flawed way, yet his teeth are perfectly straight and white. Water cascades over his face as he takes his mask off and runs his hand through his sandy-colored hair, sticking it up on its ends.

"Was that a manta ray?"

I nod as I wonder how a man could be so gorgeous. "She was beautiful," I say, slipping off my mask and then tilting back to get the hair out of my face. His eyes transfix on me.

"Have we met before?"

Panic clogs my throat. "Um... do you not remember, I'm A."

"No, I remember." He lets out a raspy chuckle. "It's your eyes. They seem familiar."

Where are my sunglasses when I need them? The curse of having the rarest colored eyes. Everyone remembers them. Even the man who caught me staring at his naked body.

I hum and try to play it off. "I'm assuming you haven't been here long and considering I've been on these islands since I was one, I'm certain we've never met."

His eyes widen. "You're from here?"

"I am." *Hopefully not forever.*

He ponders on that for a beat. "You speak perfect English. I mean, you have an accent, but..." His voice trails off.

"That's because my father—"

"Is cuckoo," Dante interrupts me, swimming up to us, he swirls his finger close to his temple. I splash him.

"I've told you, he's not crazy. Just a little eccentric." Dante's never been a fan. My father is a private man and since he home-schooled me and is very strict, many people on the island didn't take a liking to him. I've always been the link between the two worlds. "My father is American. And he was very particular that I speak proper English and French." He continues to stare at me like he's trying to figure me out. I'm not a puzzle. If I was, it'd have very few pieces. What you see is what you get. "I'm sure you didn't come here to learn about the island girl." I spread my arms out. "There are so many more interesting things to learn about here."

He opens his mouth to say something but then snaps it shut. Rather, he follows my lead, putting his mask on. The three of us swim around, Dante and I point out sea creatures to the guy. This is our normal routine, but with a group of tourists. It's weird having one person.

As the day unfolds, I thought the more I was around him, I'd see past the gorgeous body to the narcissist man who thinks he's a god, which usually diffuses any attraction I'm having. Don't get me wrong, the man has an ego the size of this island, but he seems like a genuinely likable man. And his quick glances are getting harder to ignore. To his credit, he hasn't made an advance. Most men that want something would have accidentally brushed up against my breasts, or made some remark about how beautiful I am, or extend an invitation asking if I'd like to join them for cocktails later.

Usually after their wife goes to bed.

I've never understood the culture of people coming to the island to celebrate marriage, yet the stories I could tell about infidelity are astounding. The guilt in my heart for partaking in such an abomination is my punishment. I've worked hard to prove that I'm not that person anymore. No matter how badly I wish to leave this island, it won't be for a man.

Especially not the one watching me from across the boat.

When the boat pulls into the hotel dock, relief fills my lungs. I need to keep as far away from him as possible.

"I hope you enjoy the rest of your vacation, Ryker," I say to him as he passes me on the dock while I wait for Dante to check in with the hotel excursion desk.

"You're wrong." He throws his towel over his shoulder and picks up his bag.

Our eyes meet when he stands and I feel my brows furrow. "About what?"

"I do want to learn about the island girl." I let out an awkward laugh. And to think I thought he wasn't like other guys.

"So... what? You can go home and tell all your guy friends you shagged an island girl while your wife was at the hotel getting a massage?" I snort with a shake of my head, knowing his endgame. I tip my head back as I hop into the boat. "Have a nice night, Ryker."

"You too, Whiskey."

I freeze in my spot and chance a peek back. His knowing smile sends my heart hammering. With a quick wink, he turns and walks away but stops once again. "Oh, and by the way, I'm not married."

CHAPTER THREE

RYKER

W *hiskey.* I chuckle to myself, strolling down the excruciating long walkway to my bungalow. Had I known that my hut was at the end, I might have skipped out on the upgrade.

She looked familiar, but I couldn't put my finger on it. Until she snuck a peek at me and her cheeks reddened from being caught. That's when it all came back. Seems the island girl has a little voyeuristic side to her. Even a hangover wouldn't let me forget those eyes. They're more impressive up close. Amber-colored with a glint of copper when the sun hits them. Reminds me of my drink of choice, *whiskey.*

The more reason to stay away from her.

So why the hell tell her I was interested? I swipe my room key and walk into the wood hut, dropping my bag on the floor and head straight to the shower.

I've been here three days and I've broken every rule they gave me. Train. Stay focused. And stay away from women. Fucking Jarod Meyers, this is all his fault.

You were the one who admitted to doing something you didn't do, my subconscious reminds me. I squeeze the bridge of my nose. I'm not sure who I'm more upset with, myself or Meyers. He's a talented kid and deserves another chance.

Despite my friends assuming I'm being self-destructive because Bryn broke it off, *I wasn't*. That relationship happened six months ago. I'm over it. Bryn's got a boatful of secrets I didn't need tipping over into my world. She didn't trust me enough to tell me what she was hiding, we wouldn't have worked, anyway. I don't have time for that bullshit. She was a risk to my career.

I let out a bitter chuckle. Yet, here I am putting my career in danger all by myself. Why did I feel giving him a chance at my expense was a good idea? I pick up my phone to call Coach, but throw it back down on the table. I'm in the middle of the Pacific, banished to this island. If they need to talk, they know my number. Irritated with my situation again, I pour a shot of whiskey and down it before walking out the door.

"MR. DALLAS, this way to your table." I follow the lady to a table right off the stage. "Tonight we have something special for our guests. I hope you enjoy it."

Holding up the drink menu, I glance over it at all the couples and feel out of place. A few of them glance my way so I focus on the menu, not wanting to acknowledge their looks of sympathy. Anyone who follows football knows what happened.

"What would you like to drink tonight, Mr. Dallas?" Herman, the same waiter I've had the last two nights, stands by the table, smiling.

"I'll take a Mai Tai." *When in Rome, right?*

"You will love the show. The girls" —he wags his brows— "beautiful."

"Herman, my man. I'm not supposed to be looking."

Herman and I closed the bar down a couple nights ago. He pointed out a few single workers then too. The booze made me extra chatty, and I spilled why I was here.

He shrugs. "It's the land of romance. You never know."

I laugh. If I was to partake in a little fun, there would be zero romance.

"I think I'll skip out on the fun tonight. I'm beat from a long day in the water." He walks away, shaking his head in disappointment.

After piling food on my plate from the buffet dinner, and a few surprised glances, I find my drink waiting for me at the table set for one. To prevent further stares, I contain my desire to shovel the food into my mouth. I do have manners on most nights.

Taking a couple more trips to the buffet, I'm finally full. As I sit back in my seat and finish my drink, I check out the entertainment for the night. Tahitian men and women, dressed in bright yellow outfits for the show, walk on the stage.

I hold my hand up, stopping Herman as he passes me. "I'm ready for my—" Words escape me as I recognize one dancer. My gaze wanders the full length of her body to her bare feet and back up to her honey-colored eyes.

"What were you saying?" Herman jokes, slapping me on the back. "Another drink?"

I nod without thinking, still not able to take my eyes off her. Even in the middle of a group, she stands out. Long strands of chocolate hair cascade down over her bare shoulders, past her perky small breasts, hidden behind a strip of yellow fabric, and her eyes glow against the tiki torches. *A* is naturally striking.

I really need to find out her actual name.

Our eyes catch, and she arches a brow, still smiling. I jerk my chin up in a hello. Yep, I'm staying now. I recount all the jobs she's had since the first time I saw her. Housekeeper, tour guide and now, dancer. Who knows what else. Herman places my drink in front of me.

"Herman, is her name really A?" He follows my pointed stare and laughs once.

"Is that what she told you?" I nod and he shrugs one shoulder. "Then it seems it is."

"I thought you were trying to help me with the women?"

"Not that one. You're on your own with A." He chuckles, saying her name. "Pure heart, tainted mind." He pats his temple with his finger.

What the hell does that even mean? First, Dante expresses her dad is cuckoo and now she has a tainted mind? I watch her again and it seems like everyone likes her. Needless to say, his warning only makes the intrigue with her more intense.

During the show, I force myself to stop watching her. Damn, if I haven't had to adjust my semi-hard dick from her gyrating hips at least five times. Focusing on a dude doing the same cures that. When the announcer asks for volunteers, one of the other dancers makes her way over to me. Disappointment spreads in my chest when I catch A pulling another guy on stage.

"C'mon and show me what you got?" The woman smiles, holding out her hand. I take it, readily. I'll make sure A sees she picked the wrong guy. The woman leads me to the stage and has me stand by her side until every dancer has a volunteer. I glance over at A and wink when our eyes meet. "Hey! You're with me," my partner says, jokingly.

"Sorry. I'm all yours."

She wags her brows and unbuttons my white linen shirt, taking it off with the urging of the crowd. I throw it to my table. If I wasn't secretly waging war on the guy with a dad-bod, I'd keep my shirt on. But she'll be watching.

And I already know she likes what she sees.

With a few instructions for the dance, we're highlighted couple by couple. Thankfully, A and her partner went before us. The guy was a total dud, stiff as a board. I shake my arms out when they say it's our turn. The music starts. I copy my partner's movements. We end with me shaking my hips. Someone yells, "Go, Dallas" in the dining area and I'm certain I'll be getting a phone call from my publicist about a video and how I'm failing at keeping on the down-low. The smile on A's face made it worth it.

Strutting to my table after we're finished, I don't need to look A's direction to know I have her full attention. I throw back the rest of my drink and put my shirt on, but keep it unbuttoned. *She'll come over and talk to me.* I sit in my seat, still high from the excitement, and glance back to the stage to find A.

My smile drops at the empty stage.

I dart my gaze to the sides to find some performers talking among each other, but the one person I was hoping to find isn't anywhere around.

The unfamiliar sting of rejection strikes me through my chest as I walk back to my hut.

Alone.

This is the ultimate walk of shame. And it's a first for me.

CHAPTER FOUR

RYKER

"I am not a quitter."

I did not take my team to the championship from their 0-6 season when they brought me on without perseverance and determination. Or winning two Super Bowls the following two years.

Spreading gel through my hair, I stare in the mirror, hyping myself up. Nights we lost our games felt better than yesterday. This girl has me all twisted up. I know you win some and lose some, but hell, I've never lost a girl I was interested in.

And I don't plan on starting now.

The entire day replayed in my head last night. Then it clicked. People don't hold three jobs unless they need money. And I have plenty of it and a plan.

Now, I just need to find her.

Washing down the delicious cookie we get daily, with water, I make a mental note to ask for more. Maybe even a recipe. Gail, my sugar dealer also known as my baker in New York City, needs to make me some of these. I can't pinpoint the ingredient that makes them so good, but holy shit, I need more.

The concierge smiles at me as I pass the desk. I stop and rub my jaw, debating if I should ask. Screw it. I spin in place and her smile widens when I approach the desk. "Mr. Dallas. I hope your stay is going well."

"It is, thank you. I'm searching for someone and I'm hoping you can help. Her name is A." I shake my head, knowing it sounds ridiculous out loud. She blinks a couple times. "She works here and was also a performer last night."

"And you're sure her name is *A*?"

I drop my eyes to the desk, tapping my thumb. "No. Never mind." I sigh out of frustration. Without her name, I just look like an idiot. "Oh, wait, there is something you can do for me. The cookies we get daily... can I order more?"

"Certainly. I will have them delivered to your room this evening."

I lean against the counter, flashing a smile women love. "You think I can get the recipe?"

She blushes at my gaze, looking away for a moment. "Sorry. That I can't help you with."

It was worth a shot. "Well, thanks for the extra cookies." I tap the counter and spin to leave. My phone rings in my pocket and I'm not at all surprised to see who's calling.

"Let me guess," I say, answering, walking down the winding outdoor path through the hotel.

She lets out a bitter laugh. "You know what I love doing all day?" I roll my eyes at the snark in her voice. "Getting bombarded with questions about why our golden boy is partying it up in Bora Bora while he's on suspension. Dallas, you're playing right into everyone's hands with this shit. We sent you to one of the most remote islands ever to stay *out* of the tabloids."

"Bree, I was dancing for a minute. Give me a break. You didn't expect me to come here and hide in my hut all day."

"Yes. Yes, we did." They have lost their fucking mind. I could have stayed holed up in my condo if they wanted that. "At least get people to take pictures of you working out or practicing drills. *Something* other than partying."

A voice pulls my attention away from the scolding. Standing at the front desk in a red floral dress with her hair in a bun is A. Something about her awakens every part of me. She hands them three white boxes and steps back to a golf cart to grab another box.

"Gotta go, Bree."

"Wait, Ry—"

Her voice vanishes as I hit end and shove the phone back in my pocket. I smile to myself thinking about doing *something* other than partying. And that something is standing three feet away. I wait for her to drop off the box before approaching.

"Hey, Whiskey." I glide up to her stiff body, her sweet scent making my mouth water. She slowly turns around and pastes on a fake smile.

"Orana, Ryker."

Her greeting takes me back a couple days ago. Her cheeks redden and she drops her gaze to the ground, smoothing out her dress. Seems she remembers, too.

"Mr. Dallas, can we help you?" the lady behind the desk asks.

"Nope. I'm good, thank you." As soon as my attention is off A, she slips away, hopping in the cart.

"Wait," I blurt out, jogging the couple steps to the golf cart. She looks at me, impatiently. I have two seconds to figure out what my next move is. Afraid she might drive off, I hop into the passenger seat and her eyes widen.

"What are you doing?"

"I need a tour guide."

She blinks and then points. "The excursion desk is over there."

"I know. But I need a discreet guide."

"Mr. Dallas." Her tone turns serious. "I'm not sure what you're implying, but I am not for sale."

I throw my hands up. "No. That's not what I meant." I run my hand against my jaw, irritated that I'm fumbling with my words. "I'm supposed to stay out of the public eye so I need to hire someone to take me around the island for the day. But I don't want any record of it." She stares at me and I'm sure she's about to kick me out. "I'll give you a thousand dollars."

Her mouth gapes open before she shakes out of her stupor. She squeezes the steering wheel and I can see she's fighting herself over taking the job.

"Why me?" she finally asks.

Because you're beautiful and intriguing and for some reason, I can't stop thinking of you. I hold that piece of information to myself. "Because you know about the island and I understand you perfectly."

She laughs. "You sir, are the one with a funny accent. Not us."

"Touché. But even with your island accent, I don't have to think about what you said." She blows out a breath and sits back in her seat with her arms crossed, contemplating. "And no shagging," I add, chuckling at the word. Even though if it happened, I wouldn't care what she called it.

"Why do you find that funny?"

"It's not. The word is funny. I don't think I've ever used it."

She turns in her seat, amused. "Then what do you call it?"

"Sex. Screwing. Fucking. Getting laid—"

"Oh my. You and I have totally different views on getting lei'd." Her freckled nose scrunches and I laugh. "Okay. But I have to finish my deliveries this morning. I'll meet you at your hut at ten."

"Yes, ma'am."

Her foot presses down on the gas the second my feet hit solid ground. Not until a lady behind the desk clears her throat, do I catch on that I'd been staring at her cart until it was out of sight. I shove my hands in my pockets and give the ladies a courtesy nod before turning and walking back to my hut with a little bounce in my step.

CHAPTER FIVE

ASPEN

Damn that crooked, sexy grin. I dig the heels of my palms into my eye sockets, regret that I agreed to be his tour guide multiplying by the minute. Why did he buy all twenty seats on the excursion the other day with Dante? Why didn't I question his reason for not wanting a receipt for today? It's odd. Yet, I agreed to take him. Money seems to talk louder than common sense these days.

"Aspen?"

I yelp in surprise at my dad's voice. He stands in the doorway to my private house on our property that he built for me so I could stay close to him. "Hey, Dad. You scared me."

"I see that. Finish your deliveries?"

"Yes, sir. Done for the day." I glance at the kitchen filled with dirty bowls and cookie sheets, thinking I should stay and clean up rather than going out with Ryker. But I can't back out now. "I got another job today, so I'll be home later tonight. Are you feeling okay?" He doesn't typically visit me here. He dislikes chaos and uncleanliness. And my place is always a mess from baking.

He waves me off with a grunt. "I'm fine. Just felt like going for a stroll. I haven't seen you lately with all your *jobs*, so I was checking in with you." His voice drips with disdain. Mainly because he knows why I take a lot of jobs. To leave here, someday. I push off the dining chair and walk toward him. "You know how I prefer to keep busy." My arms wrap around his slender torso and I look up into his wise old blue eyes. "I'm glad to see you up walking around."

He grumbles out of my embrace and turns to wander outside. I follow him down the couple steps and we stare out to the vast ocean in silence.

"Well daughter, don't work too hard today," he says, in a dismissing tone. I stare at him for a moment, the sea breeze slapping me across the face like his words, but he doesn't acknowledge me, so I quietly trudge back to my place. The cancer put a strain on our relationship. After getting diagnosed a few years ago, he's withdrawn from me. He doesn't know I'm trying to save money for when I'll be left alone. Without him. Before, it was to leave this prison. Now, it's to prepare.

With one last glance at the dirty dishes, I storm out of the room, irritated with life. Why did he have to get sick? Why doesn't he want help?

He's gone by the time I leave. Tears fill my eyes that I can't help him. He's so stubborn. I don't want to imagine life without him.

Pushing the outrigger canoe off the sandy beach, I place one leg in after another and start rowing as soon as I'm situated. With each row, I blow out a cleansing breath, calming my mana. My spiritual energy becoming one with the elements of the sea and air. When I arrive at Ryker's hut, I've released all the negative energy. I can't change my dad's situation, but I can make sure he feels my love.

Ryker walks out onto his private deck, smiling with only swim trunks on, his chiseled abs making me feel things I shouldn't be feeling. "Whiskey, this is a surprise." His nickname for me is both aggravating and provocative considering the first time he said it; I was staring at his naked body.

"Why do you call me that?"

His lips quirk up on one side, making my cheeks warm. *Damn smile.* "Your eyes are the color of whiskey. And I feel stupid calling you *A.* Especially when I know it's not your name. So, Whiskey it is."

"If I tell you my name, will you quit calling me that?"

He shakes his head, walking to the edge. "Nope. Too late. I kind of like it now."

What is it with men giving me nicknames? "You ready?" I relent, pointing to the empty seat behind me. He stares at it with trepidation.

"I'm concerned that thing will tip over. I mean, that seat is tiny. And I'm... not."

I bite my lip. Definitely *not.* "Big guy, are you afraid?"

"No," he says confidently, throwing his bag into the canoe. The canoe rocks a little when he hesitantly steps down into it. When he settles in the seat he says, "I appreciate you calling me big guy, though." *This is going to be a long day.*

"I'm more surprised you got that big ego to fit in the canoe." I laugh over my shoulder and then bite my lip to stop. *Who is this person?* I silently berate myself for being this casual with him. I'd never say these things to a normal customer. Except, he's not the typical patron. For some reason, he makes my heart and mouth move faster than my brain.

I square my shoulders. *I'm a professional and no amount of attraction will change that.* Moving the oars through the water with a little more oomph because of the extra two-hundred-plus pounds of weight behind me, my mind wanders to last night and him dancing. Between his carefree personality and sexy body, it took a lot of strength to make myself walk away. Yet, here we are, spending the day together.

"Do I need to help row?"

I quit rowing at the humor in his tone. *Does he think I can't do this without him?*

"Nope," I say, refusing his smug gesture to help, looking forward and rowing again while I mumble under my breath, "You sit there and look pretty."

He laughs out loud. "I'm paid a lot of money to look pretty." I pinch my eyelids shut. *Of course he heard me.* "Whiskey, I'm also paid a lot of money to see and hear everything."

With slight curiosity, I turn and ask, "Are you an ornithologist?" Maybe that's why he's here alone, he's working.

"A what?" He continues before I can answer. "No. Whatever that is."

"Ornithologist. It's a bird scientist."

"Why in the world do you think I'm a bird scientist? Do I look like one?"

I shrug my shoulders. It made sense when he said he sees and hears everything. "I've actually never met one, so I can't say what *one* looks like."

"Do you really not know what I do?" He crosses his arms and stares at me with a surprised expression. "Don't you get some kind of dossier on hotel guests?"

A charter boat full of people passes us and the passengers wave. We both wave back, Ryker's grin forced like a parent demanding their kid smiles for a family portrait. The ripple from the boat sways us and I stop my examination of his artificial expression. We've drifted in the direction we came from.

"I don't work for the hotel." I twist my body forward to row again. Shale will kill me if we don't show up soon. He owes me a favor and wasn't too happy I was cashing it in for his Jeep for an entire day since he's not able to rent it out.

"So, were you there to rob me? Did I hire a thief to take me out?"

Sarcastic laughter ripples out. "And what if you did?"

"Fuck. My decision-making skills are broken these days." A tinge of humor in his tone almost masks the underlying disappointment. The part he's trying to keep hidden. Maybe it has something to do with why he's here. After I tie the boat to the dock on the main island, I wait for him to disembark. He quirks his eyebrow in question.

"No, I wasn't trying to steal from you. I was helping the hotel since a couple girls came down with a sickness. I used to work there."

"Phew." He blows out an obnoxious breath as he stands to get out of the canoe. "I was about to hand you my wallet to get that out of the way before we started our day."

I cross my arms and stare at him in disbelief. "You mean to tell me you'd stay knowing that I'm robbing you blind?" *How ignorant of a man can he be?* The appeal is starting to wear off.

"You wouldn't be robbing me blind if I handed it to you."

"That's beside the point." Irritation spikes and his smile drops.

"Calm down, Whiskey. I'm messing with you. It's obvious you aren't a thief. Or, at the very least, not a good one. Every time I see you, you're doing different jobs."

I shrug, heading to the Jeep. "Variety is the spice of life." With a quick glance over my shoulder, I make sure he's following me.

"Spice is one of my favorite flavors," he rumbles, licking his bottom lip.

I'm sure it is. But I am not one of those spices.

The Jeep squeaks as I pull myself up into the open vehicle. He slides into the passenger side, tossing his bag in the back.

"Seems you're a jack of all trades." *Why is he calling me Jack?* My brows furrow in confusion and I blink several times. "It's a saying that you do a lot of things," he clarifies.

"Do all men named Jack do many things?"

He lets out a heady laugh. "I'm assuming no. I have no idea why they use the name Jack."

"Do you use sayings that you don't understand often?" He runs his hand through his hair and avoids my glances. I cringe. *Why can't I think before I talk sometimes?* "I'm sorry. That wasn't meant to be rude."

"No, it's okay. I'm just not used to being questioned on American day-to-day expressions."

When I peek over, he dominates the space in the Jeep. Everything about him is large, even his presence. He flips his hat backward, and rests one of his hands on his leg, the other, out the window. Everything about him exudes sexual energy.

My hand slips from the top of the steering wheel and lands on the horn. I jump and look forward, searching for who honked at me. *Wait, that was me.* My cheeks burn as Ryker laughs out loud. I groan in embarrassment and fiddle with the keys to start the engine. He flusters me just being around him.

And the day hasn't even started yet.

CHAPTER SIX

ASPEN

"Are you sure this is a trail?" He shuffles his feet in the heavy undergrowth and steps over rocks. There's a path under there somewhere. The locals would rather not have foreigners find it so they keep it in its natural state.

"You said you wanted an adventure. This is about as adventurous as you will get out here." He's physically fit enough for the climb. It's a demanding trail, though. "But it's not for the weak."

"I'm good at challenges."

Is that why he hired me? Does he see *me* as a challenge?

At the entrance, I step on a rock so I can stare him dead in the eyes. "Are you a stubborn man?"

He's amused by my place on the rock. "More like determined."

"Stubborn it is," I retort. His smile deepens with laughter. It dies down when he figures out I'm being serious. "Listen, Ryker, you have to be careful. Watch where I place my feet and hands. Don't go all rogue thinking you've got this... because you don't."

He tips his head back at my harsh words. "You do wonders for one's confidence."

"Just follow my lead." Most locals stopped offering this tour because of how difficult it is. But I love this climb. The summit is the top of my world, it's the place I go to fantasize about what's past the infinite water—the world my father hates. I shake the thunderous thoughts away. Those are his views. I want to form my own opinion someday.

As I lead Ryker up the steep trail, I peek back frequently to make sure he's following. My heart sinks when his hand slips on a wet branch, but he catches himself on the branch below.

"Good?"

A smug smile rests on his lips. "You're very distracting."

"Me?" I rest on a steady rock protruding out of the mountain. He steps next to me on the narrow rock. Our sweaty bodies are centimeters from each other. Both our grips on surrounding trees. Why did I stop right here? A quick climb from here is a resting spot. With plenty of room.

"I'm supposed to watch every step you take, but I can't stop staring at your gorgeous ass."

I gasp, surprised by his confession. And then irritation sets in. "Ryker, you're supposed to be paying attention."

"Whiskey, there is nothing I'm paying attention to more than your ass. You have a great ass, by the way."

Rolling my eyes, and without thinking, I give him a slight shove on the shoulder.

"Merde!" My voice gets lost behind the lump of panic lodged in my throat as I frantically grip his shirt. He teeters backward, losing his balance, and reaches for another branch to catch himself. He slams into the side of the mountain, grunting. "I'm so sorry."

"Damn, woman, I'm not groping your ass. No need to kill me."

When I'm certain he's back on solid ground, or rather, safely on my rock, I release his shirt and busy my hands with the dangling rope resting between us. We use it to continue the climb. My face burns with embarrassment and I focus on the rope. Here

I was lecturing him to be careful and I practically knock him down the mountain.

"Well..." I fist the first knot in the rope, needing to put distance between us as quick as possible. "... just pay attention," I blurt out awkwardly. He agrees with a wide toothy grin and we're back to square one.

"To my hands, Ryker. My. Hands."

"Yes, ma'am."

"DO YOU EVER FEEL TRAPPED?" he asks mindlessly, staring out as far as the eyes can see, lost in his own thoughts. At the top of Mount Pahia Summit, we're relaxing from our two-hour climb. We're so high up, a sense of freedom lives in the air, as if we were birds relaxing our wings from our journey. But Ryker's words remind me I'm not free at all.

I roll my head to face him, wondering why a guy like him feels trapped. He has money, looks, and the freedom to go anywhere.

"You're kidding, right?" Crossing my feet, I continue. "If you were to drive eighteen miles, would you hit the end of your world?"

His eyes soften, and I regret my words. I don't want his sympathy. "Whiskey, what's your story?"

I sigh. "You're assuming I have one."

"Everyone has a story. What do you do every day? What brought you here? Do you ever plan on leaving? Do you have a boyfriend?"

"You jumped right into the personal stuff, didn't you?" Moisture clings to his forehead. He pulls out a water bottle from his backpack, taking a long gulp then emptying the rest over his head. "You're paying a lot of money to learn about the island girl. How about we head down and I'll take you to the next spot?" I pop up, dusting the dirt off my shorts, but he stays put, staring up at me behind his sunglasses. I can't help that my eyes travel down his bare chest, sweat and water glistening all the way down over the muscular ridges in his stomach, right to...

"We can cross off boyfriend." I jerk my eyes up, meeting his knowing grin.

Why can't I stop doing that?

It's like he has a magnet there.

Shuffling from one foot to the other, and squeezing my arms across me, I shake my head. "No boyfriend." If I had one, I would be a horrible, horrible girlfriend.

"What's dating life like here?"

Nonexistent.

But I keep that to myself. "My answer wasn't enough, huh?"

Sure, I've dated a few guys, but I've never had that spark with any of them. Maybe because I've known them my entire life and they're more like brothers to me. And there's not a large pool of available men. For now, my focus is my business and making enough money to leave here. *On my own.*

"I can't even imagine what it's like. Are you in a tribe? Are you supposed to marry a certain person?"

I stare at him and wonder if I want to get into this with him. He sits, arms resting on his knees, with a quizzical expression.

"Stand up." He follows my command without question. "There are three tribes." I point at each of them surrounding the island. Then I point to what looks like an uninhabited part of the island. Except it isn't. "See that house?" He cranes his neck toward the heavily treed peninsula on the south part of the island where two houses sit. "That is where me and my dad live." I like having our places tucked away. It's peaceful. "We moved here when I was one. My dad was referred to as Popa'a, *a mainlander*. The locals didn't welcome him. But he didn't care. He craved a simple lifestyle. Becoming a fisherman and raising me was most important to him. Eventually, they tolerated him because of his small fishing business."

"You said your father was American, right?"

"Yes. My mom was French but was in America on a work visa when she met my dad. They married and lived there for years before they had me. And then we moved here." I turn my focus to the water, surprised at the words falling from my mouth. No foreigner has ever asked about my story before and I never offered it. Why is he so interested? Afraid of him asking about my mom, I add, "And to answer your question, no arranged marriages."

Before he can ask another question, I start the descent down the trail. "Guess we're done," he murmurs, following close behind.

Yes, we are.

Back in the Jeep, on the way to our next stop, I say, "Your turn."

"My turn what?"

"Who is Ryker Dallas?? Why are you here by yourself?"

He looks forward, and his eyes jump around the Jeep. He fiddles with the blower vents. It's odd since most guys have no problem talking about themselves. "I'm a player at heart. I'm laid back, carefree, and I don't like drama." He chuckles to himself. "My friends make up for what I lack. Shit, they could have at least four seasons of a drama-filled TV show."

"Sounds like interesting friends." I shift down a gear as we slow down, coming to a stop for people crossing the road up ahead.

"They are. They're all in law enforcement and here I am—" he cuts off in the middle of his sentence. I glance over and his expression becomes distant for a moment before he reins it back in. "I chose a different occupation." Why is he being secretive? I let him slide since I've yet to even tell him my name.

"Okay. Not in law enforcement. How old are you?"

"Thirty."

"We've already established you're not married… well, if you're telling me the truth. Girlfriend?"

"No wife. No girlfriend."

I find him watching me when I peer over. I lift a brow, having a hard time believing him. "Why?"

"Remember how I said I don't like drama? I had a girlfriend. But because of my job, she was hesitant to take our relationship to the next level. She was hiding something and wouldn't tell me. She called it quits. In my line of work, it was for the better. It puts my job at risk and it's not worth it."

Now I really want to know what he does.

"She must not have been the one or she would've been."

His brows furrow. "Been what?"

"Worth it."

He straightens and sighs loudly. "Maybe. But it goes both ways. If I'm not worth sharing your secrets with, you're not for me either."

I pull into a parking spot and turn the engine off. Twisting my body in the seat, I grip the keys in my palm. "Trust is a big thing for me too. Why do guys lie to get what they want?"

"Men are assholes." I wait for him to tell me something new. "But you can't live without us." There's a maddening arrogance with him, yet I find it attractive. He hunches over and glances out the dirty window. "Where are we?"

"Bloody Mary's. It's the place to be in Bora Bora. And I figured you might be hungry after that hike."

"Starving."

"Famous people come here all the time. See those signs?" I point at the enormous signs filled with rows of famous people's names. He walks over to one of them and looks it over.

"Cool," he says, not impressed. "Ready to go in? My stomach is going to start eating itself."

I hum to myself. People tend to be more excited to see who has been here. As we walk inside, he lowers his ball cap, so it's difficult to see his eyes. I tilt my head, confused by his slight change in demeanor.

"Aspen," Teva greets us when we walk in to the open-air restaurant. She stretches her arms out wide and wraps them around my shoulders. I pat her back. Someone's being over-friendly today. Her face beams when her eyes land on Ryker. "This is a surprise seeing you. Usually you're—"

"Teva, this is Ryker," I say, interrupting her, with wide eyes and a slight shake of my head. "I'm his hired guide for the day."

"Oh." I plead with her with my eyes not to say anything. It's not that I need to keep my actual job secret, I just don't want to share that with him. It's personal and close to my heart. The exact place he doesn't need to be. She waves me off. "I can't keep up with all your jobs, anyway. Ryker, welcome to Bloody Mary's."

I take a step back when they shake hands and mouth, "Thank you." Teva is Mama Doe's daughter and we're almost the same age. She's not a good friend. She's had a crush on Dante since I can remember and she blames me that he has never shown interest. But her dislike for foreigners is stronger than her dislike for me, even gorgeous ones like Ryker.

She leads us to our table. After we sit, I notice Ryker's flashing an arresting smile. I cross my legs as an ache builds. I wish he'd stop that. "Aspen, huh?"

I laugh, holding up the menu even though I know it by heart. "I didn't even notice she said my name. I was more confused that she was hugging me. But yes, that is my name."

"Did you know it's a city in the United States?"

"It's where I was born." It's the only piece of being an American I've held on to. Growing up here and learning about the rich culture, I've immersed myself as being a Tahitian. But I'm not, and there are few people that still remind me of that. It feels like my name is the only thing I have that is the real me.

"It's one of my favorite cities."

I drop the menu and lean forward on the table. "It is? Will you tell me about it?"

Hanging on to every word, I imagine myself there when he describes the mountains, hiking, and a town as unique as Bora Bora. My dad never talks about the States, but I've looked up pictures of Aspen. Although, hearing Ryker talk about it, there's life in his words rather than just pictures.

"I like your necklace."

I run my fingers over the tiny opal bead that always hangs from my neck. "Thanks." The only thing my mom ever gave me. I've tried to take it off, but the guilt attached to it always changes my mind. She might have left me, and I don't know why, but she wanted me to have it. In a way, it makes me feel closer to a woman I don't remember.

The afternoon slips away from us. He's easy to talk to. I catch myself telling him things no one knows except for Dante. Like when I dressed up like Cyndi Lauper and put on a concert for my dad and Dante.

Yeah, I regretted that word vomit.

"So, you're a big eighties music fan?" he asks with humor in his voice. "'Cause I have a vague memory of waking up to someone singing a song of hers." I cover my flushed face with my hand. So much for him not hearing my horrible voice.

"Were you even asleep?" I choke out. For someone dead to the world, he sure does remember a lot about me being there. His deep laugh fills the room. People glance our way and he bites his lip to stop, lowering his face. When he lifts back up, mischief dances in his eyes. He wasn't asleep at all. "I can't believe you laid there naked. What exactly were you expecting?"

He shrugs. "Wasn't expecting anything. I was hungover and wasn't ready to get up yet."

"You could have told me to come back later."

Nodding, he says, "I could have. But what fun would that have been?"

"Don't give me a reason to start not liking you. I thought you were different from the other assholes who come here."

He leans across the table, his eyes hardening. "Whiskey, don't confuse being nice with being a man with a dick. We all want the same thing, some of us just go about it differently."

At least he's honest. I cross my arms in front of me on the table and lean in too. Our faces inches apart, I say, "Are you saying you're being nice because you're expecting something from me?"

I swallow at the intensity in his eyes. "No. I'm being nice because... I'm a nice guy. I hired you with a stipulation of no shagging, so there're no expectations other than you showing me the island. But I'm not gonna lie and say I'm not attracted to you."

I would have rather he lied. It'd be easier for me to ignore the draw I feel knowing he didn't have the same attraction.

Someone steps up to the table, breaking the trance I'd been in. "Can I get you two anything else?" I sit back and peek up at Reva, smiling from ear to ear. She's thinking she has something to tell Dante. Except, there's nothing to tell. And even if there was, Dante and I are just friends.

"Nope, we're all done here," I answer without asking Ryker if he's ready to go. As we fight over who's paying, I remind him he paid for a tour and this is part of the tour.

When we're walking out, he rasps, "You have a habit of ending things abruptly."

I wish that had always been the case. It would've saved me a lot of heartache. Not giving in to the attractive foreigners in hopes he'll fall in love with me and take me with him. I internally groan. How foolish and naïve I was. But that's not me anymore.

"Where to now?" he asks, jumping in the Jeep.

"Feel like going swimming?"

"Oh!"

Ryker's voice startles me as I resurface. I squeeze water from my hair as I stare at him, confused. His enormous hand covers his eyes. *Wow.* I hold up my hand, comparing it to his from a distance. Dante always joked that a man's hand represents how big his dick is. I never took much stock in that theory until now. Seems he was right.

"What's wrong?" I ask, forcing myself to stop thinking of his well-endowed manly parts.

"You... uh..." He points at me with his other hand, keeping his eyes covered. "Wardrobe malfunction."

What is he talking about? I glance down and notice my left breast is out in the open, my bathing suit pushed to the side. This man is not modest, so it surprises me how he's acting. It's not like he hasn't been staring at them the entire time. I pull the triangle fabric back over.

"Ryker, you act like you've never seen a breast before."

His lips curl up under his hand. "Unlike you, I'm trying to be respectful."

I huff. "When have I not been respect—" I pinch my lips together, the memory of naked Ryker jogging my memory. He chuckles, removing his hand. His eyes sparkle under the cascade of droplets of water running down his tan rugged face. "All right, let's talk about that day one more time since you can't seem to let it go. I was doing my duty as an employee to make sure you were alive. There were liquor bottles everywhere, and you looked dead."

His face brightens at the suggestion. "Whiskey, dead men don't have morning wood."

I blink. Morning wood?

"Erection. Boner. Hard dick—"

Oh, that.

"Okay. I get it," I snicker, holding up my palm for him to stop. "You're right. It caught me off guard and I wasn't thinking clearly. Sorry for invading your privacy." It's the only excuse I can think of.

"No need to be sorry. I'm irresistible."

I want to tell him he's not.

I want to tell him he's full of misplaced self-esteem.

I want to tell him he does nothing for me.

But I can't.

And he knows it.

Instead, I dip down and swim back to the beach. He stays swimming laps. Stretching my legs out in the soft white sand, I lounge back on my elbows and watch him. Large muscular arms slice through the water in an effortless stroke. The sun looks as if it is floating on the water off in the distance, reminding me that our day is almost over. A gentle melancholy sweeps over me, then dissipates with a heavy breath.

Don't do this.

I demand my heart to stop beating for the foreigner. This isn't his prison, it's his escape from reality. And I'm not anything but an island girl being paid to hang out with him. A thick dose of perspective makes me swallow back my emotions. Bringing my legs under me, I push up to my feet as he treads out of the water. Everything about his body is perfection. Whatever he does, it includes a heavy dose of exercise.

"You have a little sand on you."

I glance down my body and chuckle. "That's like saying I'm breathing air." He steps in close to me, stealing that air.

"How about I help you get it off," he rasps.

Despite my entire being yelling yes, I force my feet to take a couple steps backward. "That would be a no."

"Are you sure?" Without waiting for an answer, he whooshes

me up into his arms and I squeal as he runs with me back into the water, effortlessly. When he's waist deep, the water covering my butt, he sinks both of us under. I swim out of his arms, putting at least an arm's length between us before surfacing.

"Satisfied?" I ask, stretching out my sand-free arms.

His grin fades, leaving behind heated desire. "Not in the least."

The air between us thickens. The waves delicately crash when they hit the beach, the only sound around us. For a few endless seconds, I'm frozen in place. The desire that I keep running from, fueled by the heat in his eyes.

He exhales and takes two long strides through the water toward me, and I hold my breath as he nears. "Keep telling me no," he whispers and falls back into the water. His eyes never leave mine.

Relief squeezes out from the cocoon of disappointment.

I don't know how much longer I can.

CHAPTER SEVEN

RYKER

There's fucking romance voodoo vibes on this island. It's the only reason I can think for asking her to show me around the island.

A second time.

She was pushing off the dock in her canoe, and I was ready to say goodbye. The words *I'll see you around* were on the tip of my tongue. I need to distance myself from the woman. But what came out surprised the hell out of me.

"Are you available tomorrow?"

She wasn't. But she was the next day.

So, here we are. Day two. Same rule—no shagging. I needed a day to train, to warm up my arm. Maybe take a few pics to send Bree to show the world I'm ramping up my training for the game in two weeks. That is where my head should be. Not swimming in the ocean, trying to get close to this woman.

I stare at her, floating on top of the water. Water frames her face and her eyes close, exposing the most perfect smooth face. Between her high cheekbones and dainty nose dusted with freckles to her lush lips, she's the most beautiful woman I've ever met. And I've dated a few international supermodels.

My fingers itch to touch her. If I was less of a man, I would have covered her mouth with mine two days ago. Her eyes were begging for it. Fuck, after seeing her tit pop out of her bathing suit, so was my dick. Seeing her hard nipple out in the open, damn it was hard to walk away. But I won't touch her while I'm paying for her to be here. I don't want to make her feel devalued as a woman. If she wants me after today, she knows where I'm at. Then all bets are off.

"Do you know how to play football?" She rolls her head to the side, letting her body sink, and she stands up. Water hits at her waist and I force my eyes to not drop to her chest.

"*Oui*. I used to play with some boys in the streets." When she mixes her French in with English, it's sexy as hell even though I don't understand what she's saying. Most of the time she's not aware she's doing it.

"I have a ball, you wanna play?"

She shrugs. "You're paying me, I'll do whatever you'd like." My mind turns dirty. *The things I'd like to do to her.* A splash hit me square in the face. "Mr. Dallas. I said no shagging."

I laugh, wiping saltwater out of my eyes. "Don't say things like that then. I'm a man. Our minds are filthy."

Her cheeks flush, and she points to the beach. "Go get your ball," she says, her voice flustered. I inwardly chuckle to myself, thinking I could make that comment just as dirty.

"Okay, stay there." I take heavy steps toward the beach and then remember she told me to shuffle my feet so I don't step on a stingray. When I step onto the white sand, I hop on the hot surface. I grab my bag and jump to the wet sand, blowing out a quick sigh of relief.

Holy shit, that's hot!

"How are we going to play football if I'm still in the water?" she asks. I pull the football out and hold it in the air, throwing my bag up onto the beach.

"We're going to throw it." Her lips twists as she comes closer to me, staring at the brown ball with brows cinched.

"What kind of football is that?" Palm up, she stretches her hand out. I give it to her and she wraps her other hand on top of it so it doesn't fall. She inspects the ball as if she's never seen one.

"I thought you said you've played before."

Her eyes meet mine. "I have. How do you kick this?"

"Kick?" Her confusion clicks and I chuckle at the misunderstanding. "American football," I clarify. Her freckled nose wrinkles. "You're thinking about soccer, with a round ball. You kick it into the goal box?" She nods. "Have you never seen an American football game?"

"I guess not."

I take the ball back and hold it up. "This is a football. We throw this instead of kicking it and someone runs it into the end zone for a touchdown, rather than a goal. There's a lot more, but that's the gist of it."

"So, in America, the football I know is called soccer?"

"Yes."

"Weird. But okay. How do you throw it?"

"Take your ring finger and put it on the second lace and then your first finger should hit the stitch line. Don't grip it too tight. There should be a little air between your palm and the ball." I lift my hand to show her. She eagerly watches. "So when you throw it, it'll spiral out of your hand." I throw it up on the beach, not too far. Her eyes widen at the perfect spiral.

"You're good at that."

The best. Her compliment makes my ego balloon, although she has nothing to compare it to. She runs up the beach to grab it. Gripping a football while wearing a skimpy red bikini is a wet dream come true. I'm glad I'm deep enough to hide my semi. She remains there, following my instructions on how to throw it. When she launches the ball toward me, the wobbly football lands at least ten feet from me.

"You could have caught that," she teases, walking toward me.

"Hold up. Stay there," I instruct while grabbing the ball. Catching might be easier when she's not knee deep in water. When I throw, she catches it. "You're a natural." I beam with my arms out. She does a small curtsy. The next few throws, her technique improves with each pass.

"Woo-hoo!" she boasts when the ball spins in a somewhat tight spiral.

"Good job, Whiskey." I spin away from her to give myself a moment. Watching her play *my game*, her excitement over it, makes my cravings for her intensify. I glance up to the blue sky and pull in a deep salty breath.

"Did I do something wrong?" She calls out from behind me. I shake my head and blow out a ragged breath. *Definitely did nothing wrong.*

"I'm going long," I say over my shoulder, swimming further out. The shallow end of these beaches go on forever. But that's okay because I need space.

"That's a little ambitious," she screams at me, making me laugh. I stand up, a good forty yards away from her. "Are you ready?"

"To swim for it," she teases. "Sure."

I cock my arm back and snap it. The perfect spiral launches through the air, straight for her. Her eyes widen and she readies herself to catch it.

She catches this and I'm marrying her.

I squeeze my fists, not able to look away. Not even as something brushes against my leg. I jump up as the ball lands in her arms for the perfect catch.

"Yes!" I snap, surprised as hell. But then my feet hit ground. A soft, rubbery ground. "Fuucckkkk!" I scream, tumbling down in the water with pain shooting from my foot up my leg. It feels like I just stepped on a knife. Pure adrenaline pushes me through the shallow water, afraid a shark bit me. *And might not be done snacking.*

Aspen rushes to me. "Ryker, what happened?" She helps me stand and I wobble on one leg. "Something bit me."

"Can you walk?"

I put my foot down and wait for the stabbing pain, but it doesn't get worse. I nod, hobbling to shore with her under my arm, helping. Once on dry land, I sit down and she inspects my foot.

"It looks like a stingray got you."

"Should you pee on it, or something?"

She freezes while cramming our towels into her bag and stares at me, both brows raised. "Ryker, it's not a snake bite."

"Well, how the hell do I know?" I chuckle through the throbbing, although it's not unbearable. Dislocating my shoulder during a game hurt worse than this. She rushes to grab everything and then runs to the shoreline to retrieve my ball.

"That was an impressive throw." She beams as she stuffs it in my bag. That was nothing. If she only knew.

"That was a more impressive catch." I'm certain had this stingray not tried to kill me, I would have kissed her.

Kissing is *not* shagging.

Within minutes she has me on the boat and headed back to the hotel. *Oh, shit.* "Whiskey, where do you plan on taking me?" I can't have this incident reported. I throw my head against the seat, thinking. Coach will flip his fucking lid if he finds out.

She glances over from behind the steering wheel. "I was taking you to the hotel doctor. Thankfully, the barb isn't lodged in your foot."

"Do you think he can look at it in my room?"

"Why must everything be a secret, Ryker?" She pins her inquisitive stare on me. "Are you hiding out here?"

Yes.

I nod and her body stiffens. "But not like you're thinking."

"What am I thinking?"

I hold my hands up. "I'm not hiding from the law or anything like that. I'm just..." I pause. Having someone look at me as a person rather than a money sign or ulterior motive has been refreshing. But if I have any chance of her keeping this secret, I need to say something. "... I'm supposed to stay out of the press. I'm supposed to be lying low."

Her gaze jumps to my foot. I'm moving it back and forth as the pain intensifies, creeping up my leg.

"Is it getting worse?"

"No," I lie. Her lips purse and she shakes her head. "Listen, I've been hurt so many times, this is nothing."

"Fine. I'll drop you off at your place and bring the doctor to you."

I wince, grinding my teeth. *It doesn't hurt. It doesn't hurt.* "Thank you."

She lets me deal with my injury in silence the rest of the way. As soon as she pulls up to my hut, I hobble over and up to the platform to a chair. I never thought five stairs would be the death of me. I watch as she runs and fills a trashcan with water. She's not very careful as water sloshes out from the sides.

"Put your foot in it."

I do what I'm told, slipping my foot in but only make it to my big toe. "Oh shit! That's scorching hot! Are you trying to burn me too?" I pull my whole leg out of the bucket.

She dips her finger in, swirling it in a circle and glances up at me with an incredulous expression. "Really?"

With my damaged ego, I grudgingly sink my foot in the hot water. "The pain made it hotter."

"The hot water will help it. Keep it soaked until I come back with the doctor." She rests her palm on my knee and flashes a sweet smile.

"You got it, nurse." I'm not ashamed to milk my injury if she stays.

I watch her hop down into the boat and speed off. It's a good thing she brought an actual boat today instead of her canoe. The pain intensifies with her not here to take my mind off it. I lean back on the cushioned chair and rest my eyes. Aspen catching my ball flashes behind my eyelids. I can't help but smile. She doesn't hesitate or flinch. She plants her feet and never takes her eyes off the ball. Fuck, she's perfect.

And she caught the damn ball.

"It looks like you'll live," she says, sitting in the other cushioned chair on my patio. She hugs her knees to her chest and smiles at me. The doctor just left and yes, I will live.

Three more hours of burning water. I've had a quick lesson on stingrays and why I should always shuffle, *never jump.*

"You have an excellent throw," she says, trying to change my bummed mood. My hands clasp in my lap and I twirl my thumbs, debating if I should tell her. On one hand, women fall at my feet knowing who I am and having her on her knees looking up at me... I can't say that wouldn't make my fucking year. On the other hand, I like her feisty personality. She's making me work to win her over. I squeeze my eyes shut. What the hell? *Win her over?* I can't forget what this is.

Temporary. There is no need to win anyone over.

"I hope I do, it's worth a few million dollars." I wince at the cockiness in my voice. Even I'm embarrassed by it. Do I typically say shit like that? "I'm a professional football player," I add to help ease the shitstorm I just spewed.

"Well, that makes sense now."

I study her face, waiting for her eyes to glaze over with either dollar signs or infatuation. Instead, I see her. Whiskey. In that silent moment that our eyes lock, we're each searching for something.

An impossible something.

She clears her throat, breaking contact. "How's your foot?"

"You don't have to stay." The words fall off my lips and I instantly regret them.

She straightens in her chair, and her expression shifts to hurt. "Do you want me to leave?"

Hell, no.

"No, but I don't want you to stay because you feel guilty."

She shifts her toes to the ground and leans forward. "I do feel bad. I took you out there." The warm breeze picks up and whips her hair through the air. As if she couldn't get any sexier, it's like someone turned a fan on for a Sports Illustrated photo shoot.

"This wouldn't have happened if you wouldn't have caught the ball," I tease, even though it's the truth. I wouldn't have been jumping up and down.

She gasps. "What! You're blaming me because of *that?*" She stands up and walks over to me, sticks her finger down in the bucket to test the temperature. She gestures for me to take my foot out so she can refill it. "Did you realize that maybe you're overpaid when an island girl can do your job?"

Her banter is refreshing. I need a woman like her to keep me on my toes. I hear the sink turn off and she comes back out. Smart-ass puts her finger in the bucket to show me it's not bad. I roll my eyes, sinking my foot again.

"I bet you used to run all over these boys playing socc... football."

Her grin grows as she recalls a memory. "Dante used to hate

when I wanted to play. His friends stopped telling him when a game was happening, afraid I'd tag along."

I can imagine her kicking ass to prove girls are as good as boys. Those were always the girls I was attracted to. I'm not sure when that changed. No, I know when it was. When beautiful women with fake huge tits would do whatever the hell I wanted them to do. I lost my craving for strong women because I had an abundance of weak ones. It was easier to deal with them when I was putting all my energy into building my football career.

But I want more. I don't want easy.

"Do you have any girlfriends?"

She cocks her hip out. "Why? Are you tired of me already?"

"Definitely not. I just figured you were the type to have a lot of guy friends and few girlfriends."

She shrugs and plops down in the chair. "I guess. I didn't have a lot of *any* friends growing up. My dad tolerated Dante, but he kept me pretty isolated from the locals." Dante was right. Her dad seems crazy. "You're thinking he was a horrible dad."

Maybe crazy, not horrible. She seems to have her shit together and loves her dad so he couldn't be that bad. "Whiskey, I'm not one to judge. My dad rode my ass my entire life to be a better football player. I was never good enough for him. Even when he was on his deathbed, he made me swear I would continue working harder."

I stare out to the calm water. A pain lives in my chest because we didn't have a good relationship. His constant push and my rebellious pull had us at odds most nights.

"What happened to him," she whispers.

Closing my eyes, I answer, "He was in a car accident. There was a complication with his surgery. I was sixteen." There are very few people that has heard this story. I've always been afraid of people taking my stories and turning them into headlines. But with Aspen, I didn't even hesitate.

When I hear the creak of a chair, I open my eyes. She steps over and sits on the table next to the chair, laying her hand on top of mine. "I'm so sorry." I don't dare move a muscle having her this close to me, touching me. Warmth from her fingers spreads up my arm.

"It's okay. My mom and I survived. I'm a huge momma's boy because of it." I can't help myself. I lift her hand in mine and kiss the backside. My lips tingle against her skin and my gaze glued to her face, tries to read her. *Can I keep going?*

She stands straight up, silently answering my question. "I have an idea to make you feel better." I wag my brows. *I know a way.* Dipping her head slightly, she adds, *"Not that, Ryker.* I'll be back." She spins on her bare feet and rushes out the front door.

After ten minutes, I splash my foot in the lukewarm water. I shouldn't have kissed her hand. She probably said she'd be right back as an excuse to get the hell out of here. Rolling my neck to crack it, I push up to change my water.

The door clicks open as I'm dumping the water and I balance on one foot. "What are you doing?" she exclaims, rushing over to me.

I hold out the empty bucket. "Water was cold."

She winces. "Sorry. It took a little longer than expected. But I have these..." She swings her hands in front of her, presenting me with five wrapped cookies. My mouth waters as I drop the bucket and reach for the sugar greatness. "I heard a rumor you enjoyed these."

I untie the blue ribbon, all the while still standing on one foot. *"Enjoy* is putting it mildly. More like addicted." I shove the entire cookie in my mouth and bite down. I hum as the sweet taste fills every taste bud on my tongue. "These are so fucking good," I say, covering my mouth full of cookie, trying not to look like a savage.

Her smooth laugh radiates through my hut as she fills the bucket with water. "I'm glad you feel better." I hop to my chair.

"Here you go." She places the bucket in front of me and stands up. "Sorry, I need to go to work. I'm in a show tonight. Will you be okay? I can have the doctor come by to check on you."

To cover my disappointment, I unwrap another cookie and shove it in my mouth. I swallow and shake my head. "No need for the doc. My foot is already feeling better. Thanks for taking care of me." I hold up the couple cookies left in my hand. "And of course, these." She walks down the stairs to her boat. "Wait, do you know who makes these?"

She bites her bottom lip. "I might."

"Can you beg them for the recipe?"

She chuckles as she steps into her boat. "I'll see what I can do, Ball Boy."

CHAPTER EIGHT

"Come here often?" I joke as Aspen rows up to my deck. My pulse races with anticipation when our gaze meets. It catches me off guard. It's a foreign reaction toward a woman.

This morning, my foot felt better, so I went for a run, but I pushed it too much toward the end. The last thing I need is to return injured. I figured soaking it in the pool would help loosen it up.

"It seems I do." She lets out an awkward chuckle. "I was just coming by to check on you."

I have half a mind to tell her it still hurts, so she feels bad enough to hang out with me today. I'd take a pity visit, but that would make me an asshole. "It's good. Seems the doctor was right, I'll live."

A flicker of hesitation crosses her face. She twists her lips. Finally, she says, "I saw you out here so I thought I'd ask. Want to go for a ride?"

It takes every ounce of self-restraint not to jump up and dive headfirst into the canoe. *Hell yeah, I want to go.* "That depends…"

She arches a brow and waits for me to continue. "... as long as there's no shagging."

The words leave a sour taste on my lips, but when it makes her smile in amusement, it makes it worth it.

"I can't make any promises."

I freeze as I'm getting out of the water, momentarily speechless. My gaze darts to hers.

She snorts out a laugh and covers her mouth with her hand. "Oh my! I did *not* mean for that to come out that way."

I hold up my hands, smiling. "Whiskey, no matter how hard you try, it's a no." I've never told a bigger lie. Not even admitting the weed was mine compares to this, because if she asks, I would pleasure her for fucking hours. *Hours.*

She's still laughing when I step into the canoe. "Just ignore me. Trying to sound cool backfired."

She has no idea how hot she looks right now. There's nothing fake about her, and I love that. "I think you're cool, no need to try. So, where are we going?"

"I somehow missed a box for my deliveries this morning, so I need to go by my house to pick them up."

"WHISKEY, THIS IS A MILLION-DOLLAR VIEW."

I thought the view to the Hudson River from my condo, back in New York City, was amazing, but it pales in comparison to this. I spin around from the double sliding glass door and glance around the studio-sized home. The kitchen takes up more than a third of the space, looking out of place. Especially the three mismatched ovens against one wall.

"My dad built my home. And he knew I loved to bake, so he created a kitchen big enough that I could run my business out of it."

I turn to where she's sitting on her couch, watching me, and tilt my chin. "Your business?" Jesus, what else does this woman do? Her carefree laugh draws me to her. *Every. Time.* I step over to the couch and sit on the opposite end. Twisting my body to face her, I spread my arm against the back.

She bites her lip, and I watch it roll out of her teeth. Sexy as hell even when she's not trying. My eyes flash up to hers when she asks, "You know those cookies you love so much?"

The shock of discovery excites me. The random ovens and the long white box on her counter. It all makes sense. "You make those?" Her face brightens with a quick nod. "Is that why you always smell like sugar?" An intense desire to taste her, to know if *she* tastes like vanilla runs through my veins.

She's my poison. *Whiskey and sugar.*

Each second I'm around her, I take in a little more, except I'm not able to get enough. I should run away from this woman, her toxic mixture will be my undoing. But I can't. What scares me the most, I don't care.

My fingertips are inches away from her shoulder, the thin strap of her white tank top has fallen to the side. I reach over and drag it up her silky tan skin, resting it on top. Every nerve ending in my body spikes to attention.

Her eyes heavy with want, I wait a beat for her rejection or a simple shift away from me. I swallow hard when it doesn't come, afraid my next move will ruin the moment. I haven't been this nervous since I kissed Penny Rose in ninth grade.

I trace my fingers up her neck as I slide closer to her, across the turquoise velvet couch. It's taking major restraint to keep this slow.

"You should tell me to stop," I beg through my hunger.

"And if I don't?" Her lips part with a mute invitation.

I pull in a ragged breath, her sweet smell filling my lungs as I cup the back of her neck. Dipping my head, my lips brush against her shoulder as I whisper, "Then things are about to happen."

"Then stop talking, Ball Boy."

She snapped the ball right into my hands. It's all about the execution now. My mouth covers hers softly at first, waiting for regret to kick in. But rather than pull away, she pushes into my kiss with reckless abandon and her body folds against mine. Her taste causes a dizzying loss of control. Fingers scrape down my scalp and I moan into her mouth.

Someone clears their throat. I jerk backward and jump across the couch like a teenager busted for making out with his girlfriend. I push off and stand at attention, meeting the cold eyes of a tall gray-haired man.

"Dad, what are you doing home?" Aspen asks, her voice jumping a couple octaves. She joins me by my side. The man's glare bores into me for a couple more seconds before turning to her.

"I didn't feel well, so I cut my fishing day short. What are you doing?"

I step forward, holding my hand out. "Hi, Mr...."

Fuck! I don't even know her last name.

His jaw tightens, and he shakes his head, knowingly. "Mr. Foley," he chides, ignoring my outstretched hand. I drop it, shoving both my hands in my shorts pockets.

"Dad, don't be rude."

He lets out a humorless laugh. "I just walked in on my daughter making out with a stranger."

"He's not a stranger." She pops her hip out, her tone hardens and he stands taller, not about to let her win this.

"Aspen, he doesn't even know your last name. What are you doing? I thought you were over this stage."

My spine stiffens in her defense at his insinuation that I'm just another affair, and I'm pissed that he's being an asshole to his daughter. She shoots me a quick look of apology before throwing him daggers with her eyes.

"I am an adult and I would appreciate it if you treated me like one. This is my house and I would like you to leave." The carefree girl I've become addicted to becomes hard and cold. Her body radiates next to me.

I keep quiet during their war of wills, knowing my voice will only aggravate things. But this is awkward. The old man turns his icy glare to me. It screams death. My death.

"Whisk—" I stop. Not the best time for nicknames. "Aspen, I should go."

"That's an excellent idea. *We'll* leave."

She grabs the white box and my arm and drags me out the door, past her fuming dad. So much for good first impressions. She keeps hold of me until we reach the canoe. If I didn't need her help to get back to my hotel, I would tell her to stay.

I give her the time she needs as we row in silence. As much as that was uncomfortable for me, I'm sure it wasn't a cakewalk for her.

When we pull up to my hut, she remains seated. I sigh, wondering if this is it. "Whiskey, I'm sorry." I stand and pull myself up to the platform.

Glancing up at me through tears, she says, "Why are you apologizing? My father is the one out of line. You did nothing wrong."

I shrug. I'm partly responsible for their fight. "Do you have to leave?"

She blows out a deep exhale. "I'd rather not. But I need to deliver this and talk to my dad." Those are tears of guilt. She has a way better attitude about forgiveness than I do because if that was my dad, there would've been blows.

"Well... Aspen *Foley*, it was nice to meet you," I say with a lightened tone, flashing a smile. It works. She softly laughs, biting her lip and a slight growl from my throat escapes. I want to be biting her lip.

"You too, Ryker Dallas."

As I watch her canoe until it disappears, I wonder if I'll ever see her again. I'd be stupid to think I'm worth fighting with her dad. It's not like we can explore these feelings we're having for each other. Whatever this is, it's always been temporary. I would be just an affair.

I drop into the chair on my deck, not wanting to do anything. My last week here will suck if I don't see her again. The words from my coach blast through my mind. *Train. Stay focused. Stay away from women.*

Should have fucking listened.

CHAPTER NINE

ASPEN

The moonlight reflects in the quiet water, rippling as I slice through it. My arms freeze mid-row, slowing my canoe. "What am I doing?" I'm the adventurous girl, up for anything, until you add a man in the mix. I've spent the last four years building my company, focusing on the prize. My ticket out of here. And I was fine without the need of a man ruffling my feathers. Until, Ryker.

The pull between us is irrational.

Undeniable.

Unforgiving.

We're both digging our feet into the ground, but the force grows stronger whenever we're together. At what point do we give in, let destiny run its course? It's like we were meant to meet. But why?

I'm stuck here, and his life is in the States.

I look to the stars for answers. They're great at guiding me when there's darkness. Except tonight, the twinkling dots in the sky are silent.

"I should turn around. Nothing good can come of this," I say out loud to the still night. A fish flops out of the water to the right of me, causing a splash. I stare as the ripple irons out backward to glass. When he flops out of the water again in front of me, toward Ryker's hut, I smile. "You think I should go, huh?"

Taking it as a sign, I sink the oars into the water and pull my arms to my chest in one long stroke. The canoe surges forward. Spotting Ryker's hut ahead, the lack of lights inside breaks my resolve. *He's not there.* Probably out drinking, erasing me out of his memory. Why would he want to spend the rest of his vacation with a girl with a crazy father?

I slow my stroke and squeeze my eyelids shut. *I'll just leave him a note, apologizing.* When I get close enough, I grab on to the dock and tie the canoe up so it doesn't float away.

The ladder creaks under my bare feet as I climb to the platform. The boat taps against the wooden supports and the noise is deafening even though it's not loud. I glance at a neighboring hut to see if anyone is watching me, my heart patters at a quick rate. This feels wrong.

"Whiskey, this is a surprise." The deep raspy voice makes me jump backward in surprise. My gaze darts around the spacious deck, searching for where it came from. But it's too dark in the corners.

"Ryker? Where are you?"

A chair scrapes across the floor, and Ryker's tall body comes into view. With only his swim trunks on, one hand cups a glass, his rugged features highlighted by the moon's light. He takes a slow drink, his dark eyes watching me over the rim.

"Right here," he finally says, wiping the excess liquid from his lips with the back of his hand. His tone is harsh and instantly I regret coming.

"I was..." My voice wavers as I point to the water, not even sure how to explain what I was doing. "I didn't think you were here."

"Yet, here you are?" He takes a couple steps closer.

I swallow. "I was planning on leaving you a note."

Two more steps.

"And what was it going to say?"

"Apologize for earlier," I breathe out. He looms over me and arouses uncertainty that he wants me here. "But I can leave if you're busy."

"Taste this," he demands, holding out his glass.

I take the glass from him but hesitate to drink, torn from conflicting emotions. They have taught us not to take drinks from foreigners. We've heard of the drugs they've put in drinks to take advantage of women. I stare at the amber liquid.

"Tell me what it is," he adds.

I shake the idea from my head. He took a drink, himself. I take a small sip. A hint of aged wood followed by vanilla left in my mouth tells me what it is.

"Whiskey." I softly smile up at him.

He shakes his head and takes the glass from me and turns to set it on the table behind him. *It's not?* "See, I thought it was whiskey too." When he turns, an intense flare flickers in his gaze, sending shivers of desire through my belly. "But you've ruined me. My thirst for whiskey now has only one taste. *You.*"

His mouth slams to mine, devouring my lips. I match the movements of his tongue and he hums in approval, churning a need to make him want me more. Heat blankets my skin, an incessant ache building between my legs. His hands grip my ass through the thin cotton material of my dress, pulling me into his hard chest and I grind my hips against him. A growl vibrates in his mouth.

"Mmm, sugared whiskey."

I tilt my head, trying to take back control of my senses and figure out what he's saying. "What?"

"My new addiction," he rasps and blows out a low whistle as he takes in the full length of my body. "You're like my two addictions rolled up in one, five-foot-two, body of perfection."

I didn't want to drink in his professed attraction, but my mind soaks it in, getting dizzy-drunk on it. My fingers play with the edge of my dress and his brow quirks up in anticipation. He watches as I slide the cotton up over my head, dropping the dress next to us. The soft breeze pebbles my bare, sensitive nipples. He doesn't look away this time.

"You're a fucking exotic goddess," he growls, ravaging my body with his stare. I step close to him and run my fingers up his muscular abs. His muscles tighten under my touch. As if afraid to touch me, he grabs my hand instead and leads me to the private pool on his deck. Step by step we immerse our bodies into the warm water. Once we're both on level ground, he turns and picks me up. I wrap my legs around his narrow waist and he walks backward until his legs hit the underwater bench. When he sits down, his hardness hits my sensitive area and I shudder.

He rubs his face with a wet hand as if in agony and pulls in a ragged breath. "Giving in to an addiction can prove disastrous."

I'm not sure what he has to worry about. This is all an illusion to him, he'll leave this island and forget about me when he returns to his reality. But this is my life. I'm the one who should be terrified.

I cup his jaw. "What are you afraid of?"

"This ineffable feeling." My lips part, surprised by the depth of his words. His enormous hands encircle me, one at the nape of my neck, the other at the small of my back. Everything aches to be closer, yet the space between us is miniscule.

My tongue darts out, wetting my dry lips. He watches with greediness, and I swallow the lump of need swelling in my throat.

Kiss me, damn it.

"I won't be able to stop this time," he warns.

I take it as a promise.

"Are you expecting a touchdown?"

A wicked grin plays on his lips. "More like winning the game."

"Then you better start playing."

The encouragement works. His lips slam to mine. The hint of whiskey assaults my taste buds as he thoroughly explores my mouth. And when he's done with that, he moves to my neck, nibbling and licking.

His hand moves down, over my ass, and I rock my hips against him. When his fingers glide on the edge of my panties, I hum in delicious agony. I lift on my knees, practically begging. His mouth takes my breast.

Fingers move my panties aside and play with my slick entrance. But in the next second, they stop.

Everything stops except our heaving chests.

He stands with me still in his lap. "Whiskey, I need you in bed. I need to taste you."

Without drying off, he throws me on the bed, ripping off my panties. He lowers his shorts and his hard cock springs free. I definitely didn't dream how big it was. Soft kisses tickle my skin as he works up to my breasts, only to retreat south again. This time, he stops at my sensitive nub. I gasp as his tongue flicks it.

"What are you doing?" I squeal, pushing up on my elbows and moving my pelvis away from his face. He stares up at me with his crooked smile and raised eyebrows. My cheeks heat, a mixture of embarrassment and desire.

"Have you never—"

I let out an awkward laugh. Are we really having this conversation? "I've had sex before, if that is what you're about to ask."

But that's not what he was doing with his tongue.

He chuckles. "Has no man ever worshiped you?" I sink back onto the bed, covering my face with my arm, morbidly embarrassed. I don't understand what he's talking about. I've been with four men and three were foreigners. The boy from here was my first and there was no worshipping anything. More like relief when it was over.

Ryker moves my arm, laying it above me. I open my eyes and he searches for something in them. Hopefully it's not experience because I don't seem to have much. "I'll show you what a real man should have made you feel. When you see stars, feel free to scream out my name." He winks. I squeeze my eyes shut. Maybe if I don't know what he's doing, I won't be as flustered. "Eyes on me, beautiful." I stare up to the ceiling and shake my head.

Please don't make me.

But for the love of God, don't stop.

I blow out a silent breath when he kisses me on my stomach and doesn't wait for me to watch him. Desire tickles my lower belly. I fist the pillows above me when his lips blow on my sensitive nub.

Each delicious second that his tongue licks, nibbles and sucks, the ache builds to an unbearable desire until finally I succumb to the pleasure. I scream out unintelligible words as my world explodes into a million stars.

Merde! Where has that been all my life?

"Looks like you enjoyed that," he says, licking his bottom lip.

"That was…"

"Rock your world amazing?"

Yes, yes, and god yes.

"Erotic," I breathe out.

He bobs his head a couple times, an arrogant grin mixed with satisfaction lies on his lips. "I'll take it. Although, I'm a little upset you didn't scream my name."

I lift a mischievous brow. "Night's still young."

He wipes his glistening mouth on the sheets and crawls up, sucking on one of my perky nipples. "I like how you think."

I push him over and straddle him after he puts a condom on. My hair falls forward in my face so I wrap it up in a bun.

"Keep it down," he murmurs and I let it fall over my shoulders. Desire darkens his eyes. His hands squeeze my hips, lifting me until I'm hovering over his cock. Slowly he lowers me. I groan in pleasure at the fullness. And I don't think he's even halfway in. My thighs trembled, and he slows, allowing me to get used to the feeling. "Fuck, you're so damn tight. Are you okay?" I nod, lowering until my inner thighs hit his pelvis. Wow. A shock wave of heat shoots up my spine touching every nerve ending along the way. I lift, needing to move, and his fingers dig into my hips, trying to keep control. Still sensitive from his tongue, when his thumb circles my clit, I surge forward.

I rotate my hips against the full length of him. "That's it, ride my cock." His groans build my confidence, so I do it a few more times. "Fuuukk," he mutters, shooting up and flipping me underneath him. His chest heaves as he pulls in a controlled breath. "You're killing me." He sits back on his knees and thrusts hard. Tiny sparks shoot through me.

"Do it again," I plead. "Please don't stop."

Who is this woman, begging?

He doesn't. Rather, he plunges wildly until it pulls me over the orgasmic cliff again. He grunts roughly as I contract around him, making the already tight fit even tighter.

He tenses and convulses as he falls forward.

With a quick nibble on my shoulder, he rolls off me. The rapid rise and fall of our chests the only movement in the room.

"Whiskey, I think I just won the Super Bowl."

CHAPTER TEN

ASPEN

"Are you and your dad cool?" Ryker asks, tracing his finger up and down my arm.

My eyes flutter closed with his touch. The three hours of sleep we got last night catching up with me. But you won't find me complaining about Ryker's wake up call. A silent alarm of deep and slow. I'd set that alarm every day.

"Yes. We both apologized. He's always been overprotective of me. It didn't surprise me what he did. But I'm sorry you had to witness it." The part I skip is he demanded I stay away from Ryker. Easier said than done.

"You said he had cancer?"

I nod.

"He looks like he's in great health. Is he in remission?"

"Yes. He's lost a lot of weight though."

"Hmm," he responds. I glance up, wondering what's on his mind. Does he not believe me? He rolls us both over, hovering over me with questions in his eyes. "Are you still going through a *stage?*"

I blow out a heavy breath, furious my dad threw that in my

face. In front of Ryker. Pushing him over until he falls on his side, I sit up, clinging to the comforter.

"That stage is in my past. You don't want the details." I draw lines in the blanket with my finger, focusing on the indentions.

"Were you hurt?"

I jerk up to meet his concerned expression. "No. It's not like that." There are horror stories of women from the island getting raped by foreign men. It's why my father taught me self-defense. I've made some stupid decisions, but I've been lucky. "When I first started working at the hotel…" I pause, hating how I'm about to sound.

"Whiskey, it's okay. You don't have to continue."

But I do. I don't want him to think he's one of those men. "I wanted to leave the island so bad that I would have done almost anything. Men promised me things." I drop my chin to my chest again, ashamed.

Ryker lifts my hand and kisses my palm. "I remember when I first entered the NFL. I thought I was the shit." I lift a brow. Seems not much has changed. He chuckles. "Oh, it was way worse. I was living high on the hog."

I roll my lips to not laugh but fail miserably. "What does that mean?"

"I was making lots of money. And I did some stupid shit. Things I'm ashamed to admit, too."

I sigh, respecting that he's trying to make my mistakes seem inconsequential. "My father was furious when he found out." Because nothing on this island stays a secret.

"You don't say? I'm slightly scared that I'll wake tomorrow morning missing a couple fingers."

I snort out a laugh and push him on the shoulder. "My dad is a big softy. He just takes it to heart when it comes to my well-being, but he wouldn't hurt anyone." Ryker rubs his chin and nods like he has doubts. "But you're different. I'm here because I want to be with you, not what you can offer me. I know what this is."

His grin turns down. "Can you tell me, 'cause I've yet to understand."

I swallow the emotional rock choking me. Saying goodbye will scar my heart, but I couldn't walk away if I tried. "Two people enjoying each other's company?" I didn't mean for it to come out like a question.

He hums and pushes up to give me a quick kiss. "I'm definitely enjoying your company." But then he leans back, resting his hands behind his head. Early dawn light filters in from the wall of windows, highlighting his perplexed expression.

"Ryker, what's wro—"

My brain catches up to what's happening outside. Daylight. I jump up out of bed, scrambling to find my panties. When I find them balled up under the dresser, I lift the soaked flimsy material and groan.

Ryker sits up. "What's going on, Whiskey?"

"I have to go," I panic, bunching them in my hand. *I am not putting these on.* I shimmy into my dress and glance in the mirror, throwing my hair in a bun. "Thank goodness I baked all my cookies yesterday. But I have to deliver them this morning." I rush outside with Ryker on my heels and freeze on the platform. *What? No, this can't be happening.* "Ryker, my canoe is missing!" My gaze jumps around the water and other huts, looking under their platforms.

"I'm sure I saw you tie it up."

"I did!"

Pinching the bridge of my nose, replaying the events of last night and how this could have happened I come up empty. There's only one thing I can do. Spinning on my toes, I shove my panties in Ryker's hand. "You hold on to these."

I laugh at his boyish grin. "I can't very well be walking around with wet panties in my hand."

"What are you going to do?"

"I'll call Dante. He'll be up already."

Ryker's shoulders drop. "Well, at least I get to keep your panties. But knowing you'll be naked under that short dress..." His hand fists tighter around my panties.

His jealousy is cute. Misplaced, but cute. "I'll keep my legs closed." I stand on my toes and pull him down for a kiss. He leaves my lips swollen and wanting more before breaking the heated kiss.

With one quick glance before I rush out the door, he says, "Definitely enjoying the company."

"QU'EST-CE QUE... Non c'est pas possible !" I dart from my seat and dash to the front of Dante's boat when my house comes into view. Floating next to the dock is my canoe. I squint my eyes and notice it's tied up. How did it get there? I jerk my gaze to Dante, looking for answers, he shrugs.

"Maybe someone found it and knew it was yours, so they returned it."

I lean against the side of the boat, tucking my dress between my legs as the wind whips it around. *His explanation is plausible.* I narrow my eyes at my longtime best friend who has played many pranks on me in the past. "Are you sure you had nothing to do with this?"

He holds up both his hands. "Wasn't me, Manu."

I study him, waiting for his tells. A yank on his ear or a slap to his belly. Neither come, so he's not lying. He cuts the engine off and we coast to the dock.

Without waiting for the boat to butt up to the dock, I stand on the side and take a quick jump onto the ramp. I rush over to inspect my canoe. None of the gear is missing and nothing seems amiss. Maybe Dante is right.

"Thanks again for coming to my rescue," I say as he starts the outboard motor.

He spreads his arms out wide. "It's a sign. The gods are telling you to stay away from that man."

Between this and the fish, if it's a sign, they're giving me mixed signals.

"And maybe, they want you to see what is right in front of you." His voice carries off in the wind the farther he gets and I wonder if I just heard him right.

Who's in front of me?

My eyes widen.

Is he talking about him?

Noooo, that is not what he said.

He must have said something else I didn't catch. We've never explored that type of relationship and never will. Ignoring that thought, I run inside my house and get to work.

"Hey hun, you're getting a late start today," my dad says from the open door. Taping a box closed, I twist my lips and wonder if that's his roundabout way of saying he knows I wasn't here.

"Yep, it happens sometimes. You sure are visiting me a lot lately," I reply without looking at him, continuing to fill another box.

"Are you still mad at me for yesterday?"

I spin in place, leaning against the concrete counter. "What part? Where you embarrass me in front of a friend? Or when you order your adult daughter to stay away from said friend?"

"The definition of friend has changed from my days."

I scowl at him. "Maybe you need a *friend*." I spin on my toes and continue working.

It'd be good for him to have some fun.

He chuckles. "Don't worry about me, daughter." *That's right, I'm not allowed to worry about him.* I grit my teeth to keep quiet. I don't have time to argue with him this morning. "I told you I was sorry."

I release the heaviness in my chest at how I'm acting. Between our fight yesterday and my canoe disappearing, my patience is running thin. I look over my shoulder and manage a soft smile. "I know, I'm sorry, too."

His eyes crinkle in the corners with his warm smile. "I'll let you get back to work."

"Thanks, Dad. I love you."

"Love you too, hun."

CHAPTER ELEVEN

RYKER

"I don't know what you're complaining about, I'm doing what I was told."

Kind of.

The jump rope swooshes by my ears each second, my calves starting to burn. Sweat covers my body and I blink away a drop that landed in my eye so I don't have to stop. I'm in a rhythm now.

"Are you really doing what you were told?" Bree's snarky voice floats out of the phone through the speaker. "Because from the pictures I've seen, what you're doing is a little more like extracurricular activity." I don't even want to ask what pictures she's referring to.

The rope catches on my foot when my mind flashes to how Aspen's wicked naked body felt beside me in bed this morning. The way she's not at all self-conscious about her body. Her petite lean build with natural breasts that fill my hand. And my mouth. It's a stark opposite of the women I'm used to with fake everything. I lean over, hands on knees, catching my breath.

"See what happens when you think of women. You lose your

concentration," she barks and then laughs. "Stuff your dick back in your pants, Dallas. You're only there another week."

I blow out a breath full of spit and sweat and grab a towel to wipe off my face. "Stop worrying about me, Bree. I'm working harder than ever, getting ready to get down to business."

"My job is to worry about you."

I pick up the phone, done with this conversation. "Talk to you later, Bree."

"Dallas," she snaps, "If I have to deal with a baby in nine months, I will castrate you myself." I toss my head back, laughing. "You laugh now, but you won't be then."

"Don't worry, if I go into heat, I'll package my meat." *Again.*

She gasps. "I can't believe any woman would fall for your ass."

"Lots of women love my ass." Messing with Bree is one of my favorite pastimes. She gets paid well to put up with me and my humor. I'd bet she's shaking her head and rolling her eyes right now.

"I should quit," she jokes.

"But you won't because you love my ass too."

I hang up before she can respond. We've played this game many times. She's not going anywhere. I turn the music up and return to my morning workout so it'll be finished if Aspen stops by. 'Cause after last night, the last place I want my dick is in my pants.

"Mr. Dallas," beams Herman as he strolls up to my private cabana on the beach carrying a notepad for orders. Herman's charismatic personality is infectious. He's the friend that will always make you laugh. I'm usually that guy, so I like him. He's not as young as most of the other waiters, probably in his fifties, and he's lived here his whole life. "I've been hearing rumors about you." He points his finger at me with a toothy grin.

Story of my life. Rumors. Except, most of the time, they aren't true. I have a feeling this one is. Especially with pictures floating around. I shrug without a care. I'm not embarrassed to be seen with a gorgeous woman.

"You're the one who mentioned this is the land of romance."

He laughs out loud and then his expression turns serious. "I also informed you to be wary of that one." His warning about Aspen jogs my memory. *Pure heart, tainted mind.* Having been around her the past few days, nothing seems off about her to me. Aspen told me the people didn't take to her dad very well. I wonder if that has something to do with his warning. I mean, her dad was scary in a sleep with one eye open kind of way.

"I like a challenge," I say, waggling my brows.

His lips thin as he sets a knee on the cushion, leaning into the private cabana and at first I think I offended him, but then he says in a hushed voice, "I like you, Mr. Dallas. Just be careful." His gaze jumps to our left and right before he stands up. My head draws back from the serious warning and I too look around, prepared to find someone spying on us. It's not like it would be the first time someone was hiding in a bush to get close to me. But, no one is paying any attention to us.

People here are more passionate than Americans. Maybe he's looking out for Aspen more than his concern for me. I'm a foreigner and according to Aspen, people here don't care for us.

I nod to appease him despite deciding to take his warning with a grain of salt. "I'll keep a watchful eye. How about a drink, Herman?"

His smile returns, he takes my order and parades down the sand singing. *Crazy old man.* I lean back and stare out to the water. A cloud hides the top of Mount Otemanu. I grin thinking about our hike. Aspen is the perfect woman. Confident, athletic, loves being outside and she's not afraid to put me in my place. Most women bow down to my every whim, afraid they'll lose their chance with me, and I'm tired of fake women. It's refreshing being with someone who doesn't know my biography by heart before they even meet me.

I glance at every canoe passing by, searching for her face. It sucks having no way of getting ahold of her. Is this what it felt like before there were cell phones in everyone's hands? *I don't like it.*

Between being up all night, the warm breeze and reggae music off in the distance, my eyelids are heavy.

I wake from my light sleep when I hear someone approach. Herman sets my drink on the table. "Let me know when you're ready for your next one," he calls over his shoulder.

Thankfully, the private grass-covered ceiling in the cabana shields the sun. After taking a quick drink, I stretch out, focusing on the water again. My slowed breaths catch in my throat when I notice a woman stand up out of the water, like straight out of a James Bond movie, and start walking toward the beach.

Not any woman. Aspen.

I sit up and watch the most beautiful woman walk through the water. Droplets of water cascade down her body, leaving her tanned skin glistening. She smiles, catching my gaze. *Holy shit.* She's wearing a barely-there black string bikini. Her dark hair is slicked back, showing off her toned shoulders. I drink in every curve of her body. My heart slams against my chest and my dick rages against my swim trunks.

Her eyes never waver from mine as she gets closer. "Enjoying your stay, Mr. Dallas?" she purrs, crawling into the cabana like a tiger about to eat its prey. She can feast on my meat any time.

"I didn't realize it could get better." *But it just did.*

Her fingers release the white fabric from the ties holding it in place so it falls, closing us in. "And now?" she asks, inching her way on top of me. Her knee rests between my legs, brushing against my hard dick. Water drips off of her onto my bare chest and I stare up into hot liquid whiskey, melting my insides. *I have to be dreaming.*

"I was wrong. So, fucking wrong."

Threading my fingers through her wet hair, I pull her lips to mine. She sinks down into me, grinding her hips. *Jesus Christ!* Her hips alone are going to unhinge me. Nope, not dreaming as I feel the painful ache of desire in my balls.

She giggles as I hoist her up and flip her on her back. Her eyes fill to the brim with unadulterated need and lust.

"Find something funny?"

Her long dark lashes flutter as her gaze tangles with mine. "I'm happy you have the same reaction I do when I'm around you."

"If you don't want me to act on that reaction, I suggest you stop moving your ass. Because I would be okay with making you scream my name out here." Her cheeks flush under her tan. I groan when she licks her full lips, a silent invitation. "Whiskey, what exactly do you want?"

I want to hear her vocalize her silent plea. Tell me what she wants. After hearing she'd never had a guy go down on her, I was happy to oblige. Hell, I'd do anything she wanted. She just needs to ask.

"Ryker," she replies, flustered and trying to hide her modesty, "... you're great at whatever you do."

I chuckle as my ego gets a boost, but that's not what I want to hear. I drag the tiny triangle of material across her tight bud, so it's out of the way. She writhes under me and her breath catches as I flick my tongue over her nipple. I glance up and she stares down at me under hooded eyes.

"Is that what you want?"

She hums. Her hushed whimpers a direct shot to my dick. I move to the other boob, lingering as I assault it with my tongue.

Holding back until she voices what she wishes me to do next is about to wreck me. This was a horrible idea.

"What next?" I murmur while I pull on the ties of her bikini bottoms, revealing her pussy. Raising a curious brow, I wait for her to answer.

Her cheeks flush. "Just keep going."

"Keep going where?"

"Down there."

I laugh at her small gesture of her hand pointing south. That won't cut it. "Say it, Whiskey."

She stares at the ceiling, biting her lip. "Kiss me down there," she whispers.

"Where? Here?" I kiss her knee.

"Ryker," she pleads.

"Oh, right here?" I move up her thigh. She spreads her legs and I catch a glimpse of her slick entrance and my mouth waters. She shakes her head, still not looking at me. I move up and kiss her inner thigh and it tests every restraint I've ever had to not dip my tongue inside her. To taste her.

Fucking say it.

"Say *lick my pussy*."

Her body is begging for relief. "Ryker, I ca—"

"Yes, you can."

My eyes drag up her gorgeous body. I find it amusing that she's not shy about her body, but she's shy in telling me what she wants.

She lets out an adorable groan. "Fine. Lick my pussy." Her voice is a quiet rasp and filled with authority that sparks something inside me, a cross between victory and a visceral reaction to her demand. That I'm meant to please her.

I devour her mercilessly. She rocks against my mouth and fingers while biting her bottom lip to hold back her whimpers. I can't get enough to satisfy my insatiable hunger for her. Her release builds, her body tenses.

Yanking my board shorts down, I grip my cock and pump in unison with the rhythm of my tongue on her throbbing clit.

Pleasure explodes through her body, and I drink in her sweet taste. It pulls me over the cliff with her and I release in my hand.

Grabbing the towel, I clean up and then plop down at her side to catch my breath.

"Wow," she murmurs. I roll my head and her chest rises and falls.

Her cheeks are a shade of pink and her hair wild from writhing under me so much. I want to tattoo this moment to memory.

She's fucking perfect.

I can't help but lean over and bite her exposed nipple. "Don't make me wait so long next time."

I consider a repeat performance but then change my mind. When I taste her again, I won't stop there. Instead of using my hand, I'll be deep inside her and she won't be able to be quiet. I slide the triangles back in their place and she ties her bottoms together.

"I'll try not to," she muses.

When she scoots out of the enclosed cabana, I reach out and grab her hand. "Why are you running out of here so fast?"

Did I just spew that? Usually I'm the one taking off. But it's the surprising sense of loss making me cling to her. *Holy shit.* I'm turning into a woman.

She looks over her shoulder and shrugs. "I didn't want to crowd your space."

"Whiskey, if I wanted you to leave, you'd know." She spins on her ass, stretching her toned legs out, her toe brushes against my hip. I pick her foot up and start massaging it, digging my thumb into her arch. She moans, leaning on her elbows.

"Ball Boy, you're spoiling me."

"My way of saying thank you for hangin' with me." I skip the part that I'm desperate to make her stay. "So, did you find out what happened to your canoe?"

"It's weird. When Dante pulled up to my dock, it was there."

My eyes widen. Herman's warnings come back full tilt. I shake the idea out of my thoughts. There has to be a valid reason. "Do you know how it got there?"

She sighs and shrugs. "Dante thinks it might have got loose somehow and drifted away. Whoever found it knew it was mine, so they returned it." See, valid reason. It's possible.

"Did your dad say anything?"

She twists her lips and shakes her head. "When I saw him, he acted like I had been home all morning."

"That's good." An image of me as a teenager attaches to a memory, and it makes me wonder if it was her dad. "One night I snuck out of the house with some friends to TP a neighbor's house. The next morning when I woke up, there was a package of toilet paper on the floor next to my bedroom door. No note. Nothing. I knew I was busted."

I hope I'm wrong. A shiver runs up my spine. That's the last thing I need... dealing with a crazy father.

She flashes a confused expression. "How do you teepee a house?" she asks, making the two letters sound like words.

I laugh, switching feet to rub the other one. "It's where you throw toilet paper all over the front of a house and their trees. It's a silly prank. Did you do any stupid stuff when you were a kid?"

She searches her memory, glancing up to the canopy. "I can't think of any. If the teenagers I knew did anything stupid, I wasn't a part of it. The most rebellious thing I did was..." She pauses, squeezing her eyes shut with an expression of guilt. "Well, never mind."

"Foreigners?" I guess and she nods, not wanting to look at me.

"Fuck, Whiskey. I'm not going to judge you for that." Her lips quirk up to a slight smile and it kills me to see how hard she is on herself. "Okay, tell me things you did do."

"My dad homeschooled me, but I could go to dance lessons and hang out with Dante once I was a little older. My dad wanted a simplistic life, so we didn't have a TV. But I shared his love of music. Specifically, eighties music."

I wag my brows, and she rolls her eyes. "What? It's a glorious memory." One I'll never forget.

I'm sure she never will either.

"When I was sixteen, I asked my dad if I could go to college so I could get a good job at one of the hotels popping up everywhere. He surprisingly said yes. Even more so, he paid for me *and* Dante to go. So, we lived on the island, Papeete, during the week on the University campus and came home on weekends. We did that for almost four years."

"You got your degree at twenty?"

Her success in life is impressive considering her environment. I doubt many people here can say the same. A lot of people here are transplants. Hell, I thought she was too. "I have a Bachelor's in Business Management. My plan was to visit the United States after I saved up enough money, but that's when my dad first got sick. Instead, I stayed to take care of him and that's when I started my cookie business."

"You're incredible."

She shies away, looking down. "Thanks."

"Do you still want to go to the US?" Hope builds that maybe I'll see her again.

"I do. But since my dad was first diagnosed, it's been an up and down battle. I can't leave him."

"But, he's better, right?"

"For now, yes."

I drop the subject because her eyes glisten. And I don't want the little time we have together spent on her focusing on her dad. Disappointment knots in my chest. What is it with this woman? I should worry about my addiction to her. She's everything I don't need right now, *but everything I want.*

CHAPTER TWELVE

ASPEN

How do you put a fire out with gasoline?
You don't. You let it burn.

I'm trying to continue my life as if Ryker Dallas didn't storm into it and monopolize my daytime thoughts and nighttime dreams.

See, gasoline.

I whimper, ending it with an exhausted sigh, knowing I messed up. Even the cookies I'm baking remind me of him. I don't think I've ever seen a man with a sweet tooth like his. I've baked him an extra dozen for the past few days. I thought he'd be sick of cookies by now, but I think it's made his cravings worse.

Even the island's whispers haven't stopped me. Dante has kept his distance and I'm not even sure why. The horrible part, I don't care because I'm too caught up in Ryker.

I swore I wouldn't do this again.

The cookie pan slams into the rear of the oven and a couple balls of cookie dough bounce off the sheet. *Calm down, Aspen.* I carefully use tongs to grab the balls from the bottom of the oven, between the hot coils, and toss them in the trash.

"I'm afraid to know what that sheet did to you." I startle at the male voice.

"Dante," I say, holding my mitten covered hand over my frantic heartbeat. He steps inside, dressed in his normal attire. Bright floral shirt with plaid shorts. At some point, he'll learn they don't match. "What are you doing here?" If it wasn't five in the morning, there wouldn't be a question.

He shrugs, a somber expression on his face. "I haven't seen you in a few days, so I thought I'd drop in to say hi."

I throw the mitten on the counter and level him with a scrutinizing stare. "At five a.m.?"

"I knew you'd be home, baking." As opposed to being with Ryker. I guess he's not wrong. I have been spending my free time with him the last three days.

Silence hangs between us, and I hate it. It's never been this awkward between us. "What have you been up to?" I ask, breaking the silence.

He leans his elbows on the counter, clasping his hands in front of him. "Nothing new. You?"

He knows what I've been up to, so I don't mention Ryker. "The Ritz increased their order by three hundred cookies a day, so I'm excited about that."

"That's cool."

I huff in irritation and pivot to the sink to wash my hands. Why did he come here if he's going to sulk? "He'll break your heart."

There it is. The real reason he's here.

I stop short of drying my hands, putting the hand towel on the counter and cross my arms. "I don't have any grand illusion that this is something more than a couple weeks of enjoying someone's company, Dante. It's no different from when you guys do it. Yet, no one bats an eye when that happens, but god forbid a woman allows herself to have fun with a foreigner." The buzzer goes off behind me. Putting the mitt back on, I pull out a sheet of cookies and drop the hot metal on the stove. The metal clink echoes in my compact place, against the hushed morning. I pinch my eyes closed, the irritation growing that it's none of his business what I do. "And it's my heart. If it breaks, then no one has to deal with it other than me."

Palms slap down against the counter and he stands up tall. "That's where you're wrong, Manu." Slapping his chest with his fist, he continues, "I feel it, too."

The air stills as he storms out the front door mumbling a string of curse words. I watch him out my kitchen window as his boat speeds away.

I smack my hand down, his words squeezing my already fragile heart. Why is he so mad? Hurting my best friend was never part of the plan. I don't understand why he's acting different with Ryker than the other foreigners I had affairs with. He didn't like it, but he didn't take it personally.

Ryker's different.

I hang my head. That's the problem. My heart won't hurt from being left on the island, it'll hurt from him leaving. But it's not Dante's problem.

It's mine.

"Whiskey, what's on your mind." After my morning with Dante, I've been in a sour mood. I almost didn't come. *Almost.* I open my eyes from the shaded lounger to find Ryker staring at me from the pool. "You've been quiet today."

It's alarming that he knows me so well already. A man has never been this attentive with me. "Dante came to visit me earlier today." There's no need to lie. "He's worried about me."

Ryker pushes up, his muscles contract, and in one jump, he's out of the pool. Water gushes down his body and I can't stop staring at him as he walks over to his towel on the lounger beside me.

He faces me when he sits down, leaning his elbows on his knees. "Will you be okay?" Does he mean now or when he leaves? As if reading my mind, he adds, "In a couple days."

I bite back the emotion wanting to surface. I will not cry in front of him. "We both went into this knowing what it was. It is what it is."

He gives a sharp nod, swinging his legs around to lie flat. "That we did." His somber tone only buries the pain a little deeper.

"What does Manu mean?" he asks out of the blue. I loll my head his direction with furrowed brows. "Isn't that what he calls you?"

I chuckle once in understanding. "Yes. It's a childhood name he gave me. It means bird. Since I'm not a native, he said the birds brought me."

He lets out a noncommittal hum. "That's interesting."

"Why?" I would think it's more silly than interesting.

He moves off his lounger and straddles me with his panty-dropping smile. Or at least, my panties drop. His finger scrapes circles around my belly button, and I tense at the tingling sensation. "Seems I am an Ornithologist."

"Wow." I snort, remembering when I asked him if that was his occupation. "That's an astute conclusion."

He shrugs a shoulder while keeping his attention on his finger, dragging it up my chest. "It's true. I'm a bird watcher. I'm very intrigued by one that has whiskey-colored eyes and has a love for water and adventure. In fact, it's so rare that one must travel to the most remote islands of the Pacific. Watching it has been the highlight of my trip."

"And now that you've seen one?" My voice cracks, emotions I tried keeping at bay make their way out.

"You never forget your first time seeing one." He leans down and presses his lips to mine. "The rush you get," he says against my lips, "it takes your breath away." His words vibrate to my core. "I'm afraid nothing will compare." He continues moving down my neck, goose bumps pebble my skin. I run the tips of my fingers up his back and his muscles twitch under them. "But do you know what I like the best?" He lifts his head, his gaze seeks mine.

I swallow. "What?"

"That she's not a mockingbird pretending to be a blue jay."

There must be a lot of fake people in his world because he's brought it up before. It makes me sad that people can't be themselves.

"But are you a mockingbird?"

A man can't be this perfect.

"I've never been so real in my life. You make it easy to be me."

"Well, then... everyone is missing out."

"TAKE ME SHOPPING," he demands as he watches me tie my dress around my neck. I glance in the mirror and my hair is wilder than normal. Last night, Ryker wanted to have sex in the pool. I know what happens in those pools, so instead, I talked him into a midnight swim in the ocean.

I made sure there were no stingrays first.

After, I fell asleep with soaking wet hair. And now, I have crazy hair.

I glance up at him in the mirror while braiding my hair. "What are you buying?"

"I want to get my mom something before I leave."

As sweet as that is, my lips pout. I don't need a reminder of his departure. I kneel on the bed. "You're going to miss this." The words are out before I can stop them. At least they came out playful rather than needy.

His eyes rake over my body, and he swallows hard. This is

what I'll miss the most. The way he looks at me. Like I'm his next breath. "Whiskey, I definitely will."

"Someday, when I come to the States, I'll look you up."

Damn it. Stop talking, Aspen.

He's probably concocting an excuse already about not being available. I'm surprised when he flashes his signature grin. He tugs on my braid. "No matter what I'm doing, I'll make time to see you."

The ache building in my chest, sharpens, threatens. It's ready to scar me forever.

I push out of his arms and slip on my dress. Shopping sounds like a needed distraction. "Okay, let's go shopping. I need to stop by my bank first."

"Why? I'll buy you anything you want."

"No, you won't." I throw his shorts at him. "That's why I want to go to the bank. To return your money." It doesn't feel right keeping it when we've gotten so close. I never want the illusion that he bought me.

He stops pulling his shorts up mid-thighs and stares at me. "Aspen, absolutely not. I hired you for a job." He pulls them up the rest of the way. They sit right below the waistband of his underwear. He snaps his fingers, pulling me out of my daze, catching me staring at the defined V of his lower belly. "Up here, Whiskey."

"I give up. I can't stop staring at you. And I'm not sorry."

He chuckles once, but then his tone turns serious when he says, "Did you hear me? I'm not taking back the money."

"Ryker—"

"No. The money's yours. End of discussion." His resolve isn't to be argued with, so I let it go. At least my conscience feels better for trying.

CHAPTER THIRTEEN

ASPEN

"I'm already having withdrawals and I'm still inside you," he murmurs with rawness in his voice as he cradles me in his arms. My legs wrap around his narrow waist. "I've never had to say goodbye to perfection." A mixture of desire and emotion from his words causes me to moan out loud.

The moon casts a glow behind him, a whisper of a breeze blanketing us in the darkness of his deck. Our bodies are slick from sweat as he's making this a marathon versus a sprint. Slow and steady as he pulls out and slams into me again.

Our last night together.

Tears keep threatening, and I blink them back, knowing it'll only make it worse. I let him in. Let him know my heart and now it's cracking. The words *maybe someday* are on the tip of my tongue, but the words sour because they're the same words I said to the other foreigners. This feels so different, yet he's still leaving with no promises of tomorrow. But I don't expect it this time, so why does this hurt so much more?

"Aspen." Too caught up in my head, I hadn't noticed he

stopped. I peer up into his green eyes. "Don't question what this is. You've left a lasting mark on my heart," he murmurs, reading my mind.

I manage a smile through the tears. "I'm sorry," I say, wiping one that escaped.

His lips brush mine and he murmurs, "Don't be sorry, I'm not," before fusing our lips together. I've never had a man pour this much emotion into a kiss. For fourteen days, my heart has never felt so alive. But now, the tempo is an unforgettable beat. The feeling, an unforgiving touch.

I can feel the crack in our hearts.

Its vibration stings my soul.

The scar is irrevocable and deep.

Goodbye, Ball Boy.

BOLTING out of a deep sleep when the alarm rings loudly from the nightstand I stretch my arm, smacking it quiet. I rub the sleep from my eyes, and force my legs to move to the side of the bed, despite wanting nothing more than to give in to my body's fatigue. The darkness outside is about to flip a switch. It won't be long until the sun's light pours in.

Another monotonous day.

The weight of loss is slightly lighter this morning. It's already been a week since I waved at him from the dock, watching him leave, taking my heart with him. And every day since, I've promised myself that we would see each other again. But today, I feel I need to move on. My life is here. Whether or not I like it. Allowing myself to live for an inconceivable outcome isn't healthy.

No matter how much it hurts.

The sympathy glances don't help either. Despite knowing the ending, at least my friends don't rub it in. Except Dante. He's the only one who reminds me that I asked for this.

Who needs enemies when your best friend reminds you daily you messed up? But truthfully, the joke is on him. As much as it hurts, I don't regret it. It opened my eyes that there are kind men out there and not just assholes that use women. Someday, when it's the right time, I'll find another Ryker.

"Are you off to work?" my dad calls out from the end of the dock. I turn my head to look at all the white boxes filled with cookies, sitting on the boat's seat. *Isn't it obvious?* I bite back the snark and just nod. He rubs his neck with an awkward expression. One I've not seen since he made me get on birth control years ago.

"You know, Dante's a good guy."

I jerk my gaze from the rope that ties to the dock up to his. "Okay?"

Where is he going with this? "I was just thinking that you two have been best friends forever and sometimes that's a great foundation for a relationship." He sounds as uncomfortable as this conversation is for me. Does he think I'm desperate enough to settle because my options are limited here on the island?

I sigh, not wanting to get into it about not staying on the island after he's gone. It's morbid and I just can't. Not now.

"Dad. Thanks for being concerned. But Dante and I are just friends. Period."

He shrugs like he gave it his best shot and turns to walk back up to his house. I blink in confusion. That conversation was weird. He's never tried to set me up. And I didn't even think he liked Dante.

. . .

"HAVE YOU SEEN, DANTE?" Rose, one of my friends I dance with at night, asks as I drop off the cookies at the front desk.

Still reeling from my conversation earlier with my dad, my expression hardens. "Why does everyone think I should be with Dante?" I snap. Her brows shoot up.

"Girl, I was just wondering if you've seen him today. He was supposed to take out guests this morning, but never showed up."

Oh.

I wince, squeezing the bridge of my nose. "Sorry. Wow, that was uncalled for."

She leans on her elbows on the counter. "No worries. But who told you that you should be with Dante?"

"My dad."

"What? Really? They don't even like each other."

At least I'm not the only one who thinks that's crazy. "I know. That's weird, right?"

She bobs her head. "Well, I kinda thought someday you would probably end up together." I slap my hand down on the counter. "What? I think everyone did. You guys are inseparable."

"Because he's my best friend. That's it. I don't have any feelings like that for him. At all." I lower my voice as a couple passes by us. "Orana," we both say at the same time. Once they pass, we bust out laughing. We hate that word. "Anyway, I haven't seen him since yesterday. But now I'm worried. He always shows up." When her lips quirk up, I roll my eyes. "I can be concerned and not in love with him," I say sarcastically.

I slide into the golf cart, heading for the next drop off. I let off an audible groan. The last thing I want to do is think about being with another man. My heart still mourns the last one. I force myself to keep moving rather than go hide in my house.

As I'm leaving the last hotel, Mama Doe waves me down from her cart down the walkway. "Aspen, girl, come talk to me."

My shoulders drop. The last thing I want to do is talk. I watch her turn and walk to her first hut. With her back to me, I'm tempted to put the vehicle in drive and act like I didn't hear her. Shaking my head, I exit, knowing she would not be happy and that never ends well.

Following behind her, I glance down the walkway that ends at Ryker's hut. I freeze as pain twists in my chests. I've resisted the temptation to row past his deck, let the memories fill my vision until I can feel him again. I squeeze my eyes shut. *Stop, Aspen.* He's not there and no matter how bad you want to feel him, it's only a memory. It's not real.

"Mama Doe, I'm really not in the mood to talk," I murmur, stepping into the bungalow. She's already started cleaning the living room.

"I got something for you," she says, eyeing me with trepidation. "But I don't know if I want to give it to you."

"I don't understand. Why would you tell me you have something for me to not give it to me?"

"Because I can see the pain in your heart, child."

I smile at the older woman because I know she cares for me and I have always appreciated it. "I'm doing better. I really am."

Her eyes drop to my clothing and sympathy fills her expression. I look down. Okay, so maybe I didn't put much thought into my outfit today. Throwing on the first thing I saw probably wasn't a good idea. I look like Dante, today. Floral tank top with plaid shorts.

She goes to her cart and pulls out an envelope from the middle. Her fingers play with the edges. It's obvious she doesn't want to give it to me, but she finally relents and holds out the letter to me.

I take it. A quick thought flickers that maybe my mom wrote me. It's addressed to Mama Doe, though. When my eyes move to the return address area, I gasp and glance back up.

"Why did it come to you?"

"Open it."

I flip the envelope over and see that it's already been opened. Inside is another sealed envelope with writing on the outside, one sentence.

Please give to Aspen.

~Ryker

CHAPTER FOURTEEN

ASPEN

You only live once.

The last line of Ryker's letter repeats in my head. What is he thinking? I can't pack up and take off for two weeks.

Can I?

I run my thumb over my printed name on the plane ticket as if I'm testing to see if it'll rub off. This would be the cruelest joke ever. The ache in my heart has slowly subsided since he left. Would I be cracking it open if I took him up on his offer? Two more weeks with Ryker is a double-edged sword. I just don't know which side will cut the worst.

He says he misses me like no other woman. His words already making the ache build again. With men in the past, I'm the one left with the broken heart while they go about their lives like I never happened. But he wants me. Enough to send me a plane ticket.

Now, given the opportunity to escape this place, I can't breathe. Who will run my business? Who will take care of my dad? I pull in a deep breath. There's a simple answer.

Don't go.

Lying back in my bed, I drop my hand holding the note and

ticket, staring up at the exposed wood-beam ceiling. I'm so confused about his expectations. What will two weeks do? Satisfy his craving? And then I get to return to my prison? What would I get out of this trip other than heartbreak? Again.

My bedroom door swings open, and I shove the papers under the quilt. Scooting off the bed, I stare at my dad, leaning against the door, studying me.

"Hi," I say, stunned.

"I knocked. You didn't answer, and I knew you were home."

I cross my arms, narrowing my eyes. "Dad. I'm twenty-five years old. If I don't answer my door, there's no need to let yourself in. I could have been taking a shower."

He holds his hands up. "Sorry for being a concerned father. You've been moping around ever since that boy left and it worries me. I heard you received a letter today, and I thought..."

I gasp. "Does anyone mind their own damn business on this island?" Mama Doe would never have said something to my father. So, who did? "I'm fine. And yes, the letter was from Ryker." The letter is personal and I'm not about to tell him what it said.

His gaze jumps to where the letter is hiding and back up to me. "I was also coming to tell you I'm seeing Dr. Patel for a follow-up. Last week I got an MRI, and he says the news isn't good."

Guilt and sadness pulls at my heart and I rush to him, forgetting the last couple minutes. "Dad. You didn't tell me you were feeling bad again." I look him up and down as if I'll see the cancer. "Please, let me come to the appointment with you this time," I plead.

"I don't want you to hear this stuff."

He never does. He's only allowed me to one appointment. The first one where he was told he had cancer. Since then, he demands that I let him deal with it. But Ryker's questions about his cancer have me curious. I should know more.

"I don't care," I say, squaring my shoulders, readying for a fight. "I'm coming."

He stays silent for a beat and then sighs. "Okay. It's next Monday at ten."

I don't question why Dr. Patel is waiting a whole week. I just nod and flash a warm smile. "It'll be all right, Dad. I'm here for you."

Wrapping my arms around his thin body, I cherish the hug, knowing a time will come when I can only dream about these moments. "You've done so great at your cookie business, I don't want you to turn your focus away from that," he whispers into my hair. His over six-foot frame towers over my five foot two one. I wish I had gotten some of his height.

I dig my head into his chest. "Nothing is more important than you."

Even Ryker.

I won't be taking him up on his offer. Being here for my dad is my top priority.

"Thank you, honey." He pulls away from me and steps off my porch. "Can you make me some of your famous red velvet cookies? It'll make me feel a lot better." His fanatical smile makes me laugh. I'd make him anything he asked for.

"Girl, you're making a great mistake. This is your chance to explore." Mama Doe says, whipping out the sheet so it'll fall flat on the bed. After my delivery this morning, the girls at the front said she was looking for me.

I tuck in a side, helping. "He's sick. I can't leave." At my dad's appointment, a few days ago, we found out his cancer has come back. But it's a slow-growing cancer. The treatments the doctor talked about have a high success rate.

"Pshh," she says, waving me off. "He's not going to die anytime soon."

My eyebrows cock up in surprise. "You don't know that. What if something happened to him while I was gone?" I would never forgive myself.

"He doesn't even act sick, child. I've seen men on their deathbed. Your dad is not. I saw him on his fishing boat this morning."

I ignore her, tucking in the sheets with a little too much force. She doesn't understand. He's fishing because that's his lifeline. It makes him happy. I glance up at her after tucking the corner in. "Did you tell him I got a letter?"

The pillow she was fluffing plops on the bed. "Aspen, do you need to ask me that?" No. Of course she didn't. She might be everyone's Mama Doe, but she's so much more than that to me. She took me under her wing when I was a teenager and helped me in areas my dad wasn't able to. Like the day I got my period and my "I'll always be here for you" dad walked out of the room with a pale face and brought me Mama Doe instead. She's my adopted mom.

I sit on the bed and exhale heavily, hating that I'm second-guessing everyone. "I figured it wasn't you."

She fluffs the other pillow and fixes them at the head of the bed. "The ears on this island can hear whispers." That's the truth. After a long pause, she adds, "You can be back in a day. If something was to happen to Rudy, I could call the boy to get in touch with you."

I push off the bed, and she grumbles, coming up behind me to fix the tousled corner where I was sitting. Standing in the threshold that leads out to the private patio, I blindly stare out to the water. Am I stupid for not going?

If I go with the attitude that it's nothing more than a trip to help me plan my future, and seeing Ryker is just a bonus, then I won't be setting myself up for disappointment when I come home. I shake my head at my thoughts. Don't be stupid, Aspen. *You said that last time.*

"You're not going."

Dante's words slice through me as if he has any say. Despite being surrounded by water and land barely in sight, I stand up from the bench I've been laying out on and jump in the water. I'm done with this conversation.

The saltwater envelops me and it does nothing to cool me off. How dare he tell me I can't go. I swim toward the boat.

Maybe I'm not done.

When I pull myself up the ladder and find Dante, he's leaning against the canopy of the boat with his arms crossed. I take a deep inhale, my one last chance at calming down. Except it doesn't work.

"That was a pretty direct statement," I bark.

He shrugs a shoulder. "It couldn't have come out any clearer." His smug attitude only fuels the fire in my chest. Why is he being an asshole?

"Oh, it was loud and clear, all right. But why do you think you have authority to demand me to stay?"

He takes a couple steps toward me, holding a commanding stance, and I move backward until the back of my legs hit the bench. The carefree Dante I've known all my life morphs in front of me. His body hardens and his jaw tics. I'm looking at a stranger.

"Aspen, I'm tired of waiting." My head jerks back at the roughness in his voice, catching me off guard. *Waiting for what?* "I've let you have your fun with the foreigners, telling myself that when they leave, it's me you'll run to."

"What are you ta—"

"Stop talking," he shouts, cutting me off. I snap my mouth shut in surprise. "I thought you were over that shit. But, I told myself, this will be another reminder for you to see who is always here for you after those assholes leave. Maybe this time, you'd come to your senses."

The tension in my shoulders ease, and I blow out a puff of air as I realize what he's saying. He's been part of my life forever. Even though he's five years older than me, he's been there for me whenever I needed him. This makes me hate that he's wondered this whole time if there was a chance between us. Could there have been? I don't know. I've never had those feelings for him.

"Dante," I say in a soft voice, "I'm so sorry. I wasn't aware you liked me like that."

His hand grips my waist, stepping into me with longing in his eyes. "And if you did?"

Oh! This is going in the wrong direction. I wrap my hand around the one squeezing my side and pull it off and then step to the side. "Dante, you're my best friend," my heart does a little flip when his jaw tics again. "I love you... like a brother."

He flexes his tattoo-covered biceps, shaking his head. "Aspen," he growls, sounding so much older than when he calls me by my nickname. "You don't understand. You are mine."

I stumble at the blunt force of his words. "Excuse me," I grit through clenched teeth. Needing to nip this in the bud, I close the distance between us and stare at him in the eyes so he hears me. "You don't own me. You never have and never will."

He chuckles once. "We'll see about that."

What the hell does that mean?

His cryptic threat sends chills across my skin. I never thought I'd reach a breaking point with Dante. But I have. "Can you please take me home?"

Instead, the asshole sits down on the bench and stretches out his arms and brings his hands behind his neck. The boat rocks a little and I'm sure it's a wave of anger flowing through me. "No." His gaze never flickers. It bores into me as I stand stupefied. Who is this guy? I break the heated stare, glancing behind him toward the beach, knowing it's far.

But not too far. Most of it's shallow anyway.

"Fine," I say, clipping my pack around my waist and twisting until it's behind me. "You stay." Taking two quick steps up, I'm in the water before he can stop me.

"Aspen." I keep swimming when he calls out my name. It's too late for apologies. "You can't run from me." My body freezes for a moment, not what I expected him to say.

"Watch me," I whisper. I don't give him the satisfaction of looking back. Rather to prove him wrong and with more determination than ever, I swim as fast as I can toward the beach.

CHAPTER FIFTEEN

RYKER

"You fucking did what?" Jasper roars from behind me, slamming his locker shut.

I crack my neck, the tension between us lingering from practice. *Why is he such a goddamn pussy when the ball isn't thrown to him?* "Nobody was talking to you Jasper." I clench my jaw, not turning to look at the nosy wide receiver interrupting my conversation.

"What were you thinking?" he continues, ignoring me. "You already missed three games to go on a *vacation*. We have one game left of the season and everything depends on it. Your head should be in the fucking game, not some island chick. You're supposed to be the leader of this team." His voice carries and I fist my hand, readying to shut him up myself.

"Knock it off, Jasp," Donnie snaps, pushing off the bench. His enormous body stands tall. Jasper comes to my side, holding his palms up in defense as if he's not the one who started the fight, yet getting in my face. Nice trick play, asshole. I step forward so we're almost nose to nose.

"I'm just sayin'... you're thinking with the wrong head, Dallas."

He slips his headphones on and walks away. I plop down on the bench, hunched over, pissed that he's right.

I groan, running my hands through my wet hair. If I could just get her out of my thoughts.

"Why d'you do it?"

I hike up a shoulder, still not sure myself. "She's never seen a football game. I don't know… it'd be cool if she could see me play." I pause for a second and let out a long-winded sigh. "And she caught my Hail Mary." I'm hoping she does it again. Sending her a plane ticket is the riskiest Hail Mary I've ever thrown. And the odds are not in my favor.

"Aww fuck." He knows how monumental that is. Football is my life. Especially that pass and this perfect woman caught it. "I didn't realize it was that deep. I'm surprised you didn't drop to your knee and ask her to marry you," he jokes.

The thought crossed my mind.

But I keep that shit to myself. "Nah, dude. I jumped up and landed on a stingray. The asshole stung me."

He winces and bites down on his fist. "Oh shit. And you're still alive?"

I throw my hands up and give him an incredulous look. "Obviously."

He slaps my shoulder with a sympathetic expression as if he understands. But he doesn't. Hell, I don't even understand my own actions. Since I was a child, football has been my only focus, yet over the last four weeks, she has consumed my thoughts. After the first week of being home, I figured it was normal. I just got home from the most amazing couple weeks of my life. But week after week, those thoughts invaded all my mental space and after one night with a bottle of whiskey and my credit card, I booked her a plane ticket. I wish I could blame it on a drunken moment, but the idea had already formed… it was the liquid courage that made me follow through with it.

"And two weeks of sex with a goddess seemed like an outstanding idea," I add for good measure. It's not a lie, but I wish that was the only reason.

He drops his chin chuckling, thinking this was a horrible idea too but being the good friend he is, lets it go. Even though the odds are slim that she'll come, I had to try.

"Let's go celebrate our win and find me a fine piece of ass in this great state of Alabama. I dig these spicy southern girls and their accents."

CLUSTERS OF PEOPLE stroll through the exit and I search each of their faces. One by one. I'm afraid I forgot what she looks like despite knowing that could never happen. Her face is seared behind my eyelids.

When the current group passes, negative thoughts flicker through my mind. She barely knows me and to expect her to jump on a plane, leaving the only place she's ever known to come see me is insane. Hope dwindles. I drop in a chair when another group comes through the doors. The intensity of my search lessens as each person passes by. I yank down my cap further to shade my face when I get a few double-takes.

An hour and a half passes after her plane landed.

She didn't come.

I dig into my pocket for my phone and lean forward, my elbows on my knees, and open my text messaging app. I've never been the Monday-morning quarterback—regretting my decisions. *But I kind of do now.*

Me: cancel dinner.

I let out an audible sigh, my finger hovering over the send button, knowing when it's received I'll get a phone call. I don't want to talk.

"You look like someone sunk your boat, Ball Boy."

The sultry voice that's met me every night in my dreams greets me. I jerk my head up and my mouth falls open in surprise. I take a couple seconds to realize I'm not dreaming as I stare into amber eyes. Jumping up like my ass is on fire, I pull her petite body into my arms. "Whiskey, you came."

She trembles, wrapping her arms tight around my waist. "Hold me tighter. You didn't tell me you lived in an icebox."

I jolt back and glance down. *Shit, woman.* I yank off my black down coat and wrap it around her, covering her long-sleeved shirt. At least she's wearing jeans. If she thinks it's cold now though, just wait till she goes outside to the twenty-five-degree biting cold.

"I bet you didn't bring any warm clothes, did you?"

She stares at me, her red plump lips a slight shade of blue. I didn't even think that she might not own a coat. "Your assumption I have clothes for the cold weather seems a misjudgment of my wardrobe. When you say it's cold outside, I'm expecting it to be like sixty."

I laugh, cupping her face with my hands. "I'm glad you came."

Her face lights up. "Me too. What are we doing?" she exclaims as she stands on her toes and brings her cold lips to mine. Yet, there's no question left on her lips as I melt them with heat from my kiss. I hum at her sweet taste. Another thing I wondered if I had imagined. Her sugary taste is still addictive as I try not to swallow her whole. Her body folds into mine, pressing against me.

She smiles against my lips. "It's good to see you too." Staring at the woman who has me under a spell, I wonder how I'll be able to let her go again.

Aspen angles her chin at the sound of a picture being taken. She looks at the person with an awkward expression before turning her gaze to me. Pictures don't rattle me anymore and I forget how intimidating it might be for someone who has never been in the public eye before.

I loop my arm around her and grab the handle of her rolling luggage. "Sorry. It's part of being a Ball Boy," I joke, making her laugh. *Damn, how I've missed that carefree laugh.*

"It's weird to have a stranger want to take your picture."

That's just the beginning.

I lead her out of the airport to the waiting car so she's not inundated with more awkward exchanges because they'll come. I've never felt the need to protect someone. Before I didn't give a shit. It comes with being with me.

But I'd like her to leave here with her innocence in place. The last thing I want is for her to regret coming.

Once inside the warm town car, she slides next to me, her body shivering. "Ryker, it's so co—" she stops mid-sentence once we roll out of the garage and light from a cloudy sky filters into the car. Her eyes widen to the size of saucers as she peers out the window. "What is that?"

Large white flakes dump out of the sky. My lips crack into a smile at the amazement in her expression. "Whiskey, that's snow." She covers her mouth and tears pool in her eyes. She leans over me to get a better view.

"It's gorgeous." It's weird she didn't even know what snow looked like. "You told me New York City was ugly."

"I didn't say that *exactly*. I said compared to Bora Bora, it's ugly." Driving over the George Washington Bridge into the city, I try to recall the first time I came to the city. Was I in this much awe?

"It's not." She beams. "It's a different beautiful." *So are you.* She turns her attention back to me. "Thank you. For bringing me here."

My eyes tangle with hers for a silent beat. I wrap an errant hair that's fallen out of her bun behind her ear and she closes her eyes at my touch. Her reactions to the simplest gestures spikes a buzz inside me. A quick glance out the window, I see we're getting close to my condo.

"Are you tired from the flight?"

Her body relaxes in my arms. I can see the fatigue in her face.

"A little. I need a shower though."

I hum, moving closer to her and nibbling her ear. "Already want me naked, huh?"

"Well, I know how much you enjoy it. Being naked and all."

"Just when you're looking," I say, winking.

THE FIRE CRACKLES near our feet. Once she met the warmth of the fireplace, she wasn't moving. So, I brought the bed to her. Her laugh echoed throughout the penthouse as I dragged my mattress into the living room.

She snuggles into my side, tugging the down comforter over us so chilly air can't get in. "I can't believe you brought this in here." My cock jumps to attention as she rubs her leg between mine.

"I make sure all my guests feel comfortable."

She pushes up on her elbow and cocks her head to the side. "Do you entertain guests often?"

I toss her under me, silky brown locks frame her beautiful face. "Only the ones with strange accents who can move their hips at supersonic speed."

She wrinkles her freckled nose, curling her fingers around my neck. "Wow. That sounds like an interesting guest."

"You should see how she rides my dick." She snorts out loud at my dirty words and her face blushes under her tan. "But you'll have to wait on that." I kiss her forehead and she looks up through long lashes. "Having you right here is enough for now. Sleep."

Her breaths slow. As she sleeps, a soft hum vibrates against my arm and I wonder if she's dreaming of me. Has she been able to move past our time together? Because this last month she has lived behind my closed eyes. I couldn't have evicted her if I tried.

"I HOPE you don't mind, I planned dinner." She pulls one of my team sweatshirts over her head. It swallows her, hanging above her knees, but it's sexy as hell seeing her in it. Flipping her brown hair out from under it, her lips quirk up.

"Not at all." She glances down at the oversized sweatshirt and holds her arms out. "I guess I should change."

"Um, no you're not. I like you in my shirt." She snickers as I draw her to me. I can't stop touching her. "We're having dinner here. And... my best friend and his wife are coming." I sigh with the last part. They invited themselves, but I could have said no. Hindsight, I should have. *Way to overwhelm her, Ryker.*

"You were that sure I was showing up, huh?"

I give her a peck on the tip of her nose. "I told you from the very beginning that I'm irresistible." I skip the part where I had my doubts and worried that the dinner would have been more of a sympathy get together than a welcome dinner.

"I can't argue that. Especially now," she jokes, pushing up to give me a chaste kiss. "I won't change, but I need to do something with this wild hair." When she pulls out of my grasp, my fingers are already itching to reach for her. *What the fuck?* This needs to be controlled before I smother her.

"I HEAR YOU'RE A BAKER," Addie says. "Or as Ryker has mentioned, his new sugar dealer."

She glances over at me from across the table. "Yeah, his addiction is out of control."

That's the truth. Except she's the addiction.

"You ready for Sunday?" Aiden finally chimes in after being quiet the entire dinner. Always the one to analyze a situation first. Aspen found out that Addie was a crime scene investigator and she's been drilling her about it so his aloofness wasn't obvious.

Aspen puts her wine glass down with her brows furrowed and asks, "What's Sunday?" In the corner of my eye, Aiden shakes his head. I hadn't told Aspen yet. I haven't had a chance.

"Our last game of the season."

Her smile grows and her voice turns up an octave when she says, "I'm going to an American football game?"

Her excitement is why I wanted to bring her here now. "Sorry, I hadn't told you yet," I direct my glare toward Aiden, "this bastard beat me to it."

Palms up with a gaping mouth, he huffs. "How the hell was I to know that you didn't tell her about the most important game coming up?"

"All games are important," I clarify.

He shrugs a shoulder and bobs his head. "You know what I mean."

"What's special about this one?" Aspen asks.

"It's the last game of the year—"

"And they have to win," Addie interrupts me, "or they're out of the playoffs."

One of the best things I like about Addie, she loves football. But she needs to shut the hell up. I don't need a reminder about the importance of winning. I give a hundred percent to win every damn weekend. There's enough pressure thrown at me from everyone else.

I lean back in my seat and cross my arms. Addie reads my irritation. She winces and mutters, "Sorry," and stuffs a chunk of steak in her mouth.

"Ryker, are you sure this was a good time for me to visit?"

"Yes. I brought you here so you could watch a game. Don't

listen to them," I wave my fork at my friends. "Every game is as important as the last. This one is no different. I have practice during the day, but I figured you could explore the city while I'm gone. Pete will drive you wherever you want to go."

"Oh," Addie quips, practically choking on her bite. She grabs a quick drink of her wine and then continues. "I can play hooky one day and we can hang out. Do some girly stuff." I narrow my eyes at her. *Addie is not a girly girl.*

Aspen smiles at her. "I'd like that."

"Ryker, can you show me where you keep your bottle opener?" I turn to Aiden, wondering why he's asking. He knows damn well where it is. He does a small jerk of his head toward the kitchen. I hesitantly get up and follow him. This can't be good.

"What's up?" I ask, leaning against the counter, crossing my arms. He reaches into the fridge and grabs a beer and holds it up.

The smartass replies, "I really needed one." I point to my other side where the drawer is and I stare at him. He cracks a smile as he opens the drawer, taking out the bottle opener. "I have some concerns." He wipes his mouth after taking a long pull. He's FBI, he *always* has concerns.

"Why? You knew I sent her a ticket. Where the hell is this coming from?"

"I see how you're looking at her. You like this woman."

I hold my arms out and try to keep my voice down. "What did you expect? I flew a woman who lives thousands of miles away here to see me because I didn't like her?"

"Are you sure you're not an out for her?"

My arms drop and irritation hardens my jaw at what he's implying. "Aiden, she's an American. She didn't need me to come here. And I don't need Addie sniffing around her for you."

"Hey," he states, pointing his beer at me and then gesturing to the living room. "That surprised me just as much as you."

"Addie will do anything to get out of having that gaggle of kids you keep insisting on."

He tosses his head back, laughing. "I think you're right. Just be careful, brother."

"You don't have to be concerned about Aspen. She's the most genuine person you'll ever meet." *The only thing I need to worry about is not getting too deep with her. She's been here one day and already has me knotted up inside.*

We both return and the girls look up at us with curious expressions. Aiden holds up his beer. "Got it taken care of."

"You two are as bad as girls needing to go to the bathroom together," Addie says, rolling her eyes. *There's my non-girly-girl friend.*

We cut the night short because Aspen can barely stay awake. Jet lag is a bitch. But it's okay with me. The quicker I can get her naked, curled up to me, the better.

CHAPTER SIXTEEN

ASPEN

"I'll get used to it."

Ryker shakes his head, worry etched in his forehead. Determined to struggle through the cold stinging my body, and make Ryker stop worrying, I yank him into the tenth coffee shop we've passed. American's like their coffee.

The heat, like a brick wall, threatens to shatter my frozen bones. "Go grab us those seats." With a tip of his head, he motions to a table by the window, looking out to the snow-covered streets, "and I'll grab a couple coffees." I nod, pulling off my hat and walking between a couple tables.

I overhear a couple girls whisper his name as I sit and seconds later glance at me with curiosity. There's a lengthy line to order so I busy myself with taking off my coat to avoid the questioning expressions. After a few minutes, I glance to the line to see how far he's gotten. It doesn't help that he stands out in the crowded room. Between his looks and his height, it's hard for anyone to miss him. He's caught more people's attention, yet his focus stays on me. He smiles and winks. You can hear the whiplash of people's head jerking my direction. My cheeks burn and I swiftly turn my attention outside.

Not used to seeing bare trees, their bones exposed, my body aches for them in these harsh elements and I wonder how they survive. I focus on the boutique shops lining the colorless street. Everything in the city seems dull during the day, yet bright and festive at night with all the lights on the buildings. Last night, seeing how the city wakes up after dark, I was awestruck. The energy fueling my soul. It was love at first sight. People crowd the sidewalks, not bothered by the freezing temperatures. Well, per Ryker, today is a gorgeous day. Sunny and not as cold as last week. I shiver again thinking about it being even colder.

"Still cold?"

Ryker's voice startles me. I swallow my groan of pain so I don't cause a commotion, holding my hand where I tried to karate chop the table.

He puts the coffee on the table and sits quickly, reaching under the table for my aching hand. "Are you okay?" His fingers softly graze over the pain.

"A little embarrassed." I chuckle. "How did you get through the line so fast?"

Humor dances in his eyes. "I know people."

I glance around the room for a second, every eye pointed our direction. "I would say so." He doesn't bat an eye at the gawking, just continues caressing my hand, giving me all his attention. "Pretend they aren't there. It's only you and me in this cozy warm coffee joint."

I can't hold in the loud laugh escaping my lips. "There is no way I can pretend we're alone. Is this what it's always like for you? No privacy, ever?"

He shrugs with little care. "I've been in the public eye for so many years. I learned a long time ago, it's better to use it to your advantage than your demise. Because if you let it, it'll crush you."

"I see that because I'm feeling awkward right now." I flick the cardboard wrapper on my coffee. My normal confidence shaken. Compared to most of these women and their perfect hair and makeup, I stand out.

"We can leave."

"No." I sit up taller, forcing myself to settle down. "This is part of you, so I'm good." It's obvious, now, why so many famous people come to our remote island. Privacy.

Ryker sighs. "You sure?"

"Yes. But... *are you sure*? I don't want to embarrass you. Look at me." I hold my hand near my makeup-less face and wild hair.

He licks his bottom lip. "Whiskey, you're all I see."

The truth in his words flash heat in his eyes. I fidget in my seat, not used to a man directing all his sexual energy on me.

"Don't second guess yourself. New York City or Tahiti, you have all my attention." He gently squeezes my hand.

"It's all these clothes," I say to change the subject. "There are so many layers." We spent the morning shopping at a place called Macy's. The building was probably larger than all the buildings put together in Bora Bora. It was intense. But I have enough winter clothes to last me two weeks.

"I can fix that," he says, wagging his brows. Thoughts of us in the shower this morning swirl through my mind. Droplets of water cascading down his broad shoulders as his mouth sucks on my breast. A low growl comes out from the back of his throat, bringing me to the present, and he cups my neck, pulling my face to his. Our noses touch. He lowers his voice, "I'm perfectly okay with having you naked the entire time you're here. Especially when your eyes light up like that when you're thinking of me."

I lick my bottom lip, and his eyes dart to my mouth. "That imagination of yours is overambitious."

He chuckles, leaning closer to my ear. "Tell me you weren't thinking about my cock filling you."

I was getting there.

I swallow, the sexual magnetism between us sparking my pulse and melting the cold inside me. My cheeks heat.

"Ryker," I say in a tangled breath.

"All these women have nothing on your natural beauty." His lips brush against my cheekbone until they meet my lips. I pop my bottom lip out when his kiss is too quick. "Drink, so you can get warm."

"Oh, I'm warm."

"Me too, babe. Me too." He adjusts his pants and glances at his watch. His smile falls.

"Is it time for you to leave?"

"Yeah, but I don't want to." He pulls out his phone. When he pushes it across the table, I lower my gaze in confusion. "I got you a phone." *Okay.* Not his phone, *my phone.* I stare at the small electronic device.

"Ryker, do I really need that?"

"Yes," he says firmly. "You're in an unfamiliar town, hell, continent, so you need to be able to call me."

"I can easily ask someone with a phone if I'm not with Addie."

"Woman." His expression hardens. "Do. Not. Ask a stranger for their phone."

I sigh and put my hand over the phone. "Fine. Show me how to use it."

After a quick overview of how to turn it on and make a phone call, I'm confident I can use it. As for all the other colorful squares, they won't ever be used. Except one, the tiny map one.

When I notice him looking at the time again, I tell him he needs to go before I get him in trouble. He kisses me on the nose. "Have fun with Addie."

"How long will you be gone?"

He flicks his wrist, looking at his watch again, internally calculating. "Today's an off day, so I'll be working out and going over some film. I should be finished by dinner. Let's plan to meet at six at my place?" I nod. "Buy something sexy for dinner tonight."

"How in the world do I wear something sexy when I have on ten layers of clothes?" I laugh, holding out my arms that feel like I'm wearing five pounds of clothes on each side.

He digs his hand in my hair and tugs, sending a tingle down my spine. "I'm sure you'll be creative."

I twist my lips. "I accept that challenge."

His phone dings and he grunts when he sees it's one of his teammates asking where the heck he's at. "Whiskey, I gotta go." He halts after just one step. "I almost forgot, give these to Addie." He pulls out his wallet and hands me two tickets to the game this weekend. "I have the other ticket for you. Tell them to pick you up. I promise next week, it's just me and you, babe."

THE SNOW CRUNCHES under our boots as we stroll the busy streets. I'm overwhelmed by how everyone is in a hurry to get somewhere. It makes sense why foreigners would always say we lived on island time. Addie's a great tour guide. And it's refreshing not having someone constantly ask, or *not ask*, to take your picture. It's hard to get used to. Am I supposed to pose? Smile? Act like they're not there?

A closed storefront catches my eye and I stop, take a step backward so I can see the turquoise and white polka dot sign and then stare inside. Empty display cases that once held pastries makes me sad.

"I wonder why the bakery closed."

A constant flow of people passes us, so it's not a lack of customers. "Places come and go all the time down here. Maybe they moved to a better location or a bigger place."

A place like this would be perfect for me. Dreams I'd talk myself out of sneak their way back into my mind and I shake them out as quick as they arrived. Why get worked up over something that can't happen anytime soon?

"Is that something you want to do? Open a bakery?" Addie asks, glancing inside, too.

I sigh. "Someday, when I leave the island. I'm just not sure where or how I'd do it. For the time being, I have to stay in Tahiti."

"Tell me about your home? After we're done having a million kids, I'm making Aiden take me."

I tell her all the best things. No need to include the things I hate. While walking, we pass a store that has a beautiful black lingerie set in the window and I have an idea. Might as well make this one layer. I pull Addie into the store.

An hour later we're outside again, braving the cold. I don't know if I'm getting used to it, or I've become numb. "This is the cutest packaging," I say, holding up the black and pink bag with black tissue. I should do a cuter box for my cookies.

"Ryker is taking me out tonight. Do you know a place I can find something?"

"Fancy?"

I lift a shoulder, not knowing what fancy is like here. "He said sexy."

She rolls her eyes. "Of course he did. He's a man. Well, I have the perfect place to get a date-night outfit."

Thankfully, not too long later, I'm defrosting my brittle bones again in a warm shop. The lights shine bright in the modern space, filled with colorful clothes against sharp lines and glossy-white walls and fixtures. The hint of music plays in the background.

"Addison, what brings you in?" A man, dressed in a perfectly tailored blue suit, approaches with his arms out wide. He wraps them around Addison and glances over at me with intrigue.

"Hey, Roberto. I'm not here for me today. This is my friend Aspen. She needs an outfit for tonight."

"Give me your coat," he demands abruptly. I shiver thinking about taking it off, but I do as I'm told, handing it to Addie.

His eyes scan me from head to toe. I stand motionless in the middle of the store. He taps his finger on his lips and I spare a quick glance at Addison. *This isn't awkward at all.* She laughs at me.

"I'll put our stuff over here." She walks to a set of chairs and drops all our bags on the floor, taking a seat on one.

Roberto clears his throat and I jerk my attention to him. He twirls his pointer finger in the air, gesturing for me to spin around.

When I complete the circle, he asks, "Where are you going tonight?"

"Um... I'm not sure." I peer over at Addie. "I guess I can text Ryker."

"Ryker Dallas?" Roberto beams. Panic builds that I shouldn't have said that.

"Yes, Roberto, it's Ryker. Don't get all starstruck," Addie teases. "Do you have a phone? You can text him."

I run over to my bag and dig for the metal device. Staring at it. "What button do I press for a text? He showed me, but..."

Roberto's confused expression jumps from Addie to me and back to Addie. She ignores him and comes over to show me. After pressing send, I stare at it, waiting for him to text.

"Did he already get the text?" I ask after a minute of no response, holding up the phone.

"His phone did, but if he's busy, he probably won't see it. But he'll check soon, I promise."

She was right. He ended up texting me moments later. I repeated the name of the restaurant to Roberto, and he immediately got to work. He hands us two glasses of champagne and flittered around the store, grabbing several pieces of clothing, mumbling to himself, *"Not too fancy."*

Once satisfied with his selection, he ushers me into the

dressing room. When he shoves the first dress in my hands, I stare at him.

"You expect me to wear this in the snow?" I hold out a dress that will barely cover my breasts and butt. Typically, I'd be on board, but hello frostbite on places that shouldn't be frozen.

He tsked me. "Don't be an Addison."

I peek my head out at Addison as he ignores me and walks away. She chuckles and scrunches her nose at him as he stands by her. "Let's just say I try to be more conservative," she snickers.

He huffs. "Try. That's the keyword."

"I'm not conservative, but I'd like to be warm," I yell over the closed door.

"I like her," he yells back. I'm sure jabbing Addie.

When I walk out I already have goose bumps blanketing me. "This isn't going to work."

His grin grows. "Gorgeous, this was to get an idea of your body. You had too many layers on. And you have an amazing figure."

"Why didn't you just ask?" I unzip the dress and step out of it, baring my body. Thank goodness I wore cute panties.

Addie gasps, covering her eyes. Roberto claps once. "I *really* like this girl. Are you a model?" he asks, ushering me into the room, handing me the next outfit.

I furrow my brows. "No. Why?"

"Just a guess. You're very confident in your body. And you could be."

"She's French," Addie adds, still covering her eyes.

"Ah, yes. The beautiful French. It all makes sense now," he replies, shutting the door.

Roberto has one rule for winter outfits. Either you show off your legs or breasts. I chose legs. But he helped with that, too.

The outfit is definitely sexy.

"I just booked your next stop." Addison and I stare at Roberto, confused. "If I know Addison, she didn't book you an appointment for hair and makeup."

"Roberto, thank you, but that's not nec—"

"It is," he interrupts, holding his hand to his heart as if I'm disappointing him if we don't go. "You're naturally gorgeous, so their work will be easy."

Addie sighs. "There's no sense arguing with the stubborn. Let's go get our hair done."

"And makeup," Roberto yells, as we step out the front door.

"He was fun," I say, sarcastically.

"Him and my best friend always gang up on me. But he knows what he's doing. He makes me beautiful in everything he's dressed me in. And you're drop-dead gorgeous in that outfit."

As we walk to the salon, we talk about my home again.

"So, does your mom and dad both live in Bora Bora, too?"

Once upon a time. "Just my dad. My mom left when I was a baby. I think she's living in the US. Well, maybe?" My voice is heavy with uncertainty.

"Have you ever considered trying to search for her?"

"All the time," I answer truthfully. One reason I wanted to come here after I graduated college was to see if I could find her. "Except, she might be here or in France."

"I could try to look her up."

My feet freeze in the snow as I suck in a heavy breath of frigid air. Someone slams into me.

"Oh, I'm sor—"

"Don't fucking stop walking in the middle of the sidewalk," the guy spits out in a heavy New York accent as he walks around me. My face burns with embarrassment and I step close to the red brick building, out of everyone's way.

"She said sorry, asshole," Addie yells out to him. He sticks his middle finger in the air without turning back. "Screw him," she waves him off, stepping next to me. "Some people are unhappy human beings. So, what do you think?"

"About that guy?" I ask, terrified.

"No. About me trying to find your mom."

Oh, that. I play with the ends of my hair. "I… um… I'm not sure." My stomach flutters with possibilities, both good and bad. *Mainly bad.* She's never tried to see me before, why would she want to see me now? But what if she does?

"I didn't mean to upset you."

"No," I blurt. "I'm not upset. It's scary. She left me. And I worry about how my father would act if I found her."

"It's totally up to you. At work, I could easily look her up."

I blow out a long-winded breath. Even if I didn't contact her, at least I would know where she is. "Okay."

"Okay, you want me to look?" she asks, slowly.

"Yes, let's find her."

CHAPTER SEVENTEEN

RYKER

"Whiskey, I'm home."

I freeze in the middle of the entryway. The words hit a spot in my chest I wasn't expecting. A peek into my future. Coming home to a family. Kids spilling out of their rooms and running for me. A wife wrapping her arms around me.

Holy shit.

I shake the image out of my head. What is this girl doing to me? It was bad enough the shit I got from the guys today, but now this? I need a drink.

Setting a tumbler on the kitchen island, I toss in a couple pieces of ice and then wiggle off the top of one of my favorite whiskeys. The amber liquid coats the ice. As I bring the glass to my lips and take a sip, over the rim I spot Aspen walk in the living room.

The drink might as well be water because every one of my senses focuses on the gorgeous woman. I slowly drop my hand, placing the drink on the counter. How did I get so lucky?

"Drinking without me?" she asks, walking up to me.

Her beauty renders me speechless.

"Wow. I don't think you've ever *not* had something to say."

My tongue coats my bottom lip as if I can taste her on my lips. "You took my breath away."

She lifts my drink and I watch intently as the glass rests on her plump red lips. I watch her neck as she swallows. She hums. "That's tasty."

My eyes roam her body again. A long-sleeved black shirt fits snug against her petite frame, outlining the curve of her boobs. The black skirt is short and fuller, sporting a leather belt that wraps around to a bow. I run my finger along her above-the-knee suede boots, to her bare skin, up to the edge of her skirt. The itch to move higher grows into a dizzying current racing through me. "The boots are fucking sinful."

"You like?"

"Like is not the word."

She chuckles.

I stare into her eyes, not used to the smoky makeup that adorns them. She blinks her long lashes. They look longer with mascara on them and makes her amber color stand out. "I'm glad you didn't hide your freckles," I murmur.

Her chocolate hair drapes over her shoulders with soft waves. I shove my hands in my pockets so I don't reach for her and wrap my hands through the silky locks.

Taking a couple steps backward, I hitch my thumb over my shoulder. "I should go get ready."

Before I bend you over the table and fuck you until the desperation radiating through my veins is out of me.

I'm proud of myself. I only stuck my hand up her skirt once in the car. When I felt satin, I knew I needed to stop before I reached the point of no return. And end up back at my place.

I tried to pick a smaller restaurant, one where the paparazzi rarely hang out waiting for their next victim. Except, as soon as we arrive, there's a gathering of people. I drop my head when I notice the flickers in the glass coming off their cameras.

"Shit."

She leans over me to look out the window. "What's wrong?"

If she thought random people taking pictures of us at the airport or on the streets when shopping was awkward, she's in for a rude awakening.

"What do you want me to do, boss?" Pete asks.

The people all wait, their fingers on the shutter-release button of their cameras, to see who exits the car.

"It's okay, Ryker. I know this is part of your world. I can handle it."

She thinks she can. But she has no idea.

These people are soul suckers.

Demanding something that will push you until you see red. They crave reaction. And will spin it however it meets their needs.

"Say nothing," I command. "Just hold on to me. Tight."

She nods in understanding. Opening the door, the minute of silence, where the vultures assess their prey, gives me just enough time to pull her out and lead her to the entrance. Her hand tight in mine, squeezes tighter as a camera is shoved in our personal space.

"What's her name?"

"Did you find her on vacation?"

"Is your head going to be in the game this weekend?"

They toss question after question at me as I usher her toward the door. Glancing over at Aspen to make sure she's okay, I'm relieved when her smile grows and she winks. She's a rock star taking this in stride, not at all rattled.

I can't help but answer the last question. "I'll be ready to win," I say to the guy, pulling Aspen into my side. Hell, if they're going to make up shit, I might as well give them something. Bree will love this.

When I lean in, Aspen's expression flashes with confusion until I press my lips against hers. Lips still warm from the heat of the car, I kiss her hard. Possessive. Devouring her taste like I've been deprived of her. My need pours fire into the kiss and I finish with both of us gasping for air.

I hadn't planned on *that* kiss.

"Damn, you've got me so wound up," I murmur as we walk in. Cheers fade with the closing of the door.

"You have a habit of doing the same to me," she says, touching her swollen lips.

The maître'd takes our coats and his eyes skim over Aspen's body. The tinge of jealousy in my chest builds and I weave my fingers in with hers, pulling her in closer to my side. She knowingly glances up with a smirk.

"What?" I shrug a shoulder. She's mine and if any asshole needs to be checked, I'll be glad to remind him.

"Your jealousy is cute."

No, it's surprising.

Beautiful women have stood by my side before, but I've wanted people to look at them with envy and lust. They were a prop more than an emotional attachment. I'm an asshole.

But Aspen's different.

I don't want anyone to imagine themselves with her by their side. It's not happening. Ever.

"Ryker Dallas." A voice bellows from a table as we're being shown to ours. I stop and glance over.

I smile as the man stands and extends a hand. "Jace Floyd, it's good to see you." I shake his hand. The crowd outside makes sense now.

"You too, man. You ready to make me some money on Sunday?"

Chuckling, I nod my head. "I sure the hell hope so." Jace has always been a betting man. We've been friends for years. When I was first drafted in the NFL, I dated an actress in one of his movies, I dropped her but kept him out of that relationship. "Jace, this is Aspen." The old man's eyes glint as he takes in Aspen. His attraction to younger women has always been obvious. Hell, look at his date, at least forty years his senior. But when you're one of the richest film producers in the world, age ain't nothing but a number.

"Aspen," he purrs, holding his hand out. She slips hers in his and he kisses the back of her hand. "It's a pleasure to meet you."

Her eyes flash wide in surprise, but she plays it off with a smile. "You too, Jake."

His laughter ripples out, and I bite my lip to hold mine in. Leaning over, I whisper, "It's Jace."

She pulls in a quick breath, her cheeks redden. "Oh. I'm so sorry. Nice to meet you too, Jace." Since she's embarrassed, I make our exchange quick. As we walk away, she asks, "Why did he find that so funny?"

"He's probably wondering where the hell you came from. He's like the top movie producer, ever. Have you heard of..." I rattle some all-time box office hits he produced and she stares at me blankly, shaking her head. "Well, I know what we're doing a couple nights while you're here. Netflix and chill."

"What's Netflix?"

THROUGHOUT DINNER, our conversation stays light. We talk about our day. She has a lot more to say than I do. But I could listen to her talk all day. Between her sultry voice and accent, it's an aphrodisiac.

My hand hasn't left her leg since we sat down at the cushioned u-shaped table. But as the night moves forward, my fingers itch for more.

With wine flowing through us, we're hidden in the dim-lit

restaurant, tucked in close at the rear of the table. I scan the room, nobody is paying any attention to us. We've already eaten and now it's the time where the waiter comes less often, only to top off our drinks.

A bottle of wine showed up minutes ago, so he's not returning soon. She brings the wine glass to her lips and hums. "This is delicious."

I hum into her neck. "It is."

Dragging my hand up her silky thigh, I stop at the hem of her dress. Her pulse races wild against my lips, spurring my fingers to go higher. She uncrosses her legs. A growl vibrates on my lips as I've never been so turned on by a woman. She giggles. "Damn, I've missed you today," I admit.

When I reach the apex of her thighs, she shudders when I press my thumb over her satin-covered clit, widening her legs slightly more.

"You want me to finger fuck you right here, don't you?" I hiss.

"Ryker." Her whisper rolls off her lips in a plea.

I sit up and gulp the glass of wine into my dry mouth. With another quick glance around the restaurant, a low groan drums in my throat as I slip a finger under the satin, dipping it in her wet pussy. Her muscles clamp down around me and her fingers grip my leg tight, she's biting back her moan.

"Are you trying to make me scream?" Her voice a bare whisper. I thrust my finger in as far as her seated position will allow. Over and over until she's panting, yet trying to keep control.

She picks up her wine glass but holds it midair when I rub my thumb against her clit again. A passerby would think we're having an intimate conversation. They wouldn't know that I'm about to set her off.

That is until I have her entire body convulsing around my finger. She almost drops her wine glass on the table but places it down without spilling. Her hushed breaths as she comes down from her orgasm has my dick painfully pressing against my strained pants.

"You're very talented, Mr. Dallas," she purrs, adjusting her dress, so it's not hiked up to her hips.

"And you're sexy as sin, Ms. Foley. But I'm just getting started, so we should go. But I think we need to leave out the back door. I don't need an outline of my hard dick plastered all over every media site tomorrow."

CHAPTER EIGHTEEN

ASPEN

The crowd's noise deafens me when Ryker runs out on the field. This week people have taken pictures of us wherever we were, but I wasn't aware of the magnitude of his fan base. When he waves to them, jealousy creeps in, surprising me. I've monopolized his attention for the last week, seeing him offer it to someone else shouldn't bother me this much. I shake the thoughts from my mind. *It's not like he's mine.* I sigh and drop my head.

Well, that thought wasn't any better.

"Look," Addie says, tapping me on the thigh. I follow where she's pointing, down to Ryker on the sideline. His smile widens when our eyes lock and he winks right before putting his helmet on.

"Hmm," Aiden murmurs, wrapping his arm around Addie's shoulders, staring at me. "He's never acknowledged a girl at a game before. He's usually in his zone."

My cheeks flush and I dart my gaze around the stadium to hide the giddiness in my belly. Thankfully, Aiden doesn't continue his probe into what's happening between us. I don't even know what we're doing.

The game begins. Between the buzz of energy from the crowd and the constant fear that Ryker will die if he holds the ball for too long, I don't understand why people enjoy this. My heart has never worked so hard to keep me breathing.

Ryker's pummeled and I can't watch. I cover my eyes with my hands and try to calm my racing heart. "You okay over there?" Addie whispers.

The crowd cheers.

I peep through my fingers and see that Ryker is on his feet. "No." I blow out a sigh, dropping my hands. "Why does he like playing this game? He's always seconds away from getting hurt."

Aiden finds my concern funny. "He gets paid a shitload of money. That's why."

"You can't spend money if you're dead," I bite back.

"How about we get drinks?" Addie intercepts, picking up on my distress. I glance to the field and notice that the offense is on the sidelines, so I nod and stand up.

I need a break.

When we reach the top of the stairs, Addie bumps my shoulder with hers. "He'll be okay. Football's a tough physical sport, but he knows what he's doing."

I guess it's not any different from swimming in the ocean with sharks. There's risk there too, and I swim around them like they're goldfish.

"So, in other news, I searched your mom's name." My mind immediately switches gears and I wait for her to continue. Her shoulders drop. "I couldn't find her." The small part of me holding on to hope that she's here in the States fizzles out. She must be in France. "But it's weird she's not even in the system. Are you sure her maiden name is Rose Burnet?"

"I'm sure. I found an old visa with her name on it."

"Hmm. I also looked for your father because I figured if I

found him, I might locate her that way. But I couldn't find your father either."

What? "Maybe he's been gone too long, he's no longer in the system," I guess. "It's been twenty-four years." I updated my passport when I graduated college, but as far as I know, my father hasn't.

She shakes her head. "If he's ever had a passport, he'd be in the system."

None of this makes sense. He has a passport. I've seen it. People walk around laughing and cheering, but they're a colorful blur of blue and gold as I think about what Addie is telling me.

Maybe I'm mistaken and my dad wasn't a US citizen. Could they both be French citizens? I squeeze the bridge of my nose.

"I'm sorry I wasn't able to help."

"I don't know… I'm, I'm so confused," I stumble over my words. "Are you able to search by a picture?" I pop open my clutch wallet and pull out the only picture I've ever seen of my mom. My father erased my mom from our house when she left. He said he didn't want to relive the betrayal every day by looking at her. But I was a teenager, desperate to have some link to my mom. So, I searched the house until I found something. A box, hidden beneath the boards in the bathroom. It had my birth certificate and our passports, and my mom's old visa. Which is why I'm certain my father is American. Along with the documents were ten of these pictures. The same one. I had no idea why there were so many, but I stole one and hid it from my dad. We seem like a happy family. I wish I knew what changed and why she left. I hold out the picture. "That's her."

Addie stares at the picture. "Is that your father, too?" I nod. "I can try to run it through our facial recognition software and see if I get a hit."

"Thank you so much, Addie. You have no idea how grateful I am that you're helping me."

She softly smiles. "I do. It wasn't too long ago I found out who my biological father was and I wasn't even aware was still alive. In my case, I would have rather not known, but that's a different story for a different time." She jerks her thumb toward our section as cheers erupt from the field. "Ready to go back?"

I roll my shoulders and puff out a breath of air. "Yes." Despite the heart attacks, I'll watch because it's important to him.

An hour later, I'm on the edge of my seat, my fingers curled around the edge. Thirty seconds on the clock and the score is tied. Ryker's team has the ball, but it doesn't look like they'll be able to score. Aiden says it's going to be a three and out. I'd ask him what that means, but I can't peel my focus off of Ryker long enough to ask.

"Looks like they're going into overtime," Addie says to my right.

Ten seconds.

My heart races with adrenaline. The ball is hiked and Ryker checks each side, pauses, and then launches it across the field, reminding me of the day he got stung by a stingray. This is a Hail Mary. The perfect spiral soars through the air and we're all on our feet, the crowd silenced as we hold our breath.

There's a pack of players from both teams eagerly ready to catch it in the end zone. The ball falls in the middle of the pile. I gasp, searching for who caught it.

Then one of Ryker's teammates runs out from the pile holding the ball high in the air. The crowd erupts and Addie and I jump in each other's arms. My gaze searches for Ryker. He runs to his teammate and jumps in his arms in celebration. As soon as his feet touch the ground, he takes off his helmet, runs his hands through his wet hair and looks in my direction. For a moment, the noise is silenced, everything on pause, except our connection. He wags his brows and blows me a kiss. Electricity crackles in the air and just like that, someone presses the play button and reporters flood him all at once to grab his attention.

"Dayumm," purrs Addie.

"Addison," growls Aiden making her laugh.

"I'm sorry, but that was hawt." She waves her hand in front of her face, ignoring Aiden. *I'd have to agree.* I thought naked Ryker was sexy, but *hello* Ryker in a uniform.

"Woman, I'm five seconds from throwing you over my shoulder and reminding you who you belong to." My brows spike, surprised by his claim of her. Dante's words slam back into my mind and I shake them out, not wanting it to spoil my mood. Addison playfully slaps him on his chest and rolls her eyes.

Her lack of response makes me wonder if I overreacted with Dante. Maybe he wasn't *claiming* me, rather telling me he wanted us to work out, just in the wrong words. But I had never heard him be so aggressive.

I put my jacket on. *It doesn't matter;* I tell myself. I'll deal with it when I'm home. Right now, it's time to find my quarterback.

A cold cement wall holds me up in an empty hallway underneath the stadium. The three of us wait for Ryker. He comes out of the press release, dressed in a gray blazer with a blue tie and dark denim jeans. His eyes flare when they meet mine and I can't stop myself from running and jumping in his arms. He hungrily kisses me, the high from his win vibrating through his body. The sound of cameras clicking doesn't even stop us. It's not until he breaks the kiss that I notice the crowd we've attracted. *Where did all these people come from?* Heat washes over me and I dig my face into his neck.

He places my feet on the ground and whispers in my ear, "Let's go."

Yes, please.

Grabbing my hand, he leads me through the reporters throwing questions out wondering who I am again. I glance back to see Aiden and Addie following. Addie fans her face, I'm assuming about the kiss. When I laugh, Aiden's attention darts to her, and she plays it off and winks at him.

The city outside Ryker's living room twinkles likes stars through the window. My rattled nerves are finally starting to settle from the last few hours. Aiden and Addison left a half-hour ago, and I need this time to wind down.

My legs are tucked under a blanket and my head rests on Ryker's shoulder as we stare out in a comfortable silence. "Is it a rush for you?" I whisper, my thoughts taking me back to the game.

"It used to be." He twists his body and pulls my legs across his. The warmth of his hand on my thigh. "But it was tonight."

"What was different about tonight?"

"You were there."

I inwardly smile. It's the same feeling I had when Ryker was watching me feed the lemon sharks. It's something I do every day with no thought. But when Ryker was there, it made me remember how dangerous it is, made me feel invincible.

"Thank you for inviting me."

This week has fueled my desire to move to the States. My thoughts are as fast-paced as the city, seeing myself build my future here. The one question that stops me in my tracks is could I do it all by myself? Taking Ryker out of the picture because I don't expect him to wait for me. It could be years. But I want this. I want this freedom.

"And thank you for letting me look at you in that sexy uniform."

CHAPTER NINETEEN

RYKER

"**A**re you sad your team isn't in the playoffs?"

The one scenario that would kick us out of the wild card game, happened. The other team won, beating us out of the playoffs.

I should be fucking furious. But I can't muster up the feelings when I know the only reason I met Aspen is because of my suspension. And now I have her all to myself this week with no interruption.

But hell if I'll admit that. *To anyone.* "Yeah, it sucks. You give everything you've got for sixteen weeks, physical and mental exhaustion. It all makes it worth it being at the top." This is the first time in four years, I'm not.

"This probably wasn't a good time for me to be here."

The sound of regret in her voice pisses me off more than not making the playoffs. I grab her hand from her lap and place it on my leg. "You being here wasn't the reason. *I didn't lose.*" My replacement lost. All three games. But that's on me. "Having you watch me play, I had fun showing off."

Her laugh fills the car. "You're definitely good at that." Her eyes shift to the side of the highway. "Where are we going, again?"

"A small town in Upstate, New York. You'll love it."

She's so fascinated with the snow, what better way to enjoy it than renting a cabin in the mountains? When I found the property, it was perfect. And after the city's disappointment with our team, it's best to leave town for a couple days to let them simmer down.

I switch the radio to an eighties channel and she immediately turns it up, singing and dancing in her seat, not giving two shits that she sings out of tune or looks crazy to the cars passing us. Between her singing outbursts and riding in comfortable silence, I've never been this content with a woman before. I don't need to pretend to be anything but myself.

The only stop we make is to get some groceries. Pulling into the snow-covered grounds, Aspen's eyes twinkle as we park in the driveway.

"It's a treehouse," she exclaims.

I have to admit, it's wicked cool.

The suspension bridge we cross to get to the front door of the two-story house, situated in the trees, has a fresh coat of snow across it. I'm as excited as her crossing it.

Her eyes are the size of saucers as she looks out from the porch at a sea of white fluff. "Let's hurry and get the groceries inside so we can come and play in the snow."

"Do you know what snow is good for?" I ask, watching her throw handfuls of powdery snow in the air and dance around it as it falls to her face. Flakes catch on her eyelashes. She looks up through them, blinking them away.

"What?"

She lets out an audible gasp as I land a snowball right in her shoulder. "Ryker! That is so unfair. You throw balls for a living." I bark out a laugh as a flicker of revenge crosses her expression before she bends over and grabs a chunk of snow.

"Whiskey, all is fair in love and war."

"Is that right, Ball Boy?"

"Give it all you got, babe," I prod, holding my arms out wide.

"If you're that confident I'll miss, close your eyes." She packs the ball in her glove covered hands. I bite back my response of *go ahead* because she could very well hit me. She lifts a brow, waiting.

"Alright," I say, closing my eyes. I'll probably regret this, but the odds of her hitting me from where she's standing is slim. I've seen her throw before. When I hear snow crunching under boots, I open them back up. "You're cheating, woman."

She flashes a sly smile but holds her empty hands in the air as she gets closer to me. "I couldn't hit you from back there."

I narrow my eyes. She's up to something. When she stands in front of me, she lifts on her toes and kisses me. I feel the smile play on her lips. As soon as I pull back, a fistful of snow falls down the front side of my pants and she runs off.

My stomach muscles tense as the cold makes its way down to my dick. Shaking my pants so the ice moves past, it's not long before it's just wet. I refocus on Aspen hiding behind a tree. Like that'll stop me.

I rush toward the tree and she half-screams, half-laughs, trying to run through two feet of snow. It doesn't take me long to catch up and I tackle her to the ground. She arches her back off the snow.

"Ryker, it's cold," she squeals.

I push some powder up her shirt as she tries to wiggle out of my grasp. "Oh, I know." I grab her boob with my glove, making sure she *feels* the cold through her bra. Except, now my hand is on her boob and I don't want to move it. With the weight of my body on top of hers, we've sunk a good six inches into the snow.

I glance around the isolated area we're in, I can hear only the buzz of snowmobiles off in the distance. "Don't you get any ideas, Mr. Dallas. There will be no shagging in the snow," she says, reading my mind. She sniffles and wipes her bright red nose with the back of her glove. "I mean, I know how sexy I am with snow-covered hair and snot running down my nose." She wags her brows.

She couldn't look bad if she tried.

"Oh, I have plenty of ideas. And they definitely include shagging." Palms on the ground, I push up until I can stand and reach out for her to grab my hand. "I think we should take our *games* inside." She hops around to get the snow off when she's back on her feet.

"Haven't you had enough losses, lately?" My mouth falls open at her jab and she erupts in laughter.

"Whiskey, those are fighting words." I bum rush her, throwing her over my shoulder and jog over to the bridge. She snorts from laughing so hard.

As soon as we're inside, the heat from the fire greets us. I'm glad I had the foresight to light it before we went to play in the snow because I'm too busy ripping all the layers off her to worry about heat.

We'll make our own.

Her legs wrap around my waist, and I blindly walk the steps to the bedroom because I can't keep my mouth off her long enough to see where I'm going.

I toss her on the king-size bed, a thick fluffy white blanket surrounds the beautiful vision in front of me. Her nipples harden as I drink her in with my eyes. She runs her hands through the fur, her breathing heavy.

"Ryker, touch me," she pleads. My cock throbs. Not yet, buddy.

I kneel on the bed, picking up one of her legs, dragging my lips up her muscular calf. She snickers when I lick the back of her knee, she tries to squirm out of my grip. I shake my head, continuing my path up her thigh.

The plush fur presses flat under me as I lie down, resting her leg over my shoulder. Her core is slick with arousal. A deep guttural growl escapes as I lick her in one long swipe. She clenches her thighs around me.

I ravish her like I'm a starving man until she's screaming my name and her body is convulsing against my tongue. I swallow her juices, savoring her taste until she's drained and gasping for air.

I grab a condom I strategically placed on the nightstand earlier, ripping it open and slipping it on before she can come down from her high. Spreading her legs apart, she lifts her ass off the bed as I slide into her.

"What was that you were saying about me losing?" I tease, pressing my thumb against her swollen, oversensitive clit. Her tight pussy clenches in a vice around me as she vibrates against my thumb. It doesn't take long to set her off again. Wetness drips down my shaft.

"Ryker... oh, god..." Her pleas ignite a feral passion inside me. I've lost all control when it comes to this woman. I lean forward on my elbows, swallowing her moans as I kiss her through the exhilarating sensual ride. Her breath hitches when I pull back, resting my forehead against hers.

"Whiskey, I..." *love you.* The words stick on my tongue as she stares up at me with half-lidded eyes. I've never even thought about saying that to a woman before. The words themselves don't scare me. I want to give her all of me. It's saying it to a woman I can't have that has me panicking.

I push up on my knees as the air that flows freely in the room can't make it to my lungs. I lick my dry mouth and start a punishing pace, gripping her hips. I'm not sure who I'm punishing, me or her. I flip her over and her heart-shaped ass slaps against my pelvis as she meets me thrust for thrust. Her moans spur me on. I glance out the window, the erotic sense that someone could be watching me claim her. See how deep I'm inside her.

She's mine.

I roar through my orgasm as it rips through me. Both our knees give out and we fall to the bed. Damn. I'm in fucking trouble.

"Is the fame why you feel trapped?" She whispers out of the blue. I don't answer right away because I'm trying to figure out where this is coming from. She adds, "When you asked me back on the island if I ever felt trapped. I'm assuming it was because you do."

I hum, remembering the liberating feeling I had on top of the mountain. "I wish I could play football without the famous status quo. But since I can't, I *guess* that makes me feel trapped sometimes."

She's quiet for a few minutes. "Being in the spotlight must be taxing."

I shrug. "It has its advantages. I won't admit it's the best, because I've hit my limits before, but I find creative ways to hide out."

Her chest vibrates with silent laughter. "I like your creative ways."

They've been the best this season so far.

I smack her ass. "Ready to go back out in the snow?"

She hops off the bed. "Yes! I thought you'd never ask," she says, excitedly, digging in her bag for dry clothes. "Can we make a snowman?"

"I have something better."

.   .   .

"Are we going on those?" Her eyes light up as we walk up to a pair of snowmobiles. Her attitude to attack everything head-on is one of her sexiest attributes. She jumps on one and surveys the entire piece of equipment.

I laugh. "Damn, woman. Hold on. Let me show you what to do."

"It can't be that different from a jet ski."

"Well, I was hoping we'd ride one together." She stares blankly at me. "Or not," I add when she says nothing. She agreeably turns her eyes back down to her ride like that wasn't even an option, making me chuckle.

With a quick five-minute explanation on how it works, she's raring to go. "Catch me if you can," she says, flipping the engine on.

I lower my goggles down and lick my lips. "Whiskey, you don't know the power of those words." Ever since I opened my eyes to hers, I've done nothing but try to catch her. What would I do if she finally held on?

"This place is perfect," she says, leaning over on the table and pressing her plump lips to mine. "I don't understand how you're single if this is how you treat women."

The candle on the table flickers in her eyes and my heart beats at a foreign pace. One that scares the hell out of me. I've fallen in love with this woman.

"Ryker, what's wrong?" She senses my rattled feelings. I'm in a no-win situation. The dose of reality hits me in the gut.

"Nothing." I shake the feeling off and take her hand in mine, kissing her knuckles. I have three days left with her, I'll be damned if I ruin it with my pity party. "I just do this for special guests that come from other countries."

She nods. "So you're afraid of commitment." Her voice is light in a teasing tone.

A year ago, that would be an absolute yes. But with all my friends marrying off, I'm jealous of their lives. I want that life too. And I'm ready for it. Except, I've fallen in love with the wrong woman.

I release her hand as the waiter puts our food down in front of us. She hums at the sight of hers. "I'm starving," she says, cutting into her steak. Another thing I'm not used to, being on a date with a woman who eats something other than a salad. It's nice not chowing down in front of someone who pushes their food aside and watches me eat the entire time.

We're sitting at a table along the window looking out at Main Street. The road's blocked off for the winter carnival, the street filled with people. It's dark outside, but the string of lights strung in a zigzag pattern over the streets gives off plenty of light.

Halfway through our meal, Aspen inhales sharply and squints, looking outside. I follow her gaze. "What do you see?"

She sits back and waves me off. "For a second, I thought I saw my dad. It was weird." *That would be more than weird.* I dart my gaze back outside, searching. There's a ton of people, but none that look like her dad from what I can see. "I mean, I know it's not him. Maybe my subconscious is feeling bad I left without telling him."

"You probably saw someone that resembled him. Have you talked with him at all?"

She hangs her head and shakes it, her guilt seeping into mine. I didn't think she'd hop on an airplane without telling her dad. As if he didn't hate me enough. "Truthfully, I've been having so much fun, I haven't thought much about home. Mama Doe hasn't called you, so I know he's okay." She chews on her inner cheek. "But this is good. I'm twenty-five years old, I shouldn't feel bad for wanting to live my life." A glimmer of hope that she might want to stay fires up in my chest. "And it's for only two weeks," she adds, throwing water on the flames.

I take a long pull of beer until it's empty, hoping she doesn't read the disappointment on my face.

"What were we doing before I had a dad lookalike scare?" she jokes.

I point to her half-eaten dinner. "Watching you eat steak like a boss."

Her smile grows. "I do like my meat."

With a low, rumbling chuckle, I yank on her chair to move her closer to me. Dipping my head into her neck, I whisper, "Any time you want it, all you have to do is ask."

CHAPTER TWENTY

ASPEN

"Hey Mo, what's your drink of choice?" I stare at the enormous man speaking to me and I angle my head in confusion. Out of the corner of my eye, Ryker drops his, shaking it. We're surrounded by five of Ryker's teammates. I'm the size of an ant compared to everyone at the table. He wanted me to meet some of his buddies. Well, the ones that didn't leave town. I try to ignore all the eyes on us from around the bar. Even if these guys weren't famous, they'd stand out. They're huge. The last three days in the mountains was a reprieve, not having everyone interrupt us every few moments for pictures or autographs. And I had Ryker all to myself.

"Is he talking to me?"

"Yes, island goddess, I am. What would you like to drink?"

"Um," I start, still confused, but order since he's staring at me. "Pineapple and rum is fine. Thank you."

"Ignore him," Ryker mutters, leaning into my shoulder. He tucks his head into my neck and takes a deep inhale, making me silently laugh. "What? I love how sweet you smell."

I rotate my body in the seat. "Why did he call me Mo?"

He twists his lips at first, followed by a devilish grin. "What are you going to give me if I tell you?"

My mouth gapes open as he tries to negotiate. "How about what am I *not* going to give you if you don't tell me?"

He licks his lower lip, flashing confidence that suggests he doesn't believe me. *He'd be correct.* I've learned I have zero willpower when it comes to Ryker, yet he's made me feel stronger in my skin, as a woman.

But my fantasy vacation ends in two days. Each second that passes is like a ticking time bomb, and it ends in devastation. Again. The past two mornings I've woken up with tears in my eyes. Dread pressing on my chest for the coming days. Even if I could stay, Ryker has mentioned nothing past my departure date. There's no sadness in his eyes over us coming to an end. That stings more. But I push those thoughts from my mind, focusing on the now. I'll deal with my broken heart when I'm home.

I thank Donnie again when he puts a drink in front of me. Since Ryker doesn't want to tell me, I ask Donnie. "Donnie, you know my name is Aspen, right?"

He smirks, nodding his head. "Mo suits you better."

"Why?"

"Yeah, Donnie. Admit your Disney fetish while you're at it," jests Hudson, sitting across from me.

"Shut the fuck up. Those movies are the bomb. If you'd ever watch 'em maybe you'd figure out how to treat a woman." He turns his attention to me, ignoring Hudson's rebuttal about how he treats women like queens. "You're the living Moana."

I blink. "Like the ocean?" Moana isn't an uncommon name on the island, but I don't know why he thinks it's fitting for me. Or what he means by the *living* Moana.

His hands fall to the sides and his eyes widen as he lets out an audible gasp. "You've never seen Moana?"

I glance at Ryker with a silent plea for help. "It's a movie about a Polynesian girl going on a journey searching for more to life than the island."

"Really?"

Did she find what she was looking for?

"Girl!" Donnie shoots forward in his chair, slapping his hand down on the table. The drinks teeter and the guys grab the beer bottles to keep them from tipping over. "We're watching that movie. Tonight." He points to Greer. "You have a theater in your crib. We're coming over."

"Oh, come on, D. She doesn't want—"

I grip Ryker's shirt to stop him. "Yes, I do."

"That's my girl," Donnie exclaims, standing. He downs his drink and slams the empty glass on the table. "Hey, beautiful, we're cashing out," he yells across the bar to our waitress. She glances up from helping another table and smiles, acknowledging his request.

I guess the party's moving.

SNUGGLED ON THE COUCH, that is larger than my entire living room, with a blanket covering us, Ryker and I dig into the popcorn Greer passed out.

"No hanky-panky over there," Donnie states, staring at us as he gets comfortable in the couch's corner. *Hanky-panky?* "Keep those hands above the blanket," he explains further when he sees my confusion. *Aww. Got it.*

Ryker laughs, holds his hands in the air. "I can't make any promises."

I slap him in the stomach. I'm not a prude, but I'm not into putting on *those* kinds of shows. Well, I say that, but we've been out in the open many times where we could've easily been caught and it didn't stop me. I shake the thoughts from my head. It's not happening *here*.

From the moment the show starts, I don't peel my gaze away once. Even the couple times that Ryker's hand slipped between my legs, I swatted him away.

I blot tears away when her family takes to the seas again. While our lives aren't identical, I felt this story in my bones, giving me hope.

"You okay?" Ryker whispers in my ear.

I sniff. The story affected me more than I imagined.

"See. That's your story," Donnie says, pushing off the couch. I manage a slight smile. The only difference, I haven't gotten off the island.

"All you got to do now, is marry that fool so you can stay." Donnie points to Ryker before strutting out of the room like he didn't drop a bomb.

Ryker's face turns to stone before he responds, "She's just here visiting, D."

I'm not sure what I expected him to say after Donnie's comment, but that wasn't it. Ryker has my full attention, but refuses to look at me. Instead, he finishes his beer, pushes off the couch and walks out of the dark room. His spot turns cold, like his reaction. What the hell did I do?

I didn't make that comment.

My vision blurs watching the rolling credits as tears pool, this time for a different reason. Swallowing the emotions back, I stand and fold the blanket. The insecurity Ryker's reaction expelled on me has me feeling out of place. The entire time I've been here, I've felt welcome. Now, I'm like an imposing stranger.

The guy's voices lead me to the kitchen. "I um…" I stop talking when the guys all turn to me. All except Ryker. He's downing another beer. "Thank you Greer for letting me watch the movie here. And Donnie, I can see why you love that movie. It was nice meeting everyone." I grip my wallet, unsure what to do next.

Donnie comes over and gives me a huge bear hug. He reminds me of a few of the guys from home and I welcome the feeling. *I wish I was back there.*

"Ready?" Ryker says in a monotone voice. I nod, following him out the door.

The ride to Ryker's place is just as awkward. He doesn't say a word.

I didn't expect the devastation to start early.

It's time to go home.

CHAPTER TWENTY-ONE

RYKER

I *didn't think this through.*

The town car stops in front of my condo and I glance up at the white skyscraper, debating if I want to get out. I can make up another excuse. I already made up a fake team meeting.

Aspen leaves tomorrow and since Donnie's comment last night, I've been avoiding her. Why? *I don't fucking know.* The word marriage was thrown out there like it's a possibility and I panicked. Yet, if there's any woman I'd want with me forever, it'd be someone like Aspen. No, it would be Aspen. And she doesn't need me to stay. She's American, for god's sake. But my knee-jerk reaction was to run.

The knot in my stomach twists tighter. I've tried to ignore it the last couple days, but the pain digs deeper, leaving a hollow crater. "Mr. Dallas, is there somewhere else you'd like to go?" Pete asks, staring at me in the rearview mirror. I inhale deep and blow it out my nose. *Man the fuck up, Dallas.*

"No. Thanks, Pete." I grip the handle and make myself pull until the door pops open. The truth is, there isn't anywhere I'd rather be than next to Aspen. Inside Aspen. With Aspen. But my ego is putting up a wall between us. People take pictures as I stand, staring at the brass front doors.

This is not manning up.

Demanding my feet to move, I make it to the elevator before I stop again. When it opens, I will myself forward.

I'm met with three packed suitcases as soon as I walk inside the door. My eyes jump around, searching for Aspen. She walks out of the bedroom and stills the second she sees me. "Where are you going?"

She chews her bottom lip, shifting her weight from foot to foot. "I figure it's best if I leave early." Her words are a punch to my gut, stealing the air from my lungs.

"Why?"

Her jaw hardens. "Why? Oh, let me count the whys for you." She holds up a finger. "You've been ignoring me since yesterday." She holds up two fingers. "You're making me feel awful for being here. Like I'm an inconvenience." Another finger pops up. "And I'd rather be a prisoner in my home than be here with you anymore."

"Aspen," I murmur, gripping my neck.

Holding up a fourth finger, she squeezes her eyes for a couple painful moments. "You call me by my real name." She struggles to get the words out. "Ryker, I need to leave. We've had our fun. It was a trip I'll never forget. Thank you for everything." She walks over to her bags and yanks the handle of one until it pops into place.

I'm ruining this. I'm ruining everything. "Wait." A knock at the door stops me from reaching for her. I ignore it. "Please let me ex—"

The knock comes again, more aggressive this time, almost a pounding. "Ryker, open up, it's Max."

What the hell is Max doing here? And why is he about to kick the door in?

I open it and Max barges in. His gaze jumps from Aspen to her packed bags and then to me. "Is that Aspen?" He jerks his head in her direction. Well, hello to you too, asshole.

My brows draw together when I say, "Aspen, this is Max Shaw." He gives her a curt nod, but his attention switches to me. He flicks his wrists to glance at his watch.

"We need to go," he orders with no explanation.

My spine straightens. "Max, what the fuck are you talking about? Go where?" He doesn't answer, rather goes to Aspen's bags and starts collecting them.

"Excuse me, those are mine," Aspen declares, rushing over to him.

"You're coming too."

"Max, what the hell is going on?"

"Grab two ball caps and put them on. There's no time to explain. We'll talk in the car on the way to the plane."

"Plane?" Aspen and I both say together.

"Now," growls Max, disappearing out the door with two of the bags. I fist my hands. Fuck! Running into my room, I grab the baseball caps, putting one on and handing Aspen the other. She looks at me, her features mixed with questions and fear.

"Max is one of my best friends. If he says we have to go, there's a reason."

"I don't understand." *You and me both.*

"It'll be okay, Whis—"

"Oh, don't start that now. Too late, Ryker." Her voice hardens, cutting me off and reminding me where we were before Max barged in. She slips on the cap and grabs her last bag, stomping past me. Well, I'd rather her be mad than scared because if Max is here, it's not good.

Aspen sits in the back seat and I hate that I'm not next to her. She made it clear I wasn't welcome. She's going to hate me when she leaves here.

Wasn't that the point?

To make it easier for her to want to leave. I was doing her a favor, because I'd pick being angry over this pain in my chest any day. I've fallen in love with the one woman I can't have. I have to break the chain she has on my heart before the links fuse. This is hard, but it'd be almost impossible if I kept the hope that we could have a future. *We can't.*

The regional airport is close, but the traffic has us stopped. "All right, Max. What's going on?" I say to silence the voice.

"I don't know, exactly."

The seat belt locks up as I whip my body around. Shit! Yanking on it only makes it tighter. Frustrated, I click the buckle to unfasten the seatbelt and release the locked belt and then buckle it again.

"What is this then? Are we in some kind of trouble?"

His gaze jumps to the rearview mirror to Aspen and then back on the road. "I got a call from Harper. She said Addison ran into her office and told her to call me with a message. Right before a couple guys in suits came in and took Addison away."

I do a double-take. I think Max has lost his shit. "What does that have to do with me? I'm the last friend to help Addison. Where is Aiden?"

He sighs. "The message was *Dallas needs the island to see station nine. Stat.*"

I repeat the message in my mind, breaking it down. Okay, so she told Max that me and Aspen needs to go to Max's house. But why?

"What is station nine?" Aspen asks from the back seat.

Max replies, "It's my house."

"My flight leaves in a few hours for Tahiti. I don't have time to fly somewhere else. I'm sure your house is lovely, though." Even in the middle of chaos, she finds a way to be nice.

His stone expression breaks with a smile. "Aspen, I'm sorry for this. Not how I usually make introductions, but there's something going on that has a good friend sending me encrypted messages that says to get you and Ryker out of town ASAP."

She sighs and whispers, "This is crazy."

I agree. I recall our week and a half together searching for anything off. Other than me acting like a prick, nothing felt wrong. We did nothing illegal. Bree hasn't called to yell at me for something I did. She wasn't happy with me bringing Aspen here, but that wasn't her call.

"Grab her suitcases," Max instructs me as soon as we pull up to the plane. I hop out of the car and open Aspen's door. She stares at me with trepidation from the back seat.

"We'll get answers soon." *And then you can leave me.*

I hold my hand out and she slips hers in it, sending a buzz throughout my body reminding me of the chemistry we have. *Fuck, this hurts.*

As we're stepping up the stairs, I murmur from behind her, "I'm sorry for being an asshole."

Her shoulders lift and fall and she nods. Once on the plane, she looks around, not sure where to sit. Max points to a set of four chairs around a table. She sits in a chair by the window. I drop into the one across from her.

My hands itch to reach out to her, so I fist them in my lap. The craving to touch her is suffocating. I stare out the window focusing on the people on the tarmac finishing their inspection.

Max sits next to me and I glance over. He flashes a confused expression; I'm sure wondering why the silence. I do a sharp shake not to ask. The plane starts down the runway. I focus on the ground, getting further and further away.

I whip my head around when Max asks, "Aspen, you enjoy your time in the States?"

Her scoff is hollow. "I did." She pins her pointed glare at me. "But I exceeded my welcome."

I growl, tightening my fist. "No, you didn't."

"Then what the hell, Ryker?"

"Are we doing this right here?" I throw my skull against the seat and look up at the ceiling of the tube we're stuck in.

"Well, it seems we have time," she sneers, crossing her arms. "Someone mentions marriage and you shut down. I don't even want to marry you."

Ouch. The stabbing pain from her admission scars me. "Whiskey, I didn't shut down. I haven't ever felt this much before. I wish I could shut it down."

Max gets up and moves to another part of the plane. *Thanks, asshole. You started this and now you're leaving me to hang myself.*

She swallows and her voice shakes when she asks, "Why did you bring me here, Ryker?"

"To prove to myself that you were an in-the-moment thing."

Her jaw tics and her eyes pool with tears as she pins me with her glare. "How'd that work out for you?"

"You weren't." You're a forever thing, but not my forever. My heart thuds against my chest in protest.

When the first tear escapes down her cheek, she pushes up and disappears into the bathroom.

"Fuuuck!" Leaning on the table, I drop my head into my hands, scraping my fingers through my hair, gripping the strands on their ends. Why did I have to fall in love with this woman?

"The heart's a bastard, huh?" Max slaps me on the shoulder and sits down in the chair next to me again.

"I screwed up."

"We all do. It's what we do after that decides our fate."

No matter what I do, it won't change our fate. "It's not that easy in my case. She's leaving. She has obligations at home. And I can't move there. I dug myself a hole and I'm drowning in it." The weight of it all is too heavy. "And now this. What's happening?"

He shrugs. "Best I can tell you is we're doing this as a safety precaution. There's a reason for the message Addie sent me, but until we talk to her, your guess is as good as mine. Tell me about your last couple weeks." I recount everything we did. I told him that Aspen hung out with Addie one afternoon. And then she was with them at the game. But I'm sure Aiden would have told me if something had happened during that time.

Aspen appears and scoots over to her seat, eyes red, but back in control of her emotions. "Aspen, did you and Addison ever talk about anything that could have led to this?" Max asks her.

She flicks an apologetic gaze to me before answering. My shoulders tense, afraid of what she's about to say. "She offered to locate my mom. I just wanted to see if she was in the US," she adds quickly.

Max nods. "Okay. What did she find out?"

"Nothing. She couldn't find her in the system." Why didn't she tell me any of this? I wouldn't have cared. "She couldn't find anything on my father either. I asked her if she could search based on a picture."

Max leans forward on his elbows. "You gave her a picture? Who was it?"

"It was all of us, my mom and dad. When I was a year old. It's the only picture of her I have. Do you think that's why? Did I get her in trouble? I didn't mean to. She could have said—"

Max holds his hand up, cutting off her panic. "It's okay, Aspen. This isn't your fault. There's nothing wrong with searching for your mom." Max bends over and pulls a notepad and pen out, sliding it over to her. "Can you write your parents' name down?"

She looks to me for answers. Oh, now you want my help? I swallow the sarcasm threatening to come out. "Max owns a security team. He might be able to locate your mom and maybe it'll help figure out what's going on."

She drags the pad in front of her and stares at the blank page, hesitating to write the names at first, but she eventually writes them on the first two lines. Her handwriting is even perfect. It's written in beautiful cursive.

Max stares at it, too. "I don't mean to sound rude and question this, but for a girl who's grown up on an isolated French island in the Pacific, you speak and write perfect English."

She folds her hands on the table and I settle back against my seat. "My father homeschooled me and was very strict on how I spoke and wrote." She chuckles to herself. "He would tell me that the island might not always be my life and wanted me to succeed in the outside world."

Tapping his finger on the table, he stares at the names. He focuses back on her. "Why did your parents move you to Tahiti?"

"My dad wanted a simple life. He was tired of hearing about the volatile political environment and didn't want to raise me here. I would ask questions, but he never wanted to talk about it. Said it stressed him out, so I would drop it."

"Was he involved in politics?"

She shrugs a shoulder. "I don't think so. He was an English professor."

Max leans back, digesting everything she's saying. The plane starts its descent from the quick flight and she tightens her seatbelt, fidgeting under his gaze.

"Who has Addison?" I ask Max.

"I don't know. Aiden's working on that. All we know is, it's not the FBI."

"Aspen, do you mind if I run your passport?"

"Not at all," she blurts, digging through her purse on the seat next to her. She hands it to him. "I have nothing to hide. In fact, you'll discover I'm the most boring person ever."

I wish. There is nothing boring about Aspen. Her whiskey eyes soften when they meet mine. A boring person can disappear. Aspen couldn't hide if she tried. Between her exotic looks and magnetic energy, she's like finding gold in a riverbed of rock.

The reality—*our reality*—is that we can't be together, so I keep my mouth shut. Why try to burn a wet match?

She breaks our contact with an eye flutter right before wincing as we connect with the concrete. Her hands squeeze the ends of the armrests, her body tenses with the jolt of the brakes. I wish I had known she hated landings, I could have helped take her mind off of it. Reminded her of my asshole ways. At least she wouldn't be terrified. Her plump lips part with a small exhale when the plane comes to a stop.

Jesus Christ. I hop up so she doesn't see what her silent moan does to me. Pressure squeezes my dick and I adjust my pants to give it some reprieve. *That's not for you,* I remind myself. Except, it's the same breath she takes when I'm buried full tilt inside her.

"Can't you guys find women I don't have to save?" Max mumbles, striding past me. I open my mouth to argue but snap it shut. He has a point. Although, we don't even know if she needs saving. *And she's not mine.*

"Are we leaving?" Aspen's sultry voice is at my side, and I twist my body toward her and take a couple steps so I'm standing toe to toe with her in the aisle.

"Tell me you have no idea what's going on." Her soft smile fades and she presses her lips together in a flat line, her expression hardens. I hate asking her this, but the reality slams against me that maybe I don't know this woman as much as I thought. She pushes past me. But I grip her arm, halting her. "My friends will bend over backward to protect you, but I need you to answer me."

She skewers me with a venomous look. *"Va te faire foutre!"* She whips her arm out of my grasp and steps out of the plane. I follow her as she stomps down the stairs.

"What does that fucking mean?"

She holds up her middle finger and keeps walking. Seems she's picked up on a few New York mannerisms.

CHAPTER TWENTY-TWO

ASPEN

I toss the phone across the bed as if it lit me on fire. Having the world at your fingertips can be dangerous. I'm sitting alone in a bedroom in Max's house—scratch that—Max's mansion, and I've yet to find out why we're here.

But the information I just found sent icy chills down my arms. I pick up the phone again, closing the internet app so I don't see his face again. Or any of their faces.

Tempted to call my father, my finger hovers over the numbers. He'd be on my side. Unlike Ryker, who seems to not believe me.

I glance up to a soft knock at the door, following a turn of the handle. The door creaks open and Ryker flashes a sheepish smile. "Hey."

I drop my chin to avoid his gaze, still furious that he questioned me. I've never told him a lie. "My answer is no."

Sighing, I turn off my phone. There's no way I can call my dad. He'd buy a ticket on the first flight out. He has enough to worry about. *Like beating cancer.*

"Sorry. But I had to ask." Shoving his hands in his pockets, his gaze jumps around the room. "This is crazy. And not my life. My friend's life... this shit is normal. I have obligations and a career that I can't get caught up in—God knows what the hell is happening here." His voice strangled with frustration.

I'm officially more trouble than I'm worth. He's already made it clear how much he stays away from drama. "I'm sorry I came."

He releases a harsh breath, and heavy steps on the carpet follow. I lift my head when his shoes come toe to toe with mine. "I don't regret meeting you. And I sure as hell don't regret bringing you here. It's what comes after that I'll always regret."

My brows furrow. "After?"

"You going home."

"Ryker," my voice breaks along with my heart. I'd rather him say I'm too much drama for him. I stand up, our chests a fraction from touching. "My father—"

He presses his finger to my lips and nods in understanding. "I didn't think it'd hurt this bad saying goodbye."

It was painful the first time. This time might cause damage to my heart. "We've definitely gotten ourselves into a predicament."

"Who knew how much this Ball Boy would like the Island Girl?" I didn't. For a few quiet moments, I revel in our embrace, knowing the end is near, but there's nothing that can change it.

He drops his hands, each gripping a side of my hips. I can't control the heat between my legs when his smile quirks to life. It's like my arousal is connected to a damn string that flicks on when his lips curl up.

"Since you told me to go fuck myself, I think you owe me a dance." He's getting better at figuring out what I said in French. His fingers add pressure. "The one where these move really fast."

I've missed his playful tone the last couple days and I need it more than ever now. But I don't feel like dancing.

I dig my face into his shirt, letting his smell cocoon me. The tension in my shoulders release. "Whiskey, it'll be okay," he murmurs empty words because he has no idea. "Feel like making some cookies?"

I draw my head back. "You're kidding, right?" *Not the best time to request cookies.*

"It'll help you relax. Max has a stocked kitchen, and he said it was cool."

"I don't want to inconvenience him any more than I already have." He waves me off before grabbing my hand, leading me out the door. Truth is, it will help. I haven't been in the kitchen for a couple weeks and I miss it. It's the one place I can tune out my problems and do what I do best.

But first, we need to talk. I stop walking, yanking on his arm, and he glances over his shoulder at me. "Wait, I have to tell you something," I swallow the panic rising inside my chest. If he needs a reason to feel better about sending me home, I'm about to give it to him. "Remember when I told you about the foreigners I had affairs with?" He nods sharply. "Well, I looked one up. Because he's a lawyer and I thought maybe he could help me."

"I told you to trust Max." He looks at the phone sitting on the bed. "Did you contact him?"

I shake my head. "No. He's dead." Panic courses through me. "I looked for the other two men out of curiosity. They're dead too." His eyes widen. "What if this has something to do with them? What if I'm cursed? Or you're in danger because of me."

He looks at me with an incredulous stare. "Whiskey, you're overthinking things. I'm sure their deaths were a coincidence."

God, I hope so.

I PAUSE, hands covered in cookie dough, at the trill of a phone. Max answers from the living room and joins us in the kitchen. Ryker sits at the bar and we both stare at Max for an update. Three dozen cookies sit on the counter and I'm working on the fourth batch. The last hour I've immersed myself in sugar and flour, but the impending question has lingered in my mind. *Why am I here?*

Max holds the phone away from his ear and a male voice screams on the other end. "It's for you," Max says, handing the phone to Ryker. He sighs and takes it.

"Aiden, what's going on?"

My fingers squeeze the dough, anticipation mixed with unease when Ryker closes his eyes and color fades from his cheeks.

"I have no idea. She doesn't either." He listens and his jaw tics as he paces the kitchen floor. "Why do they still have her?"

I gasp, holding my hand over my lips. *They still have Addison?* Ryker shakes his head at me and mouths, "It's okay." Is it? Because it doesn't sound like it. It's been hours already.

After a couple minutes, he hands the phone to Max, and he walks out of the kitchen to talk to Aiden in private.

"This is all my fault," I cry. What's worse, I don't even know why.

"We don't know that," he lies. Even if I did nothing wrong, I'm still the reason everything is happening. "I'll go talk to Max and see what's happening next."

When I hear them talking in the other room, I stay still and lean with my ear in their direction. They're too far away for me to make out the words. At the sound of their footsteps, I start messing with the dough again. They both walk in with serious expressions.

"Aspen, Ryker told me about your *indiscretions*. Mainly about them being dead." I chew on my bottom lip. "I wouldn't ask if I didn't think there might be something to it."

I peer at Ryker, and a pained expression mars his face. "Whiskey, I'm sorry. But with everything going on, I thought the more information he has, the better." I flash a small smile. He's probably right.

With a heavy sigh, I begin by telling him their names and their jobs. "After they left the island, I never heard from them again."

"They were all married?"

Tears threaten and I whirl around to look outside the kitchen window, not wanting to see the judgments in their faces. My vision blurs. "I was stupid, young and so badly wanted to leave the island. Thought if they wanted me enough..." But they never did. I was used and tossed aside like a whore. It wasn't until the third time that I felt like one.

"Aspen, I get it. Men know what to say to impressionable young women to get what they want. Did their wives know?"

"Not that I'm aware of."

Max types the names into his computer one by one, reading out loud how they died. They deemed two suicides, with the third being murdered.

"Did any of them hurt you?" he asks.

I rub my temples. I'm not proud of who I was in the past. The desperation is demeaning. "*Not really*. Chuck Adams was the last of the three. I realized that no matter what I did, these guys wouldn't help me. He tried to get a little more physical with me. Wanted me to do things I wasn't comfortable with." I keep my gaze glued to the outside.

Ryker's chair drags across the floor and I imagine him walking out of the room, not wanting to hear this, and a pain in my chest spikes. Instead, his arms wrap around my chest and he kisses the top of my head. "It's okay," he whispers.

He rotates me so our bodies are mashed together. I whisper, "Thank you." When I pull back, Ryker wipes my tears away with his thumb. "I learned how to defend myself, so he didn't hurt me. Rather, I left him with a broken nose." He flashes an amused smirk.

That was the end of trusting men to help me. Determination to do it myself fueled the success of my business.

Max hums. "And he's the one who was murdered."

The guilt I was hoping he could ease, grows like a vine inside me. "Do you think that was because of me?"

He scratches his head. "I'm not sure how something that happened thousands of miles away and they left there like it never happened, had anything to do with their untimely deaths, but we can't discount it."

My prison kept me safe from the consequences of my actions. They are dead because of me. The gods righted the men's wrong. And now this... this is my punishment. I'm just uncertain what this is.

I rush out of the kitchen to the bathroom, locking the door behind me as bile from my stomach burns my throat.

"CAN I stay in here with you?" Ryker asks later that evening, bringing my last bag into the bedroom. He stands and shoves his hands into his athletic pants. Today weighs on his body, making him appear smaller.

"You don't have to. I'll be fine." I dig into my bag to find my toiletry bag. When I find it, I walk into the bathroom to avoid watching him leave.

The lights in the bedroom are dim and Ryker's tucked into the bed, leaning against the headboard.

"But I want to," he says when he meets my questioning glance.

With a quick snort, I reply, "So it seems." I pick out a night-shirt, ignoring the heat coming from his side of the bed as he watches me change. "Ryker, I'm drama you don't need. I'm giving you an out." It's my last attempt to make him leave. Except, the words sour on my lips as soon as they escape.

He yanks back the sheets and pats the space beside him. "What I need is for you to be beside me." I sigh and walk to the side of the bed, hesitating. "I promise I won't bite."

I sit on the bed, bringing my feet under the sheets and then Ryker pulls them up over my bare legs. His fingers graze my thigh by accident and I bite back the desire.

"Whiskey, you're so beautiful," he murmurs, wrapping my hair behind my ear. "You might not believe it, but I'm glad we met."

I close my eyes, reveling in his touch. No other man has ever made me feel so many emotions like he does. "This was easier when you were being an asshole."

The look of regret etched on his face reflects how I feel about leaving him. I'm so torn inside. Guilt that my dad is sick, yet I want to stay here makes me a horrible daughter.

"They released Addison."

My spine straightens and I grab his hand, hoping she's not in any trouble because of me. "That's good, right?"

"It is. She said when she ran the picture, the system glitched. There was information for a second, but it erased before she could read anything. That's why she called Max when she saw men asking for her. But she had to give them the picture."

"That's fine. It was only a picture of my family." But it means she was being interrogated because of it. I fall against the padded headboard. "We should call whoever and tell them where I'm at. They can ask me anything."

Ryker wraps his arm around my shoulder and pulls me into his body. "We'll figure it out tomorrow. Let's try to sleep."

CHAPTER TWENTY-THREE

ASPEN

"They're here," Max says, looking out the window to the vehicle that just pulled up the driveway. Ryker and I push off the couch and stand. Ryker's hand grips mine, tight. I squeeze with a single nod, reassuring him I'm okay. But I'm far from it.

This morning Max agreed to call the CIA and tell them where I was. He wasn't on board with it, but I told him either he did it or I did.

"Aspen, think about what you'll say before you answer his questions," Max warns. "You don't want them to use your words against you." I exhale, readying myself for something I can't imagine.

"We'll be right here," offers Ryker.

"Hmm," Max says to himself when he sees the guy walking up. He opens the door wide for the man to enter. A draft of frigid air follows him in. "Richard, good to see you." Relief floods my body. *He knows him.*

They shake hands. "Max Shaw, always a pleasure."

As soon as the man's eyes land on me, they widen. "Gabriella," he mutters in surprise and then clears his throat. He straightens his spine and tugs at his sleeves peeking out from under his black suit jacket. I take a step backward as his wrinkled glare burns holes in me. My gaze jumps from Ryker to Max in confusion. Max watches the man for a beat before correcting him. "Richard, this is Aspen Foley."

"Oh, I'm sorry." He scrambles and attempts to flash a warm smile, but it seems forced. "She reminds me of someone."

"Richard, I'm surprised you're here alone," Max says, glancing outside at the lone black SUV. "The Director of CIA rarely makes house calls."

The man slides his hands inside his suit pants pockets. His attention travels back to me, making my skin crawl. I don't like the guy's aura and I'm not sure why.

"The nature of the visit is sensitive and because of national security, it's above your clearance." His voice hardens, a direct jab at Max, yet his eyes stay pinned on me.

"Ms. Foley, can you confirm that the picture Mrs. Addison Roberts was in possession of was of you and your family?" I nod and his lips form a straight line. "I'm going to need you to come with me for questioning."

"What? No," Ryker clips, taking a step in front of me. "Why can't you question her here?"

"Ryker," Max warns, shaking his head. He's telling him I don't have a choice. And I'm the one who called this meeting.

"It's fine. I'll go. I have nothing to hide." With one quick squeeze, I let go of Ryker's hand. This will be a quick visit, especially if it's about my mom. I don't even remember her. Without that picture, I wouldn't know what she looked like.

Max's house disappears in the mirror. The man doesn't talk, not really. He mumbles to himself more than anything. His controlled demeanor from earlier unravels in front of me. A bead of sweat rolls down his temple and our eyes meet for a fraction of a second before I jerk my gaze away.

Fifteen minutes in the car, yet it feels like I've been in the car with him for hours. His anger escalates each passing mile. When he strikes his steering wheel and lets out a string of curse words, I know something isn't right.

What's worse, we're not anywhere near a town. The last sign said the next city was a hundred miles away. Snow-covered trees line the freeways with vast open fields beyond them. Peering at his gas gauge, I can only hope he's on empty so we pull over soon. That hope sinks to the bottom of my stomach, twisting it. It's full.

"Where are you taking me?" I finally ask, rotating in my seat. He grits his teeth and swerves to pull over, and I grab the dashboard to catch myself from slamming into the door. The tires squeal as we come to a complete stop. Cars speed by and I glance around wondering why he stopped.

"I only have one question. Where is Tobias Paul?" The venom in his voice pierces without touching me.

Who? I jerk my head to face the man, pointing a gun at my head. Fear lumps in my throat, choking out my words, and I hold my hands in the air. "I… I don't know who that is."

"I don't believe you, Gabriella."

Blinking back the tears burning my eyes, I choke out, "My name isn't Gabriella. I'm not from the United States. I only came to visit Ryker. You have the wrong person."

He shakes his head sharply. "No, I don't."

"Who is Tobias Paul?" I whisper, tears burning my cheeks.

"The man I hired to kill you twenty-four years ago."

CHAPTER TWENTY-FOUR

RYKER

"There has to be something we can do." Even I realize how messed up this is. Taking an innocent woman into custody with no reason is unjust. What a warm American welcome I'm giving her.

Max glances up from his computer. My feet won't stop pacing across the room.

"Ryker, it's the CIA. I don't know what to tell you. Everything has to do with the picture. Did you see it?"

I growl, the reminder that maybe she wasn't here for me is a slap in the face. "No. She didn't tell me she asked Addie to help her."

Something catches Max's attention out his window, and I follow his gaze. Two black SUVs pull up the long drive. *Thank god she's back.* We both beeline it to the door. Once outside, we watch four men step out of their vehicles, none being the Richard guy. *Or Aspen.* I jerk my head toward Max.

"Where is she?" I clip.

He shakes his head. "Let me handle this."

The four men stalk up the steps to where we're standing. I pull in a deep breath of the cool crisp winter air, doing nothing to cool off my rage.

"Max Shaw?" the taller stocky man asks, pulling out an ID and flashing it. His eyes are hard and all business. "I'm Agent Oliver Wilson with the CIA. You called about Ms. Aspen Foley, that is staying here. We're here to talk with her." My brows furrow in confusion. *They fucking already have her.*

Max appraises them before answering. Probably wondering what the hell is going on too. "Ms. Foley is no longer here."

The shortest of the four, wearing thick black-rimmed glasses, pulls out a small pad and pen. "Can you tell us where she went?" His nasally voice sends an irritating buzz through my head.

What game are they playing?

Max crosses his arms and stands tall. "You guys are an hour too late. Agent Richard Devereux was here earlier and took her in for questioning. You know your boss?"

The man stops writing and looks up, wide-eyed. Another man who has yet to talk, whips around and walks down the stairs, pulling out his phone.

"Are you sure?" Agent Wilson asks.

"Am I sure that it was Richard? Or that he has her in custody?" Max shoots back in an irritated tone. I focus on the guy by the vehicle on the phone, watching him pace while talking.

"Did he show you identification?" the guy retorts.

"Richard and I have worked together in the past. It was him."

The guys stare at Max, uncertain what to say, obviously not what they expected. Which leads me to lose my shit and spurt out, "Where the fuck did he take her?"

"Sir, please calm down. I'm sure there's been a miscommunication. Whoever instructed us to come here wasn't aware Agent Devereux was assisting on the case."

I throw my hands in the air. "What case? She's not even from here."

In a quick monotone voice, he answers, "We can't answer that."

I scrape my hand through my hair and jerk aside, mumbling, "Of course you can't." I throw the door open and storm inside.

Motherfucker.

Red tape bullshit. Why can't they see that something is amiss? Hopefully, Max can get more info from the guys. He's worked with them before. I'm just some overpaid jock to them. *Shit, to most people.* I stop pacing when the door opens. Max walks in with a grim look and shakes his head.

"They're being tight-lipped on this one."

I drop my chin and close my eyes, guilt weighing me down. If she didn't already hate me for acting like a total asshole, I'm sure she does now. I can't stay here and do nothing. Max grabs my arm as I stalk past him, ripping my keys out of my pocket.

"Where the hell do you think you're going?"

"I'll go find her myself."

Max barks out a humorless laugh. "Ryker, sit the fuck down. This is the CIA. You aren't finding her until they're ready to bring her back." I pin my glare on him, clenching my hand. "How much do you know this girl? Is she worth all this bullshit?"

My fist cocks back and swings. Max ducks, grabbing my arm and twisting it behind my back.

"Quarterback, you might be fast on the draw with a ball, but don't try to hit me again," he chuckles under his breath, shoving me away. I flip him off when I adjust my skewered shirt.

"She is worth it," I clip, walking away with my bruised ego. I've never felt this way about a woman before and I can't explain our connection, but I owe it to her to help. She's here because of me. And I'll be damned if I don't return her home safe.

"Okay," he says. "And just because they're not giving me anything doesn't mean I'm giving up on finding out what the hell is happening."

Relief, yet irritation fuels my body. "You could have said that from the beginning, asshole."

Stomping to the couch, I fall into it and lean back, waiting for Max to spit out his game plan. His eyes jump to my bouncing knee. Every nerve inside me is racing to go. *Do something.*

"She's with Richard so I'm not too worried. He's a respectable guy."

I narrow my eyes and lean my elbows on my knees. "Then why did he take her without his people knowing?"

"Not sure." He blinks. "But he used to be the Head of Security for President Malone and we've worked together on a few cases. He could be protecting her," he says with an unsettled tone, doing nothing to calm my nerves.

Max and I both stand tall as the front door opens. "Found something," Stone, Max's right-hand man and the computer genius on his team, declares as he struts through the front door. "Well, at least I think I did." We follow him into the kitchen where he sets his laptop down on the island. "First, I pulled Aspen's information. Her passport and birth certificate. That looked clean... until I dug deeper. When I pulled the hospital records where it's stated she was born, there was zip about her. She wasn't born there, or they deleted her records. But that's more than I found on her parents. I couldn't find info on them anywhere. I located a couple people with those names, but either they were dead or close to it because they were in their nineties."

None of this makes sense. I met her dad, and he wasn't in his nineties.

"We don't know anything then?" I snap.

Stone holds up his finger, his smile growing. Leave it to the computer geek to find this amusing. "I didn't say that. Max told me Richard called her Gabriella when he first saw her. I did a search typing in Richard Devereux and the name Gabriella." He turns his computer around to face us. "This pulled up."

Max and I both read the article's title. *"President Malone's one-year-old daughter, Gabriella Malone, was found deceased."*

My head jerks up, confused more than ever. "I don't understand. What does this have to do with Aspen?"

"Keep reading," Stone presses, pointing to the computer.

My eyes roam over the article. Most of it, I've read before. We learned about it in history in high school and then again in government in college. There were so many rumors and conspiracy theories about what happened. I keep reading, waiting for something to pop out. It doesn't take long.

'Gabriella's body was buried in a shallow grave in a wooded area on the outskirts of Aspen, Colorado.'

My heart slams against my ribcage, confusion flooding my vision. "It has to be a coincidence. That child was dead."

Max bobs his head from side to side. "If I remember, the body was burned beyond recognition. They only confirmed it was her because they found pieces of her clothing close to the grave."

"Correct," Stone states. "And there were plenty of theories it wasn't her."

"So, what? Someone kidnapped her and flew her to an isolated island to keep her hidden?" The outlandish words that fly out of my mouth sound more like plausibility to my ears. Resting both my hands on the countertop, I drop my head between my shoulders. If someone was trying to hide her, taking her to a small South Pacific island isn't too far-fetched. Aspen's voice is clear in my mind. *"My father is extremely protective. He doesn't trust anyone."*

The hair on my arms rise. I found a buried treasure. And just like in the movies, messing with it always releases a dangerous storm. What the hell did I do?

"If it's her," Max says, emphasis on *if*, "at least Richard has her. He was the President's right-hand man. Shit, he was his best friend."

Stone snaps his fingers at Max. "He was. But most of the

conspiracy theories said that it was an inside job. No one's closer to you than your best friend."

Hearing what I was thinking makes my fears explode. The situation just took a turn for the worse. She's the one in danger. And we might have just handed her to her killer.

CHAPTER TWENTY-FIVE

ASPEN

My eyes never leave his constant movement. Methodically, he peeks through the thick curtained windows. One by one and then he checks the doors, unlocking and locking them again. Five times now and we've hardly been here an hour. Whoever he's waiting for, he's nervous.

We traveled by foot for a mile in the freezing cold to the abandoned house in the jungle after we switched cars three times at different locations. Each place deserted and had been for some time, so there was nowhere to run. He had my hands tied, and a gun pointed at me most of the time.

Yet, there's a small voice inside of me that doesn't want to run. Like it knows he's speaking the truth.

His unquestioning confidence that I'm Gabriella is tugging on a string buried deep inside me. *Why?* Who is Gabriella? And who is Tobias Paul?

"Why did you bring me to the jungle?"

He lets out a sarcastic laugh. "You aren't in the jungle, Gabriella. More like a forest." He stops moving and levels his cold ice-blue eyes on mine. They harden looking at me.

I swallow hard at his hatred. "My name is not Gabriella."

"It was." A ball of anger knots in my belly, and I want to spit at him. "You've grown into a beautiful woman. You look just like her." *Her?* His eyes roam down my body, making me shudder. "She wasn't my type, neither are you."

"Who do you think I am?"

He checks his watch before perching on a barstool across the room as if he's determined he has time before the monster appears. His fingers clutch the gun as he wistfully stares past me. A blanket of restless unease covers him from head to toe. "Who are you," he responds, not as a question but more of a statement. "You are the one person who can destroy me." He waves his gun. "I might as well put this up to my head and pull the trigger."

"Why don't you," I dare him. His eyes flash to mine.

"Because I'm going to make the man who put this in motion, suffer, first."

"Tobias Paul?" I take a guess.

He nods. "So, you know him?"

"I don't."

His lips twist as he studies me. I recognize that look well. My dad would do it when he was trying to figure out if I was lying. More often than not, he was correct, so Richard should be able to see the same thing. I'm not lying. "Where are you from? And who raised you?"

I answer to prove he has mistaken me for the wrong person. "I'm from Tahiti. And my father, Rudy Foley, raised me."

"And your mother?"

I stuff my feet underneath me, uncomfortable talking about my mom to a stranger. "She left me when I was a baby. She didn't prefer a simple island life." I hear my dad's voice as I say those words. *His words.* I don't have any idea if that is really why she left. It's just what he always told me. I sigh.

Stop second-guessing your dad.

I love my dad. He has always been there for me. And how do I repay him? Leave him when he's sick. Now, I might never see him again. Tears pool and I blink them away.

Stay focused, Aspen.

"Here's the thing. Rudy Foley and Rose Burnet don't exist." I glare at the man who's obviously trying to get me to tell him something different. But I can't. *Those* are my parents. I can't explain why they can't locate them in their system. He raises a brow. "You really didn't know they weren't your parents, did you?"

Yes, they are! "Why are you doing this to me? Who are my parents then?" I cry out, my emotions breaking through my tough facade.

"That will be answered in due time."

He has to be lying. He can't even answer my questions. "How can I destroy you if I don't know who you are?"

"Because you're alive."

I wonder for how long, though. "If you take me to the airport, I'll take a flight back to Tahiti tonight. I'll leave here and never return."

He draws in a quick breath and releases it. "It's too late for that."

I drop my head in silent resolve. It's time to escape. All those years my father taught me self-defense and martial arts, I never imagined I would need it. I just want to go home.

Although, there's one question that's been nagging me and I'd like an answer before I fight for my life. I lift my head and pin my stare on the man.

"Qui est Tobias?" Not until the question slips off my tongue do I catch that I asked in French. I open my mouth to repeat the question in English, but he answers before I can get the words out.

"He's a ghost. The military trained him to kill, and when he got out, he became a contract killer. Dangerous doesn't begin to describe him. The people that usually meet him are already dead."

The knot of fear in my throat strangles my words. *This is who he's waiting for?* "Why... why would he come here?"

"For you."

Spikes of that same fear wrap around my spine, stealing my fight from me. I'm certain my training is a five-year-old's karate chop compared to his. Is he coming to finish the job he paid him to do? My gaze bounces throughout the room, frantically searching for anything to help me escape. Darkness on the other side of the drapes makes me shiver. He could be watching us and we'd never know.

"Don't think about trying to escape," he snaps, holding his gun up.

"Why are we in the middle of nowhere if you're expecting someone to find us?"

He releases a humorless laugh. "I left breadcrumbs just in case he doesn't already have a direct link to you. He'll find us." A direct link to me? What does that mean?

I bite my lip, silently questioning if I was to escape, if I could find my way through the thick freezing black forest. The cold still stings my bones. A tremble vibrates through me. Neither situation sounds promising. I hug my knees and drop my head between my arms.

Minutes turn into hours and nothing happens. Richard remains on guard and I struggle to keep my eyes open, watching him. The quiet house is warm, but a thick layer of dust covers every square inch of the place. I catch a glint of a spider web in the corner when the heat turns on, making it sway in the air.

I was hoping he would relax in a chair, maybe even fall asleep, giving me an opportunity to escape. But he's vigilant in his post. It's useless asking questions he won't answer.

"Can I use the restroom?" I ask, my voice raw with emotion. He eyes me for a moment.

"I'm not taking off the cuffs."

I hold my hands up in the air. "That's fine. But I really need to go."

He jerks his head to a small hallway. There's only two doors, I assume they go to a bedroom and the bathroom. The first door is the bathroom. Stopping in the doorway, I lean back, glancing to the other door. The light from the living room illuminates a bed, but other than that, it looks empty.

"Gabriella, don't make me have to stand over you while you pee," Richard threatens. I squeeze my eyes shut, wishing he'd stop calling me that, but rush into the bathroom, shutting the door behind me. He is not going to watch me pee.

While it wasn't ideal, it was doable. I'm washing my hands when the lights flicker off. Everything stills in the darkness except my heart trying to escape up my throat. I turn off the running water and listen, running my wet palms down my pants.

I gasp, covering my mouth with my hands, as a loud thump hits the ground outside the door. Falling back against the wall, fear takes hold of my being, shaking it to the core. The silence on the other side of the door is painstaking torture.

Is he here? Is he waiting outside the door to kill me?

After minutes of continued silence, I blow out a breath and reach for the doorknob. Squeezing the metal handle and twisting as quietly as possible, I slowly turn it. I close my eyes for a beat, thankful it didn't make a sound. But freeze when the door squeaks as I pull it wide. Only opened a quarter of the way, I wait for a sound. Nothing.

I release the handle. Holding my breath, I wince as I move the door open the rest of the way, this time it sways with no noise.

Peeking around the door, only darkness greets me. There's a chill in the air without the heat and a shiver runs up my spine. I glance to the bedroom with a thought of locking myself in. But the hollow wooden door wouldn't protect me against anything.

Why isn't Richard making any noise?

"Richard?" I whisper from the narrow hallway.

I flinch as he replies, "I'm out here." Not expecting to hear him, I blow out the breath I was holding, leaning my head against the doorjamb. "I need you to come out here." I hesitate, trying to decipher if the tone of his voice has changed. "Now, Gabriella."

Nope, he's still the demanding asshole. I grind my teeth together and walk out into the living room. A candle flickers from a side table. It's enough to light up half the room.

And light up the man's body laid out on the floor. My throat constricts and a sharp pain shoots through my chest as I run to the man.

"Dad!"

CHAPTER TWENTY-SIX

ASPEN

Tears flood my vision, and I blink them back as I check for a pulse on his neck. "He's not dead. At least, not yet."

"What did you do to him?" I scream. Turning back, I tap my dad's cheek. "Dad, wake up. Please wake up." With a quick scan of his body, nothing seems wrong. A soft moan floats out of his mouth.

"Fucking bastard," he rasps, rubbing the back of his head. I sit back on my knees, giving him room to sit up. When our eyes meet, his body deflates as he hangs his head low. The moment of silence between us feels like I just fell in a long narrow hole. It's suffocating. "I'm so sorry, Aspen."

Richard clears his throat and my dad shoots an icy glare at him. "Well, isn't this nice? A family reunion, of sorts."

"You don't need to involve Aspen in this," my dad's voice clips. His eyes jump to my handcuffed hands and his expression hardens. He pushes up from all fours and stands. Richard points the gun at my dad's head.

"It's too late for that. Old man, you're getting sloppy in your old age. I thought this would be harder."

What the heck is going on? Do they know each other? I stand up too and flick my gaze back and forth between the two men. My dad's murderous smirk affirms my fears. He knows him.

"You figured you could get away with this, didn't you?"

He gives a sharp nod. "I did."

Richard shakes his head and tsks. "I guess I have to finish what you started." My dad's chest puffs out and he takes a step to block me from Richard. "You think you can stop me?"

"What is he talking about?" I plead to my dad.

"Yeah, Tobias, tell her."

My breath gets caught in my chest and I stumble back, slamming into the wall. I shake my head with force, an uneasy tremble flowing through my veins. "No. Tell him he's wrong. That's not your name."

My father is not a killer. He's not *my* killer.

His face twists with regret and I roll my lips in between my teeth to hold in the cry of betrayal and disgust souring my mouth.

"Tell him," I plead again, hot tears stream down my face.

"I'm so sorry."

His apology cuts a deep wound. My knees give out from under me and I slide down the wood-paneled wall until my butt hits the ground. Nothing makes sense. I dig my palms in my eyes. Past moments flash behind my eyelids. Good memories. Were they all lies?

"Tell her who she is, Tobias."

I lift my eyes, with one last silent plea that he didn't lie to me my entire life even though the truth is written all over his face. Blinking through the tears, I wait for him to say something. *Anything.* His mouth opens and shuts a couple times.

Finally, he starts with, "I love you. You will always be my daughter."

My eyes never leave his, even when Richard barks out a sadistic laugh. "Except she's not. She was not yours to take," he yells, slamming his hand down on the table, his patience running thin.

My dad doesn't even flinch. "You were..." He pauses, swallowing hard. "You were one when I kidnapped you."

My mouth gapes open, and I suck in a breath for oxygen to move through my system again. My head feels faint and I fight to stay conscious. Part of me wants him to stop. If I'm going to die anyway, I don't want to know the truth. I want to die loving my dad.

But he doesn't stop.

"Your..." he struggles to say the next word, "... father was the President of the United States. He was about to sign something into law that would put a very large industry out of business. A lot of powerful people in the world weren't happy. They hired me to kill you. With help from Richard."

"You bastard, I didn't want this. I didn't want to help! They made me. They threatened my family. It was them or *her*."

The words run together after he said my father was the President. I can't focus on anything other than that. It's hard enough to keep breathing.

"But you failed," snaps Richard. "And now you've ruined my life. Once this gets out, I'm over. Too many people are aware of her now. And if I go down, so are you."

I scream as a gunshot rings out, echoing in my ear. My father crumbles over, catching himself on the arm of a chair. "Dad!"

As I crawl over to him, he mouths, "Stay there." He grips his arm and blood runs around his fingers. Everything happens so fast, yet in slow motion. He pulls a knife out of his shoe and flings it straight at Richard. I gasp, digging my face into my arms, when it hits him square in the neck. Stomach bile threatens to come up at the sound of him gargling what I imagine is blood.

I try to block out the sounds, dreaming of the ocean. Free with nature, where there are no lies, only truths. But the only thing I can focus on is the sounds in the room. When a grunt meets a grunt, I peek up. My dad knocks Richard back, kicking the gun out of his hand.

Or, not my dad.

A killer.

"You… you just killed him," I stammer, watching him search the room for something.

He sighs heavily. When he finds a bag, he picks it up and drops it on the counter, digs through it, and pulls out a shirt to wrap around his bleeding upper arm. It reminds me Richard shot him.

"Are you okay?" Worry mixed with fear keeps me frozen in place.

I don't know him.

He groans as he tightens the shirt. "It'll be fine. It was a clean shot." I stare at him. What does that even mean? "Aspen, it was him or us. He was not letting us walk out of here alive." His voice doesn't carry an ounce of regret for what he did.

"You're really a hitman?"

The last half-hour temporarily made me forget why we're here to begin with. I guess getting shot and killing someone supersedes kidnapping someone and lying to them your whole life.

"So, do I call you Tobias or Rudy?" My voice drips with bitter distaste.

He blows out a ragged breath. "I'll tell you everything. But I need to get you out of here. Just in case Richard had help."

He digs into Richard's pants pocket until he finds the handcuff key. When he offers his hand to help me up, I narrow my eyes. "Why should I trust you? You're a trained killer." I gasp at a fleeting thought and my eyes bulge out. "Did you kill the men I had affairs with?" Pushing myself up off the floor, I pin him with my stare. "Tell me that wasn't you."

His jaw clicks. "Aspen, those pieces of scum used you. They

were a waste of skin and didn't deserve the memories they had of you."

"So, you decided they should die," I scream. "Those were my mistakes and now because of you, I have to live with the guilt that they're dead."

With no emotion, he replies, "I didn't kill two of them. They took their own life when given the option."

I blink. Who is this guy? This is not the man who raised me for twenty-four years. I'm afraid to ask about the last one, but the words fall out before I can stop them. "And the third?"

He scowls, finally showing some emotion. "I would have given him the same option, but when I found out that his current mistress was sixteen, he didn't deserve to live."

I knock the thought out of my head that I *might* agree with him. *No, no, I don't.* No one deserves to be murdered. "Who's the woman in the picture?" His brows furrow, confused. "With the three of us. I thought she was my mother."

"She was a colleague. She helped me get you out of the country." Lies. Everything was lies.

He holds up the key, stepping in front of me. "I hate you," I sob, lifting my hands. As soon as the cuffs are off, I rub my raw wrists.

He nods, dropping his head. "I know."

CHAPTER TWENTY-SEVEN

ASPEN

We both stare straight ahead as the car idles, the only sounds are passing vehicles on the highway. The rest stop is dimly lit, with a couple cars parked on the other end of the lot, closer to the bathrooms.

I've never felt so alone. Or confused. "Why?" I choke out. It's the beginning of every question I have, but the one word alone asks it all.

His fingers grip the steering wheel, the whites of his knuckles bleed through his old tired hands. "I was hired to kill you." I still can't believe someone would hire someone to kill a baby. He tilts his head toward me. "I know what you're thinking. A baby? In all the hits I've done, it had never been a child. But I never considered I *couldn't*. My heart was already stained black." He blows out a ragged breath. "The day it was to happen, you stared up at me with those eyes and said daddy. You held your arms out and that black heart was yours forever. I couldn't do it."

"Why didn't you take me back?"

"You called me daddy. *Me.*" He grips his chest. "You became something that was mine. You were in danger and I couldn't place you back in harm's way. If it wasn't me who carried out the hit, someone else might have."

"But you don't know that. I wasn't yours," I cry out, trembling.

He drops his head. "I can't say it enough. I'm sorry."

"Were you ever sick?"

Bile rises in my throat as he shakes his head. I dive out of the car and round the back so I'm not in sight. My legs give out and I crumble to the ground, heaving between tears and disgust. All the time I worried about him or had sleepless nights agonizing about losing him was all for nothing. Lies. All of it.

I hear him get out, ice that hasn't melted yet from the shade of the tree crunches under his feet as he steps toward me. When he puts his hand on my back, I swat it away and violently shake my head. "No. I don't want you to touch me." Anger replaces disgust the longer he remains by my side. "Did you ever wonder what would happen when I found out the truth?" I push off the cold vehicle, staring at him.

"I lived that fear every day. I knew it would come, but I couldn't bring myself to tell you. It would ruin the one bright thing in my evil world."

I wipe away the salty tears and sniff. He manipulated me my entire life and I can't bring myself to hate him. I'm furious, but it's because of him, I'm alive.

"I tried my best to give you a good life."

I cross my arms over my chest. "I don't know you at all."

"The only thing I care that you know is I love you."

I rub my temples, not knowing what to say. A horn in the distance makes me jump and I lean on the car to hold me up as I catch my breath. My heart races so fast, it's drumming in my ears. This is all too much.

"Breathe, Aspen," I hear right before I see stars and then nothing.

. . .

WHEN I COME TO, I'm in my dad's arms. *No, not my dad.* My head hurts from thinking. He places me in the back seat and I lay there feeling drained and empty.

"Sleep, Aspen. It's been a long day," he orders, placing a blanket over me. His deep gravelly voice has always calmed me. Now, I don't know if it still does or I'm too tired to fight. My eyes are heavy and I blow out a deep sigh, sleep pulling me under.

I JOLT upright at the sound of a car door slamming. Morning sunlight beams in through the front window. My eyes land on a guy, walking away from his vehicle a couple spaces over from where we're parked.

Wait, where am I?

I crane my neck to look out the back window at the stone building in front of the parking lot I'm in. Two American flags hang at the entrance, on each side of the FBI sign. Panic at the thought of my dad turning himself in pinches my chest.

They'll kill him.

I spin and sit forward, hoping to find him asleep in the front seat. But the only thing there is a letter and a phone. The car is idling so I wonder when he left. I sit back and unfold the letter. My fingers shake, afraid of what I'm about to read.

DEAREST ASPEN,

You'll never know how much it pains me to see you hurting. I can't apologize enough for being the cause of that. I don't regret my decision because you made my life worth living. I wasn't just a soldier. Or a killer. I was a dad. And for that, I thank you. You'll always be my little Asperanza. Stay driven and stubborn in all that you do. You'll probably never see me again, but know I'll continue to watch you from a distance.

I love you with everything inside me, even my black heart.

~ Dad

Please take the phone into the FBI building and ask for Agent Lopez. Tell him who you are and hand him the phone. There is a recording and video he'll want to see.

TEARS ROLL DOWN my face as a weight lifts off my chest. He's not turning himself in. I squeeze by eyes shut. *Shouldn't I want him to turn himself in?* He's killed people that I know. He kidnapped me. *But he didn't kill me.*

Reading the letter again, my thoughts filter back to my childhood memories. Indoor tents that were big enough to fill with all my stuffed animals, fishing trips where he would sing and make up silly stories about mermaids, the nights I was afraid of monsters always ended in tickling attacks. The memories flood back. One by one. He was a great dad, I can't deny him that.

But now, I'm stuck in a strange world, alone and confused. I have a mom and dad who have mourned me. Can I disrupt their lives? Would they want to know that I never died? I fold the letter in my hands and grip the phone so tight, my fingers hurt. What if I went on with my life and didn't tell anyone? I could drive this car and run. I shake my head at the thought, too many people are looking for me. And Ryker. He must be going out of his mind wondering what happened. But knowing the truth, he'll want to stay far away from this train wreck. The tight twist in my chest isn't helping. *One issue at a time, Aspen.*

Taking a deep breath in and blowing it out my mouth, I lean across the front to grab the keys and then open the door. The frigid air smacks me in the face, reminding me—I'm alive. I might not know what'll happen tomorrow, but I've never been one to back down from a fight. And this is the fight of my life.

When I open the heavy metal-framed door, a swoosh of hot air envelops me and I'm greeted by a security guard, directing me to go through the metal detectors.

"Are you okay, ma'am?" he asks, concern written on his face. I manage a small smile and nod although my inner voice is screaming *no, nothing will ever be okay, again.*

"Yes, thank you." He surveys me for a minute before letting me through.

I stuff the letter into my back pocket and put the phone in the bin. On the other side, I focus on my steps to the information desk.

"Hi. I'm looking for an Agent Lopez."

"Okay. I just need you to fill this out." The receptionist's soft voice helps calm my buzzing nerves, not knowing if I'm at the right place. She hands me a check-in log. I write my name and then stare at it for a second. Should I have written my real name? "Are you finished, hun?" she asks as I contemplate who the hell I am. I give up and hand it back. She picks up the phone and calls someone. Trying to calm my racing heart, I spin around and focus on the building.

A couple tables with chairs aren't far from the desk, so I turn and whisper, pointing to the tables. A sympathetic expression crosses her face. I'm sure I look like a hot mess.

I stare at the phone in my hand, flipping it over and over, wondering what's on it. "Ms. Foley, I'm Agent Lopez. How can I help you?"

I glance up at the nicely-dressed, middle-aged man, with warm chocolate-colored eyes, hands clasps in front of him. I stand up and clear the emotional knot lodged in my throat.

The words on my tongue are about to change my life. I wipe my free hand down my jeans.

"Hi. I… um…" I swallow, taking a moment, trying not to pass

out again. His eyes jump to the phone I'm squeezing in my palm and back to my face. "My name is Gabriella Malone, and I was kidnapped twenty-four years ago."

CHAPTER TWENTY-EIGHT

ASPEN

The plane's tires grind against the pavement in the unknown city, and my mind has passed the point of processing the easiest of questions. My body, exhausted from the last twenty hours of being poked, prodded, and questioned, is numb. But they confirmed it, I'm Gabriella Malone.

"Ready?" an agent asks, standing and peering at me with a bag in his grip. I blink. One word. It's a simple word, yet I don't have any idea how to answer. Am I ready for what?

To leave this plane?

To start my life over?

To meet my actual parents?

That would be a universal no.

Then again, I wasn't ready to find out that the last twenty-four years was all a lie either. But here I am, out of sorts, like I don't belong anywhere. How does one restart their life from scratch? The bag he's holding is the only thing I own.

"Ms. Foley," the agent states. I blink him back into focus.

Is that still my name?

"Yes?" I squeak.

"We're here. We should get going." *Where is here?*

"Oh." I unbuckle my seatbelt and drag my body up, standing. Ready or not, I'm being thrown into an unknown world. I follow him down the aisle and walk out the door. The bright sun and warmth surprise me, and I hold a hand in front of me to shield my face. Yellow grass surrounds the desolate private airport and in the distance, I see hills covered with trees. A stark opposite of all the cement in New York City.

"Where are we?" I step down the narrow airplane stairs, making sure not to trip.

"Austin, Texas," he replies over his shoulder. Three black SUVs await us at the bottom of the stairs. A blond woman leans against one, dressed in a plaid long-sleeved button-up shirt and jeans. She stands out from the multiple men all dressed in black suits looking serious with black shades covering their eyes. My escort places my bag in the back of one of the SUVs.

"Hi, Ms. Foley. I'm Agent Halli Hughes. I'm with the Secret Service." She extends her hand. When I slip mine in hers, she grips it with a firm shake. "Anything you need, let me know and I'll get it for you."

Can I have my old life back?

She opens the passenger door for me. I glance in the empty SUV and again at the eerie quiet airfield. Last time I got into one of these vehicles, it didn't work out for me, which was merely two days ago.

"Where are you taking me?" This time I ask before getting in.

"We were informed you know Addison Roberts?" She waits for a confirmation. I nod, wondering what Addie has to do with this. "Her aunt has a ranch here." Her tone is all business, unlike her outfit. And her answer explains nothing, but she looks at me expectantly.

Hoping I don't regret this, I get into the vehicle and she shuts the door behind me. My butt sinks into the smooth black leather that smells new in the spotless interior. Agent Hughes slides in at her side and pushes a button to start the engine. I shiver as cool air blows out of the vent right on my face. I move the vent away from me. It's warmer here than New York, but not that much.

After minutes of silence, I ask, "Have they found my dad?" I half-expect her to give me a dirty look for referring to him as my father, but she maintains her neutral expression.

"They haven't." She continues to look forward as we drive out of the airport with one SUV in front of us, the other behind. I blow out a silent breath of relief. "But to be honest, he hid you for twenty-four years, so I doubt they'll ever be able to find him."

Staring out at empty fields passing by in a blur, I wonder where he disappeared to. And if he was able to get treatment for his gunshot wound. "Thank you for being honest with me."

"I'm sure the last thing you need from me is to sugarcoat things."

I chuckle to myself. No, I have enough sugarcoated things in my life. And then my mind switches to Ryker and his look of concern as I left Max's house. "Does Ryker Dallas know I'm okay?"

Her solid tight lips, crack a smirk. "They informed him." I wait for her to continue, but she doesn't. At least he knows I'm safe.

The drive is quick and as we pull into the ranch; we drive through two black metal gates. Cows and horses graze in pastures on both sides of us. The dirt road jerks us around and we both end up laughing as we're tossed inside the cab like a salad. A puff of dirt leads us up road.

"Wow, this is rural," she says in a lighter tone than before, gripping the steering wheel.

"Where do you live?" I ask, holding on to the handle above my head for dear life.

"I travel a lot, but my home base is Washington, D.C."

As soon as we hit a cement driveway attached to a sprawling

one-story red brick house with white columns, we park and I'm instructed to stay in the car until given the okay. The men in the front vehicle step out and disperse around the property, one goes into the home. Once she gives the go-ahead and turns the car off, I hop out. A warm hushed breeze whips around me with a *moooo* off in the distance. It's very peaceful.

I wonder how long they plan on keeping me here. The front door opens and a man and woman step out. They head toward us, hand in hand.

"Mr. and Mrs. Smith, thank you for having us," Agent Hughes asserts, taking charge and shaking their hands.

"You can call us Ted and Amy," Amy says, smiling at me. Tears pooling in her eyes confuse me. "I'm sorry, I didn't expect to be this emotional." She holds her hand over her heart. I lift a brow in the agent's direction wondering why this stranger is taking me being here so personal.

"Amy, why don't you show these guys where their rooms are," Ted says, slapping her ass. She playfully twists her lips, but it pulls her out of the lull she's in, directed at me.

Once everyone is inside except me and Agent Hughes, I ask, "Why are we here?" No one knows about me, so this seems a little extreme.

"It's not one of our normal places, so it's off the grid. We can control things here. We also hoped it would be easier to integrate you where it's not so busy."

I stare at the woman. Her blond hair is tight in a bun, and she stands with confidence. I catch myself straightening my back when I'm next to her.

"Integrate? I wasn't raised with animals. I might be from the jungle, but my father taught me American ways to do stuff. I mean, not my father." I sigh in frustration, not knowing what they expect me to say when I talk about the man who raised me.

She cocks her brow. "Integrate was probably the wrong word.

More like introduce you to our world. But Aspen, this is your life. No one will question what you decide. We don't think you'll fall back into your real parents' life like you're a child who just went away to college. This is why we're here." She stretches her arms out, the countryside behind her. "Everything that happens here is up to you. At your own pace."

"Thank you."

We walk in silence toward the brick house. The warm air is humid without the hint of salt. Not like home. I clench my eyes shut, squeezing the bridge of my nose. *Not my home anymore.*

"Agent Hughes, do they know?" I whisper the one question that gnaws away any positive thoughts I'm having. She glances over with a confused expression. "That I'm alive?"

"First thing, please call me Halli. Second, they're being briefed tomorrow." She stops walking and rotates her body to face me. Her expression turns more serious. "Aspen, this situation is unprecedented. But like I said, I'll be honest with you. You need to ready yourself for a shitstorm. You are about to change history books. Not only did your parents mourn you, but so did the country."

That explains Amy's reaction. The panic buzzing morphs to solid stone, weighing on my chest, suffocating me. "Whoa, breathe Aspen," she blurts, wrapping her arms around my waist. I pull in quick shallow breaths, fighting to not fall into the tunnel of blackness as my vision hazes. I hold myself up with my hands on my knees. "That's it. *Maybe* I shouldn't have been so honest."

I puff out a laugh and stand when the lightheadedness eases. "No, I need honest. My entire life has been one colossal lie."

"You have life experiences that are yours. Tell me about Aspen. What do you like to do? What was it like growing up on a beautiful island? What are your dreams?"

She's right. Nobody can take away my memories. Those things

are mine. We both lean against columns, facing each other, and I tell her a few stories about growing up and my life.

"You owned a business?"

Owned is the keyword. My smile drops thinking about how I'm disappointing all the hotels. They depend on me to provide them cookies.

"*I did.* Not anymore."

"No one can stop you from going back if that's what you wish."

I let out a humorless laugh and direct my gaze to the horses in the distance. For years I planned to leave the island that imprisoned me, and now that I'm not going back, I'm having regrets. I'm scared of the unknown. And there are so, so many. It's ironic that my prison feels safe to me now.

"I don't know what I want. It's just all I know."

Taking the three steps up to the porch, a swing sits off to the right. I sit in it, letting the warmth of the sun saturate my skin for a while longer and swipe my foot to sway me back and forth.

Memories of Ryker keep popping up in my thoughts. Through the midst of the unknowns, his chiseled face is clear as day. Telling myself that he won't want to deal with all this hasn't helped diffuse the feelings I have for him. The second I stepped out of Max's house, he probably washed his hands of me. I'm not good for his image.

"After we get settled, there is a Target up the road a few miles. We'll go pick up any essentials you need. Aiden Roberts had your bags sent from Max Shaw's house, so you do have those waiting for you inside."

"Target?"

She gasps in surprise. "You've never been to Target?"

I shake my head, and she puffs out an exaggerated sigh. "You were raised with animals," she jokes and then laughs at herself. She's a bit odd. "Oh! We can pick up some groceries and you can bake some of your famous cookies."

"They're not famous," I chuckle at her attempt to make me feel better.

"Yet."

"You haven't even had one."

Her eyes gleam. I like her better when she loosens up. "Let's fix that. I have a major sweet tooth."

I sigh. *So does Ryker.*

"HOLY COW!" Halli beams. I tilt my head, confused by her choice of words.

"Does it taste like meat?" Picking up a warm sugar cookie off the cooling rack, I take a quick bite, afraid the extract turned bad. Relief that it tastes normal and not like bovine settles my panic. That would be embarrassing.

She stuffs the whole cookie in her mouth, licking away the crumbs left on her lips. "Nooo. Have you never heard that phrase? It's delicious," she mutters with a full mouth. "This is the best cookie I've ever had. What's in it that makes it different?" She grabs another one and eats it in one bite. She wasn't kidding. Major sweet tooth.

"It's a secret," I lie.

It's not. It's the Tahitian vanilla extract from one specific tiny farm in Tahiti. His process is a secret, but he produces the purest, richest vanilla I have tried.

Oh no! I drop my head with guilt, smacking myself in the head. I'm the one who pushed him to produce more. My order makes up more than half his stock each month and now with me not there, his business will suffer. I make a mental note to call him at some point. Maybe I can get some shipped here.

"Guys, come in and grab a cookie," Halli says into her sleeve.

Good thing I brought a larger bottle of extract with me. If

there's anything about my life for certain, it's baking. "I want to open a bakery," I blurt.

"Sign me up for a dozen a week." Halli moans, eating another cookie. "Wait, make that two dozen."

"What smells wonderful in here," Amy says walking into the kitchen with her nose in the air.

She glances around the messy kitchen and I'm about to apologize but Halli exclaims, "You have to try these cookies. I swear they have crack in them. I can't stop eating them." She jerks her head toward me and asks in a worried tone. "They don't have crack in them, do they?"

I scratch my head. All these unfamiliar words are baffling. "Crack? I... I'm not sure what that is."

"Drugs."

I laugh out loud, wondering how I'll ever learn the lingo. "No drugs, I promise."

Amy takes one and splits it in half before taking a bite. She hums and waits to finish before saying, "This is fantastic, Aspen. Is it just a sugar cookie?"

"It is."

The looks on their faces give me hope that I can offer something different. "Can I bake you guys some other pastries?"

"You can make whatever your heart desires," Amy says. "As long as I get a piece."

I throw my hair up in a messy bun, already planning the menu. I spend the rest of the day making one dessert after another. As fast as the oven will allow me to bake. I'd do anything to forget about my life right now.

With Amy's blessing, I search her kitchen for platters and put all the pastries on the island. By the time daylight disappears, I have the kitchen cleaned and a buffet of colorful sugar treats. I squeal with delight at how it looks. A variety of cookies, Firi Firi (a Tahitian fried donut), coconut cake, and a new recipe I'm trying out—Whiskey cupcakes inspired by Ryker. *I couldn't help it.*

When I walk into the living room a few agents are relaxing on the couch with Amy and her husband, watching TV. Halli's on her computer, sitting at a small desk in the corner of the room. I clear my throat and everyone turns their attention to me.

Twisting my shirt in my hand, I'm suddenly worried that they'll hate everything. "Um, do we want to eat dinner first?" I say, not even sure what that would be since I've been hoarding the kitchen all day.

"No," Halli and another agent say simultaneously. I need to learn their names. They introduced themselves at one point, but I was still in a state of shock.

"You've been killing us with the wonderful smells," Halli says, jumping up and making a beeline toward the kitchen. The other agents pop up from their seats and race her to the kitchen.

"We better hurry before Hughes eats it all," one of them says.

I chuckle. "Oh, that will be happening."

They stop in their tracks at the sugar explosion. Halli gasps, bouncing on her toes. "Where do I even start? Everything looks amazing."

I shift my body as gentle hands rest on my shoulders. "Wow. That is a piece of art," Amy softly says, gazing at the island and then to me. Her warm smile is one I always imagined a mom would give her daughter. "I'm sure they taste as good as they look."

"I hope you like them."

"Well, it looks like if I don't get in there to get a plate, there won't be any left."

"You snooze, you lose, babe," Ted says with a pile on his plate.

"Geez, here I thought you were getting enough for me too." We both laugh as he shakes his head like that's a crazy notion.

I anxiously stand back while they test everything. "Oh, my

gosh. I'm going into a sugar coma," Halli says. "I'm not sure I can be your detail if I'll be around this stuff all the time. I have no willpower."

I jerk my head back and furrow my brows. *What did she just say?* "Detail? Like a guard? You're only temporary, right?" The five agents stop mid-bite and stare at me.

"Aspen, why don't we all go sit in the living room," Ted says, placing his plate on the kitchen table. The seriousness in his voice concerns me. I agree and follow him, with the others behind us. I wait for someone to talk.

Halli clears her throat, putting her plate on her lap. "All Presidents have the option of continuing the use of Secret Service after their term. The same goes for their spouse and children under sixteen."

"Well, I'm not sixteen," I add quickly.

"Right. But this is an extenuating circumstance. It's been strongly advised that you accept our services. Our country mourned you. When they find out you're alive, it will be hard for you to go anywhere without getting bombarded. You'll need help. At the least, in the beginning, until we make sure you aren't in danger anymore."

My baking high just crashed. I drop to the arm of the cushioned chair, my head into my hands. "I left one prison and now I'm in another."

"Try not to think of it that way. You can do whatever you want, we just want you to be safe. And I was totally kidding, I would love to be your detail. I may just have to work out twice a day."

I flash a smile at her, but I'm not happy. When I was with Ryker, the number of people who felt they had a right to take his picture and stop us while we were out was insane. I tried to not let it bother me because I was with him, but now it sounds like that will always happen to me.

"There are crazy people in this world," Amy says. "Just ask Addison. None of us want to see you harmed. Especially after all you've been through."

I nod. "I'm just going to go to my room. I need some time to think."

"I'm here if you need to talk." Amy stands and wraps her arms around me.

"Thank you," I murmur and walk down the hallway to my room in silence.

THE TEARS HAVE DRIED, but the despair still lurks. Between feeling anxious and worried that my actual parents won't like me and now finding out that my life will never be mine again, I've had to stop myself from trying to find my father to hide me again. I shake the ridiculous thought from my mind. That will never happen.

"Come in," I say, at the soft knock at the door. The door opens and Halli walks in wearing bright turquoise silk pajamas. Her white-blond hair is loose, falling halfway down her back. She looks like a totally different person. Younger.

"Are you doing okay?" The bed dips where she sits.

"This is all so heavy and I feel alone," I admit, rolling to my side to face her. "I've lost the man I called my father. I've lost the man I had major feelings for. And now there's no one left."

"If it helps, you have me."

I sigh. "That's another part of the problem."

"I won't take that personally." She playfully huffs. "Things will slow down, Aspen. Just take it a day at a time. It's all you can do."

"Can you get me some rum?"

Tonight's a good night to drown my sorrows.

CHAPTER TWENTY-NINE

RYKER

"C'mon brother, do me a solid."

Aiden sits back in his seat and stares at me while taking a slow pull from his beer, enjoying the groveling I'm doing a little too much. He's still pissed off about the CIA holding Addie.

"Jaxon?" I plea to one of my other best friends.

He holds his hands up in the air. "Don't look at me, I don't know where she's at."

I drop my head. There's one man at the table that knows and he's being an asshole right now.

"Maybe it's better you don't know," Max chimes in. "She has a lot going on right now." Figures, Max is the voice of reason.

My shoulders rise and fall. He's probably right. But fuck what's right at the moment, I need to see her so I can catch my breath. The pinch in my chest hasn't subsided even after finding out she's safe.

"She's the one, huh?" Jaxon asks and I lift my gaze back up.

Shrugging, I answer, "She's the only woman I see myself with. The only woman that drives me batshit crazy. She's the only woman..." My words fall short because she is the *only woman* I want. When she caught my Hail Mary, she also caught my heart.

"Sounds like the one to me," he replies. "Welcome to the land of no return."

They all cheer to that, clinking their bottles. I scrape the hairs on my jaw. "We've only known each other for two months." My attempt to drive a stake in what I'm feeling is pointless. Saying it out loud, or repeating it to myself nightly, isn't working.

"So, why don't you let this play out?" Aiden asks, sitting forward on the table. "She won't be in hiding forever." But if I wait, will it be too late?

I grit my teeth. "Because I need in on the play. I need to be a part of the game."

Aiden rolls his eyes. "Always the player. I'll see what I can do."

I just have to make sure I don't fumble.

"BE READY TO GO BY TEN," Max clips in my ear, skipping the greeting when I answer my phone. Shooting up out of bed, I pull my phone back to check the hour. Midnight.

Shit, I wouldn't care if it was four in the morning.

"Where is she?"

"Just be at the plane by ten." The bastard hangs up. Sometimes, I wonder how he landed the fun, outspoken girl of the group.

I throw off the sheets and find my suitcase. With a quick glance at my schedule, I see my next couple days are free. Anything past that, Bree won't be happy.

Packing takes a whole fifteen minutes and now I'm lying in bed, wide awake. I don't have a clock that ticks, but I swear with each passing second I can hear one. It could be the thumping of my heart.

I hope she doesn't hate me. It's been six days since I've seen her. Six days since her life has been flipped upside down. What if she blames me?

By morning, I've run every scenario through my mind. Hours of different ways this could play out. The last time I looked at my clock, it was five and I couldn't do it anymore. I got up and showered, walked to the corner coffee joint and jumped in an Uber to the airport.

So what if I show up a couple hours early? I flick my wrist to check the time. Okay, three hours early. When I walk into the hanger, Max's pilot sees me and his smile grows.

"Hey, Ryker." I take his extended hand. "Max told me to expect you early."

I chuckle. Am I that predictable? I take a sip of my lukewarm coffee and shake my head. Not out of my friends. I'm the spur-of-the-moment type of guy compared to their rigid and controlled lifestyle.

The pilot directs me to the sitting area. "It's warm in there. And you can get some more coffee if you'd like."

As if I need more. I was hoping to get some sleep on the way to wherever we're flying. The sole reason I got this cup was because I needed something to do to waste time.

When my phone rings, I half-expect it to be Max, making sure I made it. But Bree's name flashes on the front. I groan out loud. She was livid when I vanished last week to Max's house. Wait until she hears who Aspen is. I haven't told her, but I will right before it's announced. With the pictures of us out there, she'll be swarmed with questions. The least I can do is warn her.

"Hey Sunshine," I answer. Silence on the other end has me glancing at my phone. She's still there. "Bree?"

"Please tell me you're at the airport to say hi to a friend."

Standing taller, I slowly glance around the empty room. How the fuck does she know where I'm at?

"Hell woman, you put a tracker on me?"

"I should," she snaps. "It seems your Uber driver was a fan. She snapped a picture of you walking into the airport and posted it already on every social media site she can. Where is Pete? And why are you there?" Her voice escalates with frustration. Damn nosy people.

"It was a last-minute trip, and I didn't want to get Pete up at the ass crack of dawn."

She groans. "You're going to *her*, aren't you?"

"Don't be jealous," I joke but then wince when a growl comes across the phone. I guess Bree's not a morning person.

"Ryker." She tries to control her tone. "I have a terrible feeling about this. About her. There's something you're not telling me."

I sigh. "There is. But I can't tell you right now." She starts to interrupt, but I cut her off, "Soon, Bree, just not right now. I can't. But I'll give you fair warning."

"Give me fair warning? Is this going to be big?"

A sarcastic laugh escapes my lips and I sit back in a chair, staring up at the ceiling. Catastrophic big. And yet, I can't stay away from her.

"Let's say, you'll be busy."

CHAPTER THIRTY

ASPEN

Tap.

A noise at the window pulls my attention from the TV. I stare at the curtain-framed window from my bed, darkness blankets it from the second-story bedroom and I wonder if I imagined it.

Tap.

Tap.

My heart beat picks up at the realization that I did, in fact, hear something. I glance at my bedroom door, debating if I should get Halli. It'll probably be something stupid like a tree branch hitting the glass and would only make me look silly. Instead, I scoot off the bed and slowly put one foot in front of the other, and then drop to the right of the window so I'm not in plain sight.

Tap. I startle and cover my yelp with my hand. This is ridiculous, I'm on the second floor. No one can get up here. Peeking around the drapes, I peek down at the lit yard and relief fills my lungs. A grin spreads across my face when I see Ryker waving his hands in the air. Butterflies flood the fear in my belly, staring at the gorgeous man wearing dark jeans, a gray sweatshirt and a backward ball cap with his signature sexy crooked smile.

I can't believe he's here. Another tap snaps me out of my dreamy state. He points to the window and puts his palms up. Oh, yeah, he might want to talk instead of staring at me, like I am him. I slide open the window and I'm met with a cool breeze. The sheer curtains dance to my sides. I stretch my head outside when he disappears and my eyes widen when I see him climb a ladder leaning against the house.

"I'd tell you to drop your hair, but wrong princess," he jokes, coming into view. I roll my eyes, he's been hanging around Donnie too much. I'm not a princess, more like a secret no one wants to deal with. Our faces are inches apart, my unknown world falls into an abyss of darkness as I focus on his face. For a moment, everything seems right. "You going to invite me in?"

"Oh, sorry. Yes," I say, stepping to the side to allow him space to crawl through the window. "How did you get past Secret Service? And where did that ladder come from?"

He slides in and stands tall, hovering over me. Would I seem too eager if I dive into his arms? "I know people." He wags his eyebrows and I laugh at his typical arrogance, taking a step backward so I don't act on impulse and attack him out of desperation.

"Then why did you just sneak into my room?" Not that I'm complaining.

He shuts the window and turns toward me with a mischievous grin. "Your people trump my people and I was afraid they wouldn't let me in."

"I'm glad you're here." My voice is soft.

He pulls in a ragged breath as his eyes roam over my body. Heat flickers in his eyes, lighting my entire body up with just one look. He takes two quick, long strides and pulls me into his chest. His lips fuse to mine and I melt in his arms, not even caring how desperate I seem. I am desperate.

He moans into my mouth and breaks the kiss. "Sugared whiskey. My favorite flavor." My heart hammers looking at his eyes gleam like I'm truly his taste of choice. "You've been baking." I nod, smiling, but then it falters when his expression morphs to regret. "I'm so sorry, Aspen."

"It's not your fault."

He jerks backward and steps around me. I can feel the tension as he brushes by and it rocks me at my core.

"How can it not be? I put all this in motion. I brought you here."

The pain in his voice makes my stomach coil. I swivel on my heel, angry that this is putting a wedge between us. Even if we don't work out, I can't have him thinking he ruined my life. He didn't. He's made me feel more alive in four weeks than my entire life. "No. Richard Devereux put all this in motion." Ryker drops his chin, gripping his neck. "I don't blame you at all." I plead with him to understand, to drown out the concern filling his thoughts.

"Is it true? Are you President Malone's daughter?"

The words have yet to come out of my mouth. Vocalizing it, confirming it to be true gives me serious anxiety.

He twists his body, so it's flush with mine, towering over my petite frame. My eyes flutter shut as his fingers brush through my hair. "Hey, stay with me." A tear escapes down my cheek. The pad of his thumb wipes it away. "Open your eyes, babe."

I draw in a shaky breath. "Yes," I whisper, never having spoken a word that holds so much weight. It's hard to breathe. He softly smiles, touching his forehead to mine. His touch soothes my anxiety.

"I'm here if you need to talk."

I roll my head against his. "I can't. Not yet." Admitting it is one thing, talking about it would bring on a full-blown panic attack. Like Halli said, one day at a time. Today is not that day.

"I get it."

"How about we pretend we're at the treehouse. Just you and me," I sigh. He rubs his jawline as his lips quirk to the side.

"You're a little too loud for that." My mouth gapes and my cheeks warm with memories of how he can make me scream. Arousal pulses between my thighs. "But I'm up to the challenge."

Ryker's eyes bulge and he dives behind the bed at the sound of a soft knock on the door. I cover my mouth to stop from laughing as I can see his feet sticking out the end. "Your feet," I half-whisper, half-laugh. He tucks them under the bed.

I open the door, Halli stands there in bright pink silk pajama bottoms and a matching button-up shirt. She must have a rainbow of colors in the same pajamas. "Orana, Halli."

Stupid, stupid, habit.

Her lips pull up in a grin. "I was just checking on you before I went to bed. I thought I heard something."

"Sorry. I opened my window to let some fresh air in, but it was colder than I thought." I try not to sound rushed, but I can't help it. "Have a good night."

I keep hold of the door so she can't walk in. "Okay," she says, her eyes looking past me for a quick second. "You have a good night too." As I'm shutting the door she adds, "You too, Ryker Dallas."

He sits up, wrapping his arms around his legs, looking like a kid caught with his hand in the cookie jar. "Seems my people called your people."

"So it seems." I lick my bottom lip, shifting from one foot to the other, thinking about what Halli interrupted. He pushes off the ground to stand up. "What now?"

"I guess you don't need to be that quiet," he draws out, lunging for me at the same time. I bite back my yelp as he tackles me to the bed.

He digs his face into my hair and takes a long slow sniff,

making me giggle. "You have no idea how intoxicating you are. I'm already getting high."

"You and that sugar addiction."

"It's more like an Aspen addiction," he replies. I gaze into his eyes, looking for truth. Second-guessing what everyone tells me, is not what I want to do.

"I feel like my life is distorted. What you see is not what you get. It's like this wild distortion. Two worlds colliding, creating this warped reality. I'm questioning everything and everyone," I admit. He deserves to know where my head is.

"I see only you, and that hasn't changed."

I don't agree with him. Everything has changed.

"Are you going back to the island?"

A fresh round of doubt creeps in. Why didn't he ask me to stay here, with him? Is he here just to relieve his guilt? When he leaves, is this it for us? Is this goodbye? We seem to be good at doing that.

And if the answer is yes, I can't hold it against him.

I'm a disaster.

Why would he want to be with me?

"I... I don't think so," I stumble over my words, having no clue what I'm doing. "If I stay, will you..." My voice loses its confidence, afraid of his answer.

He licks his bottom lip and quirks up his brow. "Finish what you were saying, Whiskey."

I twist my lips, hating when he makes me say exactly what I mean. He knows what I'm asking.

"Will I see you again?" I breathe out. The air around us stills as if his answer will be the only thing to give me life. A rejection will be another blow, but at least I'd understand.

"If I could stay away from you, I would've done it the moment I left the island." He opens his mouth but then snaps it shut. My heart sinks deep into that void of hesitation. "But you need time to figure out your new life before we can give us a true shot."

I drop my chin, knowing he's right, but it doesn't stop the disappointment. "Are you here out of guilt?"

His hand lifts my chin to meet his eyes. "You think I'd sneak past Secret Service, who have orders to shoot first then ask questions, because I feel guilty?"

"I come with a lot of baggage."

"Whiskey, you come with an island of baggage and I still don't care. You told me once that the right woman would be worth it." He shifts forward, pressing his lips to mine. "You're worth it." His words take a direct path to my heart, warming it. "I just want to give you time to figure stuff out. And you have a shitload of stuff to figure out. But I'll be here, waiting. I promise."

"I'm scared."

"Of what?" He pushes up on his arm, reaches over and tucks a lock of my hair behind my ear.

"Of everything." My chest heaves as panic builds. I glue my gaze to the white ceiling. The vulnerability in my voice scares even me.

"Aspen, live life like an adventure. You are the strongest woman I know and since I've known you, you've attacked every challenge thrown at you." I close my eyes and a tear rolls down my temple. They ripped away my strength with my past life. With the lightest touch, he wipes it away. "I mean, you wrestle sharks. How much more badass can you be?"

He makes me laugh. "I've never wrestled a shark." Although, I'd rather be swimming with hungry sharks than swimming into the unknown.

"No, but if you did, I'd bet on you."

I tuck my body into his. "How long are you here?"

"Only tonight," he murmurs. Disappointment spirals through me. "I'm sorry. I'd stay longer if I could, but I have obligations and you have a family to meet."

"Thanks for reminding me." They know about me now. Halli

told me they flew to Austin today and they're waiting for when I'm ready. I'm not even close. The pressure is insane. "What if they don't like me?" My number one fear rolls off my tongue.

He tsks like that's absurd. "They already love you."

I wish I could believe that.

Changing the subject, because I don't want to think about what happens in the coming days anymore, I say, "I went horse-back riding yesterday."

His grin fades for a beat as he changes his focus, but he ends up nodding in understanding. "I bet it was different riding here than the island."

"The major difference was riding on a saddle. I prefer bareback."

My brows furrow, wondering why his lips stretch from ear to ear. Maybe he's glad I did something I love to do.

"So do I, Whiskey. So, do I."

"It's so much more freeing. For both of us." A horse can't enjoy having a metal thing in his mouth. Ryker sucks in his lips, attempting not to laugh again. "You like to ride bareback?"

What is so funny?

"I've never, but I've always wanted to try." He rolls on top of me, his eyes filled with a mixture of amusement and heat.

"I thought you said you prefer it?" What am I missing?

"I do. Especially with you." He's finding this conversation way more entertaining than it is. And by how hard his bulge is pressing into me, arousing too.

"Ryker, does bareback mean something else?" I ask and then moan when he presses his cock against my swollen clit.

"It means I want to slide my dick inside you, bare." He kisses me in the crook of my neck. "Whiskey, you make me a needy man."

"What do you need?" I reply in a tangled breath.

"You. Always, you."

The energy that has always attracted me to him, surges and crackles in the air. As if the heat was burning us, our arms flail to strip each other's clothes off for relief.

Except it doesn't come when we're both naked. Our chests heave as I sit in his lap, his hardness sits at my entrance, begging for consent.

"Are you on birth control?" His words tangle in his throat, his restraint hanging on by a thin thread. Now is not the time to get into the story of my dad demanding it when he found out my indiscretions, so I just nod. I slide down his shaft, swallowing the moan from feeling all of him. His nostrils flare and his growl is low as he grips my hips to stop me from moving.

"Give me a second," he breathes, closing his eyes for a moment. His Adam's apple bobs as he swallows thickly. "This is more than I expected. Fuck, I'm going to come too fast." When his eyes open, pure unadulterated lust flashes up at me. Both of his hands squeeze my breasts and I grind my hips around him. Seeing his restraint slipping spurs me on and I rotate my hips, riding him in quick thrusts. He licks his thumb and presses it on my swollen clit and I swallow my moan knowing Halli is close by. My whimpers turn into dizzying breaths as waves of ecstasy crush me.

Still buzzing from my high, he flips me over, his hard body on top of mine. He thrusts a couple of times and I moan at the new position. So deep. Fingers trail down my arms until he reaches my hands. Intertwining them, he pins them above our head. The tips of my sensitive nipples brush against his hard chest as our bodies become one. I tremble, the intense sensations overwhelming. The liquid movement of our heated dance is erotic. Consuming.

Perfect.

He plunges wildly, and I yank a pillow over my face as my moans gain traction. His body convulses, and he falls over me, ripping away the pillow and replacing it with his needy mouth devouring mine.

As our chests still rise and fall while we come down from the most intense lovemaking, he rolls his head to the side with a slow smug smile.

"What?" I giggle.

"Bareback is definitely the best."

"You know you don't have to leave that way, right?" I stare at him as he pops open the window. "They already know you're here." I mean, we ate breakfast this morning with everyone.

"Shh. Let me live a fantasy of mine."

I bite my lip at how cute he is. Crazy. But cute. "And what fantasy is that? A night creeper?"

He pauses, straddling the window, and looks back at me. "No. A spy who infiltrated a heavily-guarded mansion to find the one thing everyone has been searching for. But it's worth the risk."

"And what is that?"

"The King's daughter." He wags his brows. His tale is shockingly close to the truth. "But now, I have to escape because she was too loud, and she alerted the guards. So, I must leave, Whiskey. It's been fun while it lasted." My breath catches and he laughs at my expression.

I was not loud.

The pillows have permanent bite marks that will forever hold my moans. "Oh, wait!" I rush to the bedside table, grabbing my phone. "I need to give you my number."

I've yet to learn my new phone number so I search for it. "Here, give me your phone," he demands, impatiently.

I hand it to him and he plugs his number in with a few quick strokes and gives it back. "There. Call me."

He winks and then glances at the bedroom door behind me as if someone is about to come in. I look over my shoulder but the door remains shut with no sign someone is on the other side. When I turn back, he's already climbing down.

With the phone to my chest, I watch him run across the lawn like he's being chased. Ryker's playful side is one of the many things I love about him.

My heart squeezes.

Yes, I said love.

Later that afternoon, still on a high from seeing him, I text:

Me: Can't wait to be 'loud' with you again.

CHAPTER THIRTY-ONE

ASPEN

"Halli?" I knock on her open door and wait for her to look up from her bed. She's reading something on her computer.

"What's up?" She replies, closing her computer and putting it on the bedside table.

"I want to go back to the island."

Her head tilts as she tosses around what I said in her head. "Like... forever?"

"It's tempting," I joke, half-heartedly. "But no. The box that came for me yesterday wasn't everything. I need to go back. Also, I'd like to tell everyone goodbye. It doesn't matter that my dad lied to me, those people back on the island are still my people."

Today, Secret Service found out that if my father wants to find me, he can. Receiving a box here sent the Secret Service into hysteria. Somehow, he found me and sent a box of personal stuff from home. Pictures, jewelry, and knickknacks that I've collected over the years filled the box. No return address, but he sent it from the States. At first they were hell-bent on taking me somewhere else, but if he wanted to get to me, he's proven that he would have already done it by now. Running from my dad isn't why we are here.

"I'll have to go with you."

I was hoping she'd say that. I don't want to do this alone. And she's the only *somewhat* friend I have. After getting the box, it reminded me I can't put this off anymore. To move forward, I need to be at peace with my past. And I need to do this before meeting my parents.

"You're only saying that because you want to go to Bora Bora."

She puts her palms up. "I'm not complaining, that's for sure."

THE SALTY AIR GREETS ME. Although, it's only been a month everything is different as I step foot into the boat that takes us to Bora Bora from the airport.

Couples surround us, a mixture of exhaustion and excitement on their faces as they take pictures of themselves on the way to paradise. Me and Halli sit at the back of the boat.

"You doing all right?" She yawns and puts her sunglasses on, leaning back against the padded seat.

"It's weird being here."

This has been my home for twenty-four years, except right now it feels like I'm an intruder.

The boat engine fires up, and we're on our way. Not long after, Otemanu comes into sight. I tap her leg and her head lolls over. "My house is right past this town. We have to get a water taxi because they won't drop us off there."

I let out an audible gasp, and Halli sits at attention. Jumping to my feet, I rush to the other side of the boat to get a better look. No, no, no.

"What is it?" she asks.

I blink back hot tears as I stare at the blackened and charred remains where our houses sat just three weeks ago. I ask the driver in Tahitian what happened. *A fire a week ago.* Who would do this?

"What happened?" Halli asks as the boat continues to pass my destroyed home.

"He says there was a fire. Were you aware of this?" I jerk my head toward her with an accusatory stare.

She shakes her head. "I would've told you before we came." Her gaze darts around the boat, surveying each person before coming back to me and lowering her voice. "Although, I'm not surprised."

"Why? Who would do this?"

"Think about it, Aspen. Tobias—I mean Rudy—would want to cover his tracks. That means he needs to erase his presence." *And mine.*

I wipe a tear from my cheek and plop down on the bench. "But these were our houses. Our lives." *Our fake lives.* All my belongings minus the box he sent me are in ashes.

The boat pulls up to the first hotel and I realize we don't have anywhere to stay. *This is great.* I watch the first three couples exit the boat while the two workers unload their bags.

"Um… Halli, we have a problem." I could have called Dante and crashed with him, but I'm not comfortable with how we left things. We need to talk though. I can't leave my best friend, no matter how much of an asshole he was. Wait until I tell him about my dad, he'll flip. He always thought he was a little strange.

"Oh," she says, figuring it out. She finds her phone in her purse. "No worries, I'll get it taken care of. What hotel should we stay at?"

I tell her about one of the cheaper hotels that usually has rooms available. I relay the information to the guys once she gets confirmation of our hotel.

Staying with the bags while she checks in, I tilt my face away from workers as they walk by to avoid them recognizing me. As if on autopilot they say, "Orana." I bite down on my lip to stop myself from saying it back. They don't care if foreigners ignore them. Most of the time, we preferred it.

We locate our hut on the beach and Halli stands outside, spinning in a slow circle, digging her feet into the white sand. "Wow. Everything is so breathtaking."

It's definitely hard to breathe.

I'm stuck between reality and make-believe. It's an odd sensation. I close my eyes and breathe in the humid, salty air. Waves roll onto the beach and I try to clear my mind with just my senses. But I'm easily distracted when I sense Halli move past me. I sigh, giving up.

Instead, I follow her in. "What's the plan for today?" she asks, opening her bag.

We're only here for three days. That means tomorrow is our only full day, and I promised her I would show her the island before we left. Despite the jet lag, we need to get busy today.

"I'd like to go by the house first. See if anything is salvageable that I want." Pulling out a pair of tennis shoes, I end up staring at them, losing myself in a memory of when I got them.

"Those make your legs look hot," murmurs Ryker from the bench inside the store.

"How do tennis shoes make legs look hot?" I tilt my foot in different positions, testing the fit as I stare at myself in the mirror.

He pushes off the bench and stands so close behind me, his chest hits my back. "It says you're athletic. Shows off your thin ankles, next up, your gorgeous lean, muscular legs. Makes the eye keep moving up to see more, like your gorgeous ass." His fingers scrape up my leggings, under my long cardigan until he has a handful of my butt. He squeezes and I squirm in his grasp. My cheeks already heating.

"Ryker," I warn.

"And then all I can think about is removing them first so I can strip

the rest of your clothes off so you can wrap those gorgeous legs around my head."

I swallow the knot of desire in my throat. "Sold."

I chuckle at the memory, blushing at the one that came an hour later when his words became actions. Until my memory reminds me he hasn't answered my phone calls or text. Why would someone give you a phone number and not answer? His phone is attached to him so that can't be his excuse.

I shake the anger from my mind and shove the shoes back into my bag, grabbing a pair of chucks instead. He said he had obligations. I try to give him the benefit of the doubt, but as the days continue without a word from him, it's hard to.

"What do you have against those shoes?" Halli jokes, slipping her gun in the holster hiding it under her shirt. She's right. The shoes didn't do a damn thing. Changing my mind a second time because, truthfully, the tennis shoes are a lot more comfortable. I slip them on, ignoring Halli's questioning gaze.

"*Allons-y!*" I snap for us to leave, rushing past her out the door.

"I'm glad I learned French." She listens, following me out. "For those times you pop in a word or phrase every now and then."

"Sorry. I'm not aware I'm doing it most of the time," I explain as we walk. "But at least I know to talk in Tahitian if I don't want you knowing what I'm saying."

"Well, maybe I know Tahitian too."

I narrow my eyes. "Do you?"

She shrugs. "I'll never tell." Walking to the edge of the dock, she stares out at the water. "I can't believe this was your back yard. It's paradise." I try to see at it through her eyes, but the emotional link is still raw. It was my prison.

"Perception changes when it's all you have. Your picture and mine are different." She slowly nods, trying to understand. She won't no matter how hard she tries.

The boat glides into the dock. "Aspen!" Ari yells from behind the steering wheel. I smile and wave. Well, if Dante hasn't heard I'm here, he will soon. We wait for the passengers to disembark before we step into the boat. Ari glances at Halli and then asks me where I've been in Tahitian. I laugh when she rolls her eyes.

"I'm moving to the United States." His eyes widen. "I've come back to get some things."

"Manu, I heard you and Dante got in a fight, but this is taking it to a whole new level." I shake my head at the stupid nickname. Dante might have started it, but it didn't take long for it to stick with all his friends.

I drop on a bench. "I'm not moving because of Dante."

"It's that American, huh? The one that throws balls."

"No, Ari, it's not," I say with more agitation in my voice than necessary. "Do you mind dropping me off at my dock?"

He blinks at me. "You know it's not..." Running his hand through his black hair, he thinks about how to tell me.

Helping with his unease, I reply, "I saw. What happened?"

"Happened in the middle of the night, a week ago, yesterday." *Right after I turned myself in.* Maybe Halli was right. "Lit up the skies real fast. By the time they could put it out, it was all burned to the ground."

"What has Dante said about it?"

He shakes his head like I did something wrong and then ignores me. Instead, talking to a couple that just boarded. Typical bro code, or whatever Dante used to call it, means he's not giving me anything.

Once on the water, Halli asks, "Who's Dante?"

"He's the reason I left."

She does a double-take. "Wait. They briefed me that you left the island to visit Ryker?"

I sigh, putting my crazy windblown hair up in a bun. "I did. But I was teetering on this line of whether or not I should go. Dante's my best friend and we got in a brief fight before I left and it pushed me to go." I feel bad about how we left things. And by how Ari is acting, he's still not happy with me.

THE SALTY AIR mixes with the smell of charcoal. The smell burns my throat and eyes. Once the scene is in front of me, a sob escapes and I cover my mouth as I fall to my knees. Sand softens the fall, but it's the destruction that hurts my body.

"Why?" I cry out to no one. The only person who can answer, I won't ever see again. Halli gives me a couple silent minutes to myself before squatting down, wrapping her arm across my shoulders.

"You still want to do this?"

A snapping twig up the hill catches our attention and both our heads jerk up. She pulls out her gun, keeping it hidden behind her. Searching the wooded area behind where my house used to be, we don't see anyone. Had she not heard it too, I would have thought I'd imagined it.

We stand up and she steps in front of me. "Come on out," she says, spreading her feet apart and holding her gun out. "Or I can start shooting and you better hope I miss." I dart my gaze to her.

"What are you doing?" I whisper-yell, lifting my hand to stop her, but then decide otherwise since she's pointing a gun. Fear that it could be Dante spikes as I frantically search where she's staring. Or nosy island kids. She's taking her job to keep me safe way too seriously. No one here would hurt me.

"One... two..." she counts.

Merde! "Dante, if that's you, please come out," I beg.

I gasp as a man steps out from behind a tree. Not Dante. He holds his hands in the air. Wearing a white polo and a pair of khaki shorts, he's too pale to have been on the island long. He could be lost, but why was he hiding?

"Who are you?" demands Halli.

He replies, "I was hiking and ended up here. I think I'm lost."

Halli shakes her head. "That's the only lie you get. Next one, you'll end up with a bullet in your leg." Before I can argue with her that he could be telling the truth, she continues. "Think long and hard about what you're going to say next. I already know that you were on the plane with us."

My gaze jumps from the man to her, back to the man trying to remember if I saw him on the plane. I don't.

A smile quirks up on his clean-shaven face. "You're thorough, Special Agent Hughes. Call me impressed."

"I'm about to call you dead," she retorts in a flat voice.

"Okay, okay. I'm Agent Jason Roth with the FBI."

"Throw your ID toward us. Slowly." He does what she says. "Aspen, grab his ID." My eyes never leave his as I inch to where he threw it. He stays in place, not moving a muscle. He already knows she'll shoot if necessary. When I get back by her side, she instructs me to take her phone out of her pocket, take a picture of his ID and text it to another agent.

"Agent Hughes, we're on the same team, can't we settle this without getting others involved?" My finger hovers over the send button, and I glance up at her, waiting.

"Are you trying to save your ass, Agent Roth?"

He sighs. "Yes."

At least he's being truthful.

"How do I know you're legit without calling it in?"

"You don't. I was hoping you could trust this face."

Her lips purse. His attempt to make light of the situation fails. She sends me a sharp nod, and I hit send. He drops his head and murmurs, "Fuck."

"Why are you here?"

When he turns his attention to me, a light bulb goes off. "You're trying to find Ru—Tobias," I stutter. Will I always be on their radar? The idea twists in the pit of my stomach.

"When we saw you were coming to the island, we wondered if you were meeting him here." Now, I understand why he burned down this place. They'll never stop looking for him. But it makes me furious they're using me.

I let out a hollow laugh. "You think I want to see the man who kidnapped me?" The phone dings in my hand and Halli nods when I glance to her for direction. I read out the text that he checks out.

"Can you put the gun down now?"

She lowers her gun, putting it back in the holster. Snatching his badge out of my hand, she scans it before walking it to him. "You know as well as I do, he wouldn't be here. So, why are you really here?"

Tight-lipped, he answers, "We're covering our bases."

I ignore the two staring each other down as I turn my gaze to the burned ruins of my home. Stepping on ash, I kick pieces of wood and walk over blackened furniture. The three stoves left standing in the middle of the destruction seem out of place.

I fist a handful of ash, letting it pour off my hand. I loved this tiny house so much. It was mine, the only thing I could call my own. I have so many happy memories of it. *You still have those memories*, my subconscious reminds me. This is all à propos when you think about it. It's the finality of the life I thought was real. In a couple years when the jungle takes over this spot, it'll be as if we never happened. We'll be whispers in the night, stories told to visitors.

An overwhelming need to leave washes over me. "I'm ready to go. There's nothing here." I storm back to the dock without waiting for the other two and sit at the edge. Hanging my head, I again try to calm my inner spirit with the islands' aura.

I groan out when every minor noise distracts me. Instead, I stand and rip off my clothes, thankful I put on a bathing suit, and dive into the water. Halli calls my name right before the water envelops me.

The silent water helps clear my mind as I focus on my strokes. Stingrays glide against the seafloor and I brush the top of one. I've named plenty of them in the past. I smile to myself as I push forward.

When I surface, the sun warms the layer at the top and I let it surround me as I float, taking in long deep breaths. An engine from a boat gets louder and I know it's our ride, but I can't make myself move. I'm finally at peace. The water is what I'll miss the most.

"Are you going to float your way back," Ari jokes from the boat, idling by. *I guess he's talking to me now.* He waits for me while I swim to him. Helping me up, he tosses me a towel as I wring out my hair. We're the only ones on the boat. I glance to the dock to where Halli and the other agent are standing.

"Wait, don't go yet." He eyes me with a lifted brow. "Where's Dante?"

"He's gone."

My eyes widen in surprise. "What do you mean, gone?"

"There're rumors that he's the one who started the fires."

My head shakes almost violently. "No. He wouldn't do that. People have it wrong. It's my dad who did it."

He shrugs. "Someone witnessed him there and now he's gone."

"Probably because you guys forced him to leave by spreading lies," I defend him, pacing the boat. "You don't understand. My dad is a horrible man. He's the one who did that." I point to our destroyed land.

He runs his hands through his hair. "I don't know what to tell you, Manu. I hate that he's gone too, but…" His words trail off.

My dad's lies weren't supposed to destroy another life. I fall onto the seat, confused. Where would he go? If he didn't do it, why would he leave?

. . .

WHY AM I trying to make sense of anything? Nothing is as it seems.

"Why are we here?" Halli asks.

I pull the glass door open to the only bank on the island. Halli and the FBI agent follow me. Nothing screams something is wrong like having people follow you everywhere. I wanted to avoid the stares, but with these two it's inevitable.

I stop walking, and Halli bumps into me. Spinning, I glare at the two of them. "Can you guys wait outside? I'm closing out my bank account."

Halli's eyes scan the tiny dingy bank where only two people are working behind the desk. Other than that, the place is empty.

"Aspen, I don't think that's a good idea," Jason says. I guess we're on a first name basis now.

"Well, I don't recall inviting you here to begin with," I snap back.

"It's fine," Halli says, pushing him back out the door. "We'll be waiting out here for you."

As the door closes, I hear him arguing with her. I roll my eyes as I walk to the counter. Ideas of how to ditch him come to mind.

"Aspen, it's good to see you," one teller says. "What can we help you with today?"

"I need to close my account."

She does a courtesy nod and starts typing. After a quick check of my ID, even though she's known me since I was a child, she prints out a check. "You just need to sign right here." She pushes a paper to me and points where I need to sign to close out everything. When she hands me my check she says, "Wait here, I have one more thing for you."

I watch her disappear into the back room. The other worker smiles at me and I return it, but wonder what else she needs to give me. The room is stuffy and warm as they only rely on a fan in the corner of the compact bank to circulate the air. Glancing down at my check, I gasp out loud and whip around.

"Um… there's been a mistake."

I've deposited every cent I've earned. And before I left, I knew exactly how much I had because I deposited the money that Ryker gave me.

This is not that amount.

Jacque comes out from the back, and I wave the check at her. "Something is wrong." She takes the check and looks it over, but hands it back.

"What's wrong with it, Aspen?"

My eyes bounce around the bank like some manic person. "That's way too much money."

Like an extra two zeroes at the end too much.

She laughs. "Your father said you would say that." She holds out a sealed envelope, my name scribbled across the front. It's my dad's handwriting.

Not wanting to open it here, I take it from her and fold it in half with the check and stuff it in my purse. It feels like my purse weighs a million pounds.

Or make that two million.

"All set?"

I nod, hurrying past them down the street. The last thing I want to do is tell them what happened without reading the letter first.

"Aspen, are you all right?" Halli asks, running to catch up with me.

"Yeah. I'm just exhausted. Can we go rest?"

She doesn't question me, but she knows something happened. As soon as we make it to our hut, I dash to the bathroom and lock the door. With a quick deep breath, I sit on the toilet and tear open the letter.

. . .

ASPEN,

If you're reading this, you have cleared out your account. The little extra money is yours. I never spent a dime of the money they gave me for your hit, plus the interest. It wasn't mine to spend as I didn't deserve it. But you do. Think of it as restitution for me stealing your life. I still have no regrets. Go spread your wings, Manu. The world is yours now.

Love,

Dad

THE BRIEF LETTER feels like a life's worth of words. I need to dissect each sentence again.

A little extra? No. A lot extra.

Money for my hit? I don't know how I feel about having the money that someone paid him to kill me.

Stealing my life and no regrets? Do I deserve this money? Is it even legal?

I jump at a knock at the door. "Aspen are you okay?"

Leaning over, I turn the knob and pull the door open. As soon as Halli catches sight of my tear-stained face, she kneels. "What happened at the bank?"

I'm not sure if I should show her the letter, but I'd rather find out now if the money is illegal. I hand her the letter and check.

Her eyes widen when she sees the amount of the check. "Wow. You really did great at your cookie business."

I chuckle. "Read the letter. Is the money legal?"

After reading the note, she answers, "I'll make some calls."

CHAPTER THIRTY-TWO

RYKER

"Thanks for coming with me," I whisper into Bree's ear as we walk through the doors to the Make-A-Wish Gala. A charity near to my heart, no matter how screwed up my life is, I'd never miss this. I wish Aspen was here though.

"I know how much this means to you," she replies, resting her head on my shoulder.

I nod, remembering the reason I'm here. Garrison Reid. My best friend. My teammate since peewee football. When we were Juniors in high school, they diagnosed him with a rare form of leukemia. Watching his life drain from his eyes in front of me was the worst part of my childhood. But for a moment in time in his last days, it was as if nothing was wrong and we were back to being carefree assholes living the life. Make-A-Wish sent both of us to an NFL football game, front row seats and passes to meet the players after.

That day changed my life. Even at the young age of seventeen, I knew what the wishes meant to people, and I made a promise to Garrison to do everything in my power to help the charity in his name.

We stop as a camera snaps a picture and continue walking as if we hit a speed bump in the road. I'm so numb to the process, it doesn't faze me anymore. Stop. Smile. Walk.

As the night progresses, I hate that my mind can't stay in this room. Ever since I returned from seeing Aspen a couple days ago, I can't concentrate on anything. It's ridiculous. The intense desire to be with her is killing me. I don't know if I should have offered to be there by her side as she navigates through the toughest thing she'll ever go through or give her space. I chose to give her space, but fuck if I'm not regretting it now.

Clapping and an elbow to my side brings me to the present. I clap along. "Stop clapping," Bree whispers through a clenched teeth grin. "This is for you."

Oh, shit. I paste a smile on my face and give a quick wave. My body temperature spikes and I can feel sweat break out on my back, but I try to remain calm.

"We thank you for your donation, Mr. Dallas," the speaker says. I smile and tap my hand over my chest. As soon as the speaker moves on to the next donor, I lean over and murmur, "What did I miss?"

"A whole montage of how you helped five families this year with their wish from your donation."

Shit.

She sighs. "I hope she's worth it." Her voice drips with disappointment and I grit my teeth, biting back the words that want to slice her open. She might be my public relations assistant, but she's replaceable.

I don't need her two-cents opinion on Aspen. She's not up for discussion.

"Sorry," she whispers, dropping her chin. "I worry about you."

"When it comes to Aspen, don't," I clip, not able to hide my irritation. Tight-lipped, she turns her attention to the speaker. When her eyes fill with tears, I feel like an asshole.

It's not the time or the place to have this discussion, so I let it go. It's better we not have it now with emotions running high.

"WE NEED TO TALK," I say to Bree.

She kept quiet the rest of the night. We just left the gala and the awkward silence between us needs to end. *Right now.* She unfolds her arms from her rigid posture in the seat next to me, clasping them in her lap as she stares at me with expectation. I don't know what she thinks I'm about to say, but sorry isn't one.

"She is worth it," I say with finality so there are no more questions, and then add, "now, we're moving on to how to deal with the situation." Aspen told me she'd be meeting her parents this week, so news will hit the fan any day now. Bree's body doesn't relax, her hands twist in her lap. "Is this a problem, Bree?"

She stares forward, and I can tell she's saying so much more in her head than what is coming out of her mouth. After a few moments, she shifts her body toward me, her knee bumping mine through the slit in her dress. "Ryker, your priorities haven't been straight since you met her. You're off in la-la land or disappearing and I'm having to pick up the pieces."

I nod, not being able to argue with that. She's right.

"And… she's not good for your image."

The fuck?

She ignores my gaping mouth and continues. "You've dated international models and celebrities. It's always gotten you a lot of press. Kept you in the spotlight. It's helped you have constant exposure, which helps get you endorsements. She's a nobody."

I can't help but laugh at how wrong she is. Running my hand across my stubbled jawline, I notice Pete in the front seat, shaking his head. *I hear you, brother.*

Now, I'm at an impasse. I was ready to tell her about Aspen

and who she really is, but Bree's just made a hard stance and I don't know if I can trust her to be on my side anymore.

We pull up to Bree's condo and she glances at me with a questioning expression. "Bree, it's best if we part ways. It seems we have different outlooks for my future."

"Ryker—"

I hold my hand up, stopping her. "I'll make sure this doesn't reflect badly on you with your company." I glance at Pete and he gets out of the car. When he opens her door, I keep my attention forward ignoring her pleading glances. It's too late for that.

Once Pete gets in the car, he twists his body to peer back at me. "If it's any consolation, you did the right thing. Aspen's good for you, even I can see that."

I flash a tight smile. "Bree knows it too, but she's too worried about her cash cow. I'm done being the puppet."

"I DON'T KNOW YOU ANYMORE," jokes Donnie.

I flip him off, not in a joking mood. I lift the cold beer bottle to my mouth and I swallow down the entire contents in one gulp. I don't have to wait long for the waitress to arrive with another. I watch her as she walks away, ignoring many requests from other patrons asking for another drink. The place is wall to wall people, yet I can snap my fingers and I'd grab the attention of a waitress, just like that.

This is what fame brings me. People notice me. And I didn't get that shit because of who I was dating.

"Can you believe she said I got to where I am today because of who I was with? What the hell?" My muscles clench, still pissed she insinuated that. I wash the sour taste off my lips with another ice-cold brew.

"Fuck her. She's the type of woman who thinks behind every strong man is a stronger woman."

I bob my head. "Well, I can kinda understand that," I say, my thoughts trailing to Aspen and how much of a strong personality she has. "But I didn't get here today because of a woman."

He drinks to that. "So, have you talked to Mo, lately?"

I shake my head, leaving out that I haven't talked to her in almost a week. I keep telling myself to be patient. But I was stupid to not get her phone number. I figured she would have texted me by now. As far as Don knows though, she went home after visiting.

He sits forward on his elbows, putting all his weight on the table. It creaks and my eyes widen, waiting for it to give. But it doesn't faze him at all. It wouldn't be the first table that he has broken.

"Let me get this straight. You and your PR chic got in a fight about a woman you're not even talking to? And you fired her?"

There's no way to explain it that he'll understand. "That's a minor piece of the picture, Don. I don't want to get into it." Donnie and I were both drafted the same year, so we're close. When you rely on a man to keep you from getting wrecked, it forms a bond. So, when he respects me enough not to push, I'm grateful as hell.

"Did you hear Jasper might go to Tampa?" he asks, changing the subject.

Now, that just brightened my day.

CHAPTER THIRTY-THREE

ASPEN

I stare at my reflection in the full-length mirror. Will I be what they imagined? Running the brush through my hair again, I can't help but feel it's not perfect. *I'm not perfect.* I'll disappoint them somehow.

Since we got back from the island, I've researched my parents, readying myself for the meeting. I look like Beatrice, my mom. So much so that I thought I was looking at a picture of myself when she was younger. Except the eyes. She has dark warm-brown eyes. David, my father, has green eyes. I have a mixture of the two.

Halli steps into the room right as I swipe the brush through my locks again. She replaced her normal relaxed attire with black slacks and a white button-up blouse.

"Don't you look professional today," I say, attempting to add humor into the serious moment.

She shrugs one shoulder, smiling. "I guess I have to work sometime." As if she hadn't been working the last few days. She has these guys on such a detailed schedule, she knows when they pee. Nothing gets by her. Not even Ryker. "You look great, Aspen." She reaches for the brush to pull it out of my tight grip. "Just try to relax. In these situations, there's no right or wrong. Let things happen, naturally."

"In these situations? This happens often?"

She sighs. "Unfortunately, this isn't the first time. It's the most public, though."

"That is not making me feel any more relaxed." I spin in place and walk to the bed, plopping down on it. My feet slide into the black booties and I stand, holding my arms out wide. "Do I really look okay?"

"No."

"Non? Qu'est-ce qui cloche?" I panic, glancing down at my black sweater, dark jeans, and boots.

She squeezes my arm, pulling my attention to her. "Nothing is wrong. I was kidding."

My eyes narrow at her. "You're not funny."

"I never claimed to be." She laughs, slipping her arm through mine. Having her around the last week has helped me navigate the unknown. The agency knew what they were doing sending her. "Yes, you look perfect. Are you ready?" She leads me to the door. "You've got this, Aspen. If you need to take a mental break and remove yourself from the situation that is totally understandable. Shoot me a *glance* and I'll make an excuse for you to leave. This is on your terms."

The closer we get to the living room, I shake out my hands and my feet freeze right before we enter. A flicker of apprehension courses through me, but then the sound of warm laughter fills the air. It's her. *My mother.* The sound is confusingly calming. Halli stares at me, as if giving me all the time in the world. I offer a small smile of gratitude and nod that I'm ready.

She pulls her arm out to straighten her shirt and stands at attention. We walk in and all talking ceases as eyes turn toward us. *Specifically, on me.* The air thickens making it hard to breathe, my body heats as my nerves bounce off each other. When Beatrice's eyes lock on mine, tears flood her eyes as she pulls in a sharp gasp. Both she and David stand up from the couch, but only Beatrice walks over to me. I can't take my eyes off her.

Dreaming about what it would be like to meet my mom was always in the back of my mind. This isn't the picture I had in that dream. I can't imagine the torment she went through. Her hand shakes as she raises it and touches my face with the soft tips of her fingers.

"You're beautiful," she whispers before catching herself. She yanks her arm back, holding it down with her other as if she can't help herself. "I'm sorry."

I shake my head at her apology. "It's okay. I'm sure I kicked you a few times," I reply, pointing to her belly.

Did I really just say that?

She laughs, breaking up the awkward buzzing in my mind.

"Yes. Yes, you did. I'm Beatrice and this is David." She gestures to him. He smiles as he joins us and stands by his wife, wrapping his arm around her shoulders. He's taller than I expected. Much taller than her. *And me.*

"Hi. I'm Aspen." I blow out a shaky breath. "Wow, this is weird," I blurt out, staring at the two people in front of me. *They made me.* I wondered if there would be some sort of natural connection, but staring at them, they are complete strangers. It's more when she talks that I'm pulled in.

"It is," he says, looking between his wife and me. "But hell, weird or not, I'm happy to see you, kid."

Beatrice's body shakes, and she lunges toward me, wrapping her arms around me. After the surprise shift, I relax into her warm embrace and hug her back. Silent tears find their way down my cheeks. Time stands still. Nothing seems to exist except the fact that I'm in my mother's arms. I've longed for this my entire life.

"I'm so sorry," she repeats over and over, her voice a whisper washing over me like a protective blanket. Except it's suffocating. I've tried not to think about how a one-year-old child was taken from her parents. I've tried not to wonder if they deserved what happened because they couldn't protect me.

But the vicious questions have invaded my dreams the last few nights. I don't want the built-up animosity in my head to ruin what I want in my heart.

I pull out of her arms to take a breath and wipe the tears off my cheeks with my fingers. My eyes jump from hers to Halli.

Help.

She does a sharp nod, and with no hesitation, grabs my hand. "Mr. and Mrs. Malone, we're going to take a break." My gaze drops to the floor with guilt.

"It's okay, Aspen," David says, with a naturally commanding voice with sympathetic undertones.

As soon as we're outside, I drop her hand and stare up to the sky. It's easier to breathe out here. Re-collect my thoughts. Minutes of silence pass before she says, "You okay?"

"I was doing okay until she kept apologizing." I walk over to the porch swing and sit, pushing off with my boot. Halli leans up against a rail, putting her hands in her pockets. "Her apologies evoke feelings I don't want to have. Negative feelings." Halli opens her mouth to say something, but I add quickly, "But I understand why she was saying it."

"Did you know she wrote a book after they lost you?" I shake my head. The quick internet searches was mainly to see pictures of them. I'm still learning on how to do searches. "I suggest reading it to understand what happened and the emotional and mental turmoil they went through. It'll help you get a better picture. I have a copy for you when you're ready to read it."

I smile at my new friend. "You think of everything, don't you?"

"I try." I love that she's not bashful at all. "I'll let you have a couple minutes alone."

"Halli." She stops and glances over her shoulder. "Thank you for being here for me."

The door opens again minutes later and David steps out to the patio. His perfectly-styled gray hair makes me wonder what color it was before. He waits for an invitation before continuing. I tilt my head to the empty spot next to me. His smile widens, and he takes two large steps to the swing. It creaks when he sits down and he clasps his hand in his lap, twirling his thumbs. His feet are flat on the ground so he pushes us at a slow, steady swing so I pull my feet up under me.

"I hope I didn't offend either of you by leaving," I offer.

With a gentle tone, he replies, "This is difficult for all parties involved. Beatrice is trying her hardest to contain her emotions, she let them get away from her."

I wring my hands in my lap. There is so much I want to say, yet it never seems like the right time. We need to get over this awkward bump to move on.

"Can I be honest with you?"

I can't stop the laugh that slips out of my mouth. "I wish everyone would."

"It will take a lot of patience from both sides. I'll try to reign her in when she's smothering you, but I can't make any promises." He chuckles, making my lips curl up. He drops his head and fiddles with his wedding ring. I watch him spin it around his finger. "How was life on the island?"

"Simple." The word slips off my tongue with no thought. It's funny how life spinning out of control puts things in perspective. My prison was at least stable.

His gaze looks out to the pasture. "I tried the simple life. Back when I graduated college, I moved to St. Thomas. Thought living off the money I earned from doing dive tours and enjoying the island life was for me." I turn in my seat, surprised. Nothing in his demeanor says laid back. He exudes and talks with authority and I can already tell he commands attention as soon as he walks in a room.

"How long did you stay?"

He tugs on his ear, trying to hide his grin. "Two months." I laugh that he's embarrassed. Although, it doesn't surprise me. "Hey, don't laugh." He nudges me with his shoulder. "I thought I was meant for simple. I found out I wasn't. And so started my political path."

"That's a big leap."

He shrugs. "That was always the plan. I was just... tired. Between my father's expectations and school, I needed a break." I understand. I came here with a fantasy that this place was so much better than my island life. *Look how that turned out.* "So, what did you do on the island?"

"Well... Ryker told me I was a John of all trades?" My voice lifts. *Did I say that right?* David laughs.

"Aww, the famous Ryker Dallas. I saw a picture of you two." He playfully waves me off and I duck my chin, not wanting to talk about this with him. "We'll talk about that later." At least his reaction is less brutal than my dad's. "Jack," he clarifies and I snap my fingers and nod. I knew it sounded wrong. "You held a lot of different jobs then?"

"I enjoyed staying busy, so I would take extra jobs here and there. But I had one primary job. I owned a cookie business."

"An entrepreneur," he boasts. His reaction of approval spurs a sense of worthiness inside my chest. "Where did you sell them?"

"I sold them to all the hotels. At first, the hotels would by a basket from me each day to sell in the snack shops. But then guests would ask where they could get more. Eventually, all the hotels ordered one for every room, for every night."

David's eyes widen. "Wow. That's fantastic."

"Thank you. I was excited at how quick it took off."

"You should be proud." He beams.

"Yeah. But now..." I pick at invisible lint on my jeans. "I don't know what I'll do."

"Let me ask you first, do you want to stay in the US? And it's okay if you tell me no," he adds.

"I do."

"Then, why not pick up where you left off? Aspen, the possibilities are endless here."

I let out a humorless laugh. "You make that sound so easy. I don't even have a pla—" I stop talking, afraid he'll ask me to live with them when he hears I have nowhere to live. I'm not ready for that conversation. I can afford to go anywhere so I don't need their help, but finding where I want to live is more the question.

"Aspen, listen, we're not expecting an overnight relationship. This is a work in progress." He points to me and him. "This is exactly what I want. Us talking and getting to know each other. That's it."

I like him already.

"I'm going to go in. Beatrice has peeked out the window at least ten times already, and if I'm out here when she peeks again, I'm in trouble." I glance to the window and the curtains move back quickly, making him chuckle. "She really would like to talk to you, too, if that's okay."

I nod, placing my hand on his that lays between us. "I'd like that. Thank you. And I've enjoyed this." He lays his other hand on top of mine and squeezes before he stands.

After he goes inside, my anxiety spikes again, and I already miss his calming aura. Because I know with Beatrice, it'll be anything but.

CHAPTER THIRTY-FOUR

ASPEN

The creak of the door has me shifting already in my seat. She takes two steps outside, closing the door behind her. Her eyes bounce to mine with hesitation. She crosses and uncrosses her arms and then she chuckles. "I just don't know what to do."

"Do you want to sit down?"

That's all the invitation she needs before she beelines it to the swing. "I'm sorry—"

"Please stop," I interrupt, reaching out to cover her hand that's sitting on her lap. "I don't need you to apologize. Let's just talk."

She pulls in her lips and nods. "I can do that. Heck, my kids tell me I never stop." Her shoulders deflate and she drops her chin at the mention of my siblings. The last thing I want is for her to walk on eggshells around me.

"It's okay. Tell me about them."

"You have two brothers and a sister. Mila, Carson, and Liam. They're all so excited to meet you too." I blow out a shaky breath. *Nothing like being thrown all in.* "When you're ready. They understand this is a lot for you."

"Everyone keeps asking me if I'm ready. I don't know if it's the best idea to wait until I'm ready. That might never happen. It's better to get it all out now so we can move past this awkward phase."

"I can appreciate that given the circumstances." I peek over when she stops talking. The wrinkles around her eyes deepen with her smile when our eyes meet. "I still can't believe you're here." Her eyes water as she loses control of her emotions. She blinks back her tears and waves her hand in front of her. "I'll just warn you now that I'm a hot mess."

I laugh out loud. "My dad used to call me that." I flinch when I realize what I said. *How much crueler can I be?* The man kidnaps me and hides me away for years and now I flat out call him dad in front of her. "I mean..."

She shakes her head and pins me with her stare. "I'll stop apologizing if you stop worrying about hurting our feelings talking about your past. Was Rudy good to you?" Her voice breaks, afraid of the answer. Tears well up that she referred to him as I know him instead of his real identity.

"He was."

"That's all I care about then. We can't change what happened and I'm grateful he wasn't able to go through..." She pauses, swallowing the words she doesn't want to say out loud. "I'm indebted to him."

"I'm not only worried about how you guys will feel, I'm confused about how *I* should feel. I should hate him, right?" My nose tickles as tears threaten to let loose. I sniff and chuckle through my tears, pointing at my face. "See, hot mess too."

Her comforting smile calms the panic inside my chest, giving me hope that everything will be okay. I need all the hope I can get. "You can't force your heart to feel something it can't. Despite everything, he's your dad, Aspen. You had a good life before it was turned upside down."

I nod, wiping a tear. "I did. I mean, I was already planning on leaving the island, but it wasn't because of him." I was *staying* because of him. I'm still furious that he lied about being sick, even if I understand why he did it. I always felt like I was missing something out in the world. Who knew it was a complete family?

"Does it feel weird calling me Aspen?"

She squares her shoulders like I just said something outlandish. "Why? That's your name." I close my eyes as a rush of emotion surfaces. How she can take in stride the evil cast on her family and make me feel at ease seems almost superhuman. *I couldn't do it.*

"Thank you," I cry out, scooting across the swing, and wrap my arms around her shoulders. Her gentle embrace cocoons me and I revel in the moment. *I have a mom.*

Clearing the emotions from my throat, I sit back up. The air is still, unlike yesterday's breeze. The shade on the patio wanes as the sun lowers in the sky and its light warms my legs, inching up my body. I run my fingers over the warmth.

"While I was waiting impatiently to take my turn with you," she says, breaking the silence, and I lift my chin giving her my attention. "They gave me the most delicious sugar cookie I've ever tasted." My cheeks flush at the compliment. "And don't think I'm saying that because you made them. Amy didn't tell me where they came from until I begged her."

I wrinkle my nose and smile. "Thank you."

"She told me you're a baker. Tell me about it."

Leaning my elbow on the backside of the swing, I rest on my hand and tell her about my business. She gives me all her attention, slipping in questions here and there. Her genuine interest makes me giddy. I can't help the excitement in my voice.

We're laughing about a story I told when David joins us on the patio. "This is what I love hearing." He claps his hands once, his eyes jumping between the two of us. "Bea, it's probably time for us to go."

Everything went so much better than I expected. I don't want it to end.

"Do you have to?"

"Do we have to?"

Beatrice and I reply at the same time, ending in a round of laughter. When I glance up at David, tears pool in his eyes and he shakes his head. "No, we don't." He blinks back his tears and rolls his shoulders, attempting to hide his emotions. "How about we take this back inside and plan on having dinner delivered?"

The suggestion of food makes my stomach rumble. Food and nerves don't mix so I haven't eaten since this morning. "I think my stomach agrees." I chuckle.

DAVID'S A PLANNER. Is it really a surprise though? I mean, he was the leader of the United States. By the time the stars are out in full, he had planned the entire week. With my blessings. Since we were up late, they stayed since Amy has plenty of room.

I'm meeting my siblings tomorrow. A mixture of fear and anticipation wrap around my spine, keeping me awake. If they're anything like David and Beatrice, there's nothing to worry about.

I like them already.

That feels weird to say. Should I love them?

My head jerks toward my window when I think I hear a tap. Ryker? I throw the covers off and run to the window, shoving the curtains open. My eyes roam the empty lawn. Zero movement anywhere.

I rest my forehead against the cool glass. Why would I run here even if he was here? He has yet to answer my calls, and it's been a week.

No, I'd lock his spy ass out.

Total lie.

Closing the curtains, I decide ice cream is the answer. *Isn't it always?* The hallway is dark, leading to a dimly lit kitchen. The warm glow from the lights under the cabinet give off plenty of light so I can see what I'm doing without making a noise by running into things.

I sit at the farmhouse-style table. Ted and Amy's house is very modest. Comfortable. Ryker's house is immaculate and modern. Clean lines with a lot of silver, white and black. I glance around the room, lifting the first spoonful of ice cream to my mouth. Blue and neutral colors fill the area.

"Can't sleep, either?"

I gasp, holding the pint of ice cream to my pounding heart. Beatrice is dressed in a blue flannel two-piece nightgown with pink flamingos. Her dark hair flows over her shoulders. "Mind if I join you?"

"Not at all."

She grabs a spoon and sits by me. I put the pint on the table between us. "What's the flavor of the day?"

I roll my eyes. "Vanilla."

She tilts her head in confusion. "I figured you would like vanilla."

Not that vanilla. It seems I'm a vanilla snob. "My cookies that you tried are vanilla, but they taste nothing like your vanilla here in the States."

She brings a spoonful of ice cream to her mouth, turning the spoon upside down before pulling it out. "Ever try to make ice cream with your Tahitian vanilla?"

"I haven't. But that's an excellent idea."

After a couple minutes of silence, she asks, "Why the ice cream at midnight?"

"It's a tradition in Bora Bora." The lie comes out to easy. She sits back against the chair and surveys me. Am I that obvious or does she have that mom intuition with me already? "Okay, it's not. There's just a lot on my mind."

"Are you nervous about meeting your brothers and Mila?"

"Yes, and no. But that's not why I'm down here."

She hums like she knows. "Does this have to do with a famous quarterback?"

Okay, so she knows.

I drop my eyes while I scoop another bite of ice cream. Guilt that I'm worried about my relationship rather than focusing on the larger picture creeps in. I should direct all my attention to the mountain in front of me, versus the ant hill.

Except the ant hill has erupted, and the ants are stinging me. It's hard to ignore.

"If you ever want to talk..." She sticks another spoonful in her mouth.

I have wanted nothing more than a mom my entire life and now that she's sitting right by me; I don't know what to do.

I nod, not yet ready to spill my soul to her. I have her DNA, but she's still a stranger. "Thank you."

"We'll get through this. Just know that both David and I are extremely grateful you were brought back to us. But it'll take time. Never feel guilty."

With that, she stands and gently places her hand on my head. She pauses like she's combining our energy through her touch. It's not until she moves her hand that I feel the loss. She's right.

I won't be lost forever.

CHAPTER THIRTY-FIVE

ASPEN

"Can you do that hula dance stuff?"

"Liam," scolds Beatrice, shooting glares at her youngest son—my older brother by two years.

He shrugs, casually sitting back on the couch. "What? It's cool."

I smile at the younger of the two brothers staring at me with curiosity. At least he's talking to me. The oldest sibling, my sister, has yet to say two words.

"It's okay," I respond to Beatrice before turning to Liam. "It's not called the hula in Tahiti. It's called Ote'a, or Ori Tahiti. But to answer your question, yes. I used to do shows at the hotels."

"It's weird hearing you talk," jokes Carson about my accent.

"That's what you think is weird?" I burst out, making the two brother's laugh out loud.

Liam, Carson, and Mila got to the ranch a couple hours ago. The brothers welcomed me with tight embracing hugs, Mila, not so much. She stood by David during the introductions. Beatrice warned me she would be the most hesitant as she's the one who took my death the hardest. She's nine years older than me and felt partially to blame. She was ten. There is no way she was even remotely responsible.

My gaze jumps to hers every so often and the second our eyes meet, she looks down. I always wondered what it'd be like to have a sister. Now, I wonder what'd it be like to have one that liked me.

"So…" Carson starts, and I glance over to him. "… what's up with you and Ryker Dallas?"

Beatrice groans. "Can you two not ask such personal questions?"

"Mine wasn't *that* personal," Liam retorts.

"They're not together anyway," Mila chimes in. "He's with Bree Kensington."

Everyone turns to me. The knife Mila just stabbed in my heart, twists. Her expression switches to surprise.

Her hand covers her mouth. "You didn't know. I'm so sorry, Aspen. I didn't mean—"

"Enough," Beatrice barks, glaring at her daughter.

My lips twitch as I try to smile. The room's silence echoes in my ears as they wait for my reaction. Nothing like meeting your long-lost family and going through heartbreak at the same time. Watch out world, there's an emotional disaster in the room.

"Why do you say that?" I choke out, needing a reason.

She hesitates, regret written on her face. She knots her hands in her lap. "They were pictured together at a gala the other day."

"Mila, you know as well as I do that pictures in the media mean nothing."

David inserts hope.

She winces and shrugs a shoulder. "They seemed pretty close. I mean, it's going around town they're together."

"Can I see it?"

She pulls her phone from her rear pocket and searches. When she lifts her eyes up, her lips twist. "Are you sure you want to see it?" At least her intentions don't seem malicious.

I slowly nod. It's more like I *need* to see it.

She walks over and holds out her phone. I don't need to look at the picture for long to see what she's talking about. Bree's tucked into his side and looking up at him with a longing glance, and he's smiling down at her.

I shoot up out of my chair. "Je reviens de suite !"

As I rush out of the room, I hear Carson ask, "What did she say?"

David answers, "She needs a minute."

Smack in the middle of the pain, my lips quirk up finding out David speaks French.

My feet smack the ground as I walk outside. With nowhere to go, I let my feet guide me. Walking along a wooden fence, I follow a narrow dirt path sandwiched between dead grass.

The sun hangs high in the sky. Normally, I would enjoy its warmth, but my thoughts are burning a hole in my body on their own. I was foolish to think we would work. No wonder he hasn't called. He's been busy with his *obligations*.

My life is... in purgatory. I'm in between lives. There are so many unknowns. I don't even have a place to call home. Why would he want to be a part of this?

A horse neighs ahead, his beautiful red mane shakes as he sticks his head over the fence. When he does it again, it brings a small grin to my face.

"Hey, big guy," I say, approaching him with my hand out. He nudges it with his velvety nose and leans down, allowing me to run my fingers along his head. When he nuzzles me in the face, I giggle through the tears. "Wow, you're a sweetheart."

Thoughts flicker through my head about Ryker and our bareback conversation and where it led us. It was perfect.

A second in time of perfection doesn't outweigh the other seconds of imperfection. That's where I'm at right now.

A life of imperfection.

Uncertainty.

Tears roll down my cheek and the horse senses it, placing his head on my shoulder. "I swear, it's not you." I laugh, scratching his neck.

"Seems you got a fan." I jump backward from the horse, surprised at the voice. "Sorry, I didn't mean to scare you," Mila says.

I blow out a breath and wipe the tears from my cheeks. "That's okay."

"Aspen" —her gaze drops and she kicks some dirt around— "I'm sorry I brought up the picture. I figured you would've seen it by now." She lifts her head and I appreciate the sincerity in her voice.

"It mainly caught me off guard. I mean, he was here last week, telling me he would wait for me. He wanted to give me space to figure my stuff out."

Our definitions of space are very different.

"Wait, he was here last week?"

I share her shock. Why would he be so genuine and then go out with someone else a couple days later? If that's dating life here in the States, I don't want to date anytime soon.

"Please tell me that's not what normal guys do."

She laughs with a shoulder shrug. "Well, there are definitely some that do. But you learn to weed out the assholes."

I lean against the fence. "But he's not an asshole," I murmur. Why am I still defending him? "That or he's fantastic at hiding it."

"Have you tried to contact him? The paparazzi are always trying to spin things so it fits their narrative. Maybe he isn't with Bree." She doesn't sound convinced, but she's trying.

"I've tried. And I think I'm doing it right. He hasn't answered or texted me back."

"Do you have your phone? I can check it, if you'd like." I pull out my phone from my pocket. Waiting for Ryker to call or text, I can't part with the darn thing. She glances at the texts and lifts her head. "You did it right. You can't screw up a text. Unless you send it to the wrong person. Been there, done that. I wouldn't recommend it." She laughs. "Where did you get his number?"

"He put it in there himself, last week."

She hums and then hands me the phone. "If I knew him, I'd be able to give you a better idea of what he's like. I've only heard he was a player."

I'm surprised she doesn't already know. "Yeah, he's a football player."

She snorts. "Not like that." When I furrow my brows in confusion, she tries to stop her laugh by sucking in her lips. "It's another name for a guy who likes to date around."

"Oh," my voice deflates.

"But that doesn't mean he is. Rumors are part of our lives. I've been pregnant like at least five times." My eyes widen and drop to her belly. "I haven't been, but hell, if I gain like five pounds or just ate Mexican food and I'm bloated, there's always a horrible picture that makes me look pregnant."

This is what I have to look forward to?

Red horse nuzzles the top of my head again, messing up my hair. I step forward, out of his reach, and pat my hair down.

"Are you ready to go back up? I mean, I'm all for staying here talking, the two of us, but the guys were pissed I ran you off."

"Sure."

As we head back up toward the house, she asks, "Speaking of being in the public, have you seen what they're saying about you?"

My steps slow. People took tons of pictures of us, but why would they be talking about me? He's the famous one.

Her grin grows. "Don't worry, none of it's bad. But for the last couple weeks you were a hot topic."

"Really?"

She nods and rattles off a few things they were saying.

Who's the new supermodel Ryker Dallas is with?

Where did the gorgeous woman come from?

Did Ryker Dallas find himself a lover while suspended?

"And the list goes on… but you get the picture."

My cheeks burn from embarrassment.

"Why do they care so much?" I ask, appalled that this is some people's career, to talk about other people's lives. And now his rejection is out there too.

"You were with New York's number one bachelor." No wonder his ego was so big.

"*Were* is the key word," I mutter.

She wrinkles her nose with a mischievous grin. "Well, I can tell you that those same people think he downgraded."

I shouldn't be happy. Nope, not at all.

But it feels *somewhat* satisfying.

CHAPTER THIRTY-SIX

RYKER

I drown the rest of my beer before answering my phone, caller ID show's it's the front desk security. Flipping my wrist, I glance at the time, I'm not expecting anyone. Especially at ten o'clock at night. And if it's Donnie asking me to go out, I'll flip my lid. There's a reason I'm not answering my phone. I want to be left alone.

"Mr. Dallas, Ms. Bree Kensington is here to see you."

I haven't drank enough for this.

I pinch the bridge of my nose, debating if I should send her away. We haven't talked since I fired her a week ago, so I can't imagine what she wants now. "I'm not leaving," I hear her say in the background.

"Ma'am, please be quiet."

Shaking my head, I say, "Send her up."

I grab another beer from the fridge, having a feeling it'll be needed. Maybe she's here to apologize for making it seem like we were a couple at the gala. It was intentional how she was posing. She of all people knows how to stage a picture.

I'm sure Aspen has seen them already. It's probably why she

hasn't called me. I blow out a harsh exhale. Getting wound up before she gets here isn't the best idea.

A few minutes later, the knock comes. When I swing the door open, she stomps into my place like she owns it. I do a double-take, staring at her like she's lost her mind. She spins and stares back.

"Shut the door, Ryker."

I push it shut and the click echoes around us. "What the hell are you doing here, Bree?" *And demanding me to do stuff.*

She squares her shoulders and puffs out air through her nose. She's still dressed from work. I can't figure out if she came from happy hour or if she was working late. "First, I'm sorry. I over-stepped."

I fold my arms across my chest. "You think?"

"I don't need your sarcasm. I was wrong." Her voice loses its initial steam. "It was my job to maintain your positive public image."

"I don't need the fucking definition of a PR manager, Bree. But tell me, what image were you shooting for when you posed with me in those pictures at the gala? Because we both know you made it appear we were together."

The paparazzi wanted to know if I fired her so we could date. Every single time it came up, it took major self-control to not drag her through the mud for doing what she did.

I throw my hands up when she doesn't answer. Her silence is her answer. "Whether or not you believe me, I thought I was help-ing. I wasn't aware how much you cared for her," she finally admits. She whips around, her heels clicking on the hardwood floors as she walks over to the bar and spins the chair around to sit in it. I stay put, watching her from across the room.

Does she think she's staying?

"Well, I'm glad we cleared that up. You can leave now." I jerk my gaze toward the door.

"Ryker, sit down."

What is up with this woman and her trying to control me? "You seriously didn't just command me to sit down? I am not your goddamn dog." If Bree hadn't been part of my life for the past eight years, I'd pick her ass up and throw her out myself.

She huffs. "Please?"

"I'm fine right here. What exactly do you want, Bree?"

Her spine straightens. "I want you to hire me back." Happy hour. Because she's delusional.

Yep, more beer. Laughing and shaking my head, I walk to the table I placed my beer on and take a long gulp.

"Ryker, the news about Aspen is out."

I pull the bottle away from my lips as my heart slams into my chest. I knew it would happen any day.

"When?"

"There was a press release just over an hour ago."

I fist my hand, the overwhelming desire to protect her growing, despite her not talking to me. I can't imagine meeting my parents for the first time and it being broadcasted for the world to see. The world who will ask so much of her until there's nothing left.

"People haven't connected the two of you. *Yet*. But it won't be long."

"I don't fucking care about me," I growl, pinning my heated stare on her. Are we back to this? "Why do you care? You're not my PR manager anymore." She slides off her seat and steps over to stand in front of me.

"You're right, I'm not. But you still don't have one and right now is the worst time to be without one. I can help."

"How?" I stand taller, pinning her with my stare. "By telling people we had a quick fling, and I had no idea who she was. Is that how you'd spin this?"

"I'd tell people whatever you want me to tell them." She

reaches out and puts her hand on my shoulder. "Ryker, I was a bitch and I'm sorry. But we've been through a lot the last eight years and I've always had your back. You've never questioned what I've done in the past and I let that control get the best of me. But I can help you. Even if she's by your side."

I narrow my eyes at her. Bree always has a game plan. She's meticulous in everything she does and that's why I've always trusted her. *Until now.*

She yanks her hand off me and drops her gaze to the floor for a moment. "I did one thing wrong. One thing, Ryker. And now you don't trust me?"

One thing that was a dick move and might have cost me the woman I love.

"Trust is the most important thing in my world of shady people. Once it's broken, it's hard to fix."

"Okay." She nods and her body deflates. I watch her stomp to the bar to grab her purse. She takes a second to gather her wits before she turns around. "I get it. But you need someone. And fast. I'll text you a few recommendations that would be a good fit."

I run my fingers through my hair, groaning. Reverse psychology at its finest and it's definitely grabbed hold of me. I'm being an asshole. She's right, we have been together long enough that I should see she's trying to make this better and I will need someone to help derail the train wreck coming.

I blow out a breath, hoping I don't regret this. "You win. You can come back." Her shoulders perk up and her smile pulls at the corners of her mouth.

"Are you sure?"

No. "Yes. But no more tricks."

She holds a hand up in the air. "Promise. Now, why in the hell didn't you tell me about Aspen," she barks, getting right to business.

"I was going to. The night of the gala. But then you—"

"Gotcha," she stops me, holding up her hand. "Okay, so this is huge, Ryker. The President's daughter?"

"Tell me something I don't already know."

She steps over to the couch and plops down, crossing her legs. "Have you talked with her since the press release? How is she holding up?"

Following her into the living area, I sit down in the chair and stare up at the ceiling, my hands on my head. "I haven't talked with her in days."

She shifts in her seat and I don't have to look at her face to know her eyes are popping out. "What? So, are you guys not together?"

I tell her everything, which is pretty much nothing since we haven't talked. Replaying our last visit, I still don't know what I did wrong. Other than her seeing the pictures, but that didn't happen until a few days after I left her room.

My gut twists in knots thinking I've lost her. And it's not like I can go see her. They'll lock the place down like Ft. Knox.

Bree listens to me ramble about how screwed up this whole situation is.

She rolls her neck and then checks her calendar. "Okay. You're out of town all next week, so I'll get in touch with Aspen's PR person. Find out what she's saying about you because you'll be a topic of discussion on her end too."

The last place I want to be is flying around the US doing keynote speaking and guest appearances. But I can't back out now. "Make sure all the talk shows I'm doing, Aspen is off-limits."

"Already noted," she says, holding up her phone and shaking it. "I'll update you as soon as I hear something from them. For now, stay on the down-low."

Laughter bubbles up inside me. "You know what happened the last time you told me that."

"You never listen," she says in a teasing tone.

CHAPTER THIRTY-SEVEN

ASPEN

One week of intense crazy.

My world has turned upside down, inside out, and any normalcy I was holding on to is no longer anywhere close to normal. The news broke about me five days ago, and every second since has been stolen from me. I can't catch my breath most days.

I long for the island, the wall of water keeping me hidden. At least my prison there didn't suffocate me. Publishing houses have contacted me to write a book. And movie deals are coming in.

The world has gone crazy.

I'm afraid to leave the ranch. Reporters camp outside the gates. In. Freaking. Tents. David and Beatrice tell me it will eventually die down. The only positive to being held hostage here is I've had some quality time with everyone.

Today, though, I'm stepping in front of all the crazy. They have advised me they'll never go away if I don't give them something. So, reluctantly, I agreed to hold a press conference. In an hour, I'll spill my guts to a world of strangers. My stomach sours and I swallow back the nausea.

I can't get sick. I can't get sick.

Merde! My mouth waters and my body's heat spikes. I dash to the bathroom and empty my stomach. Mila comes running in and holds my hair out of my face. Well, at least I won't be spilling my guts in front of the nation, literally.

"Nothing says sisterly love like holding my hair so I don't get vomit on it," I joke, wiping my mouth with the washcloth she hands me.

She flashes a sympathetic smile as I fall against the cool tiled wall, taking a breath. "This sucks, there's no other way to describe it. I hate this for you. But we will all be there with you, standing behind you if you need us."

"You can finish anytime you wish," Halli says, standing by my side, right inside the gates. "Just give me the look."

"Well…" April, my PR rep, interrupts and Halli sends her a warning glare. "Try to get out everything we went over before you duck out." She seeks Halli's approval, and she does a curt nod in return. "Remember to find the reporters we discussed. We've already approved their questions."

I bite my lip, repeating in my head what I'm supposed to look for.

Lady in a red scarf. Man with a red tie. Woman in a purple dress.

The black solid-metal gates open. I draw a deep breath, taking step after step toward my new life outside these gates. One that I have to expose to the public. I have to let them in the dark space in my head that makes my limbs shake when I enter it. I've never felt so vulnerable or flayed open. This feels like salt being poured on an open wound.

But I can do it. I've come this far.

Beatrice and Mila each slip their hand in both of mine and

squeeze. And the guys stand behind us. A line of security people flank our sides and walk out first.

"Thank you," I whisper to both, keeping my head held high as we walk toward a small podium. I pause when I take in the scene.

Holy smokes.

There are rows of chairs, filled to the max with reporters, but that's not it. Police, with machine guns, stand at attention behind the rows of chairs. Their focus is on the crowd of at least a hundred people, cheering and waving signs behind the roped off area.

Nobody warned me about this. I squint to read some signs. Most say *Welcome Home.* When David goes up to speak, it reminds me that I'm next. My eyes jump from person to person looking for my marks.

Red tie.

Purple dress.

Where is the red scarf? A woman waving her hands up and down catches my attention in the back field, but I quickly return to searching for the damn red scarf. My eyes freeze on a man with black hair in the front of the crowd, standing right by a police officer. His lips tug to a smirk when our eyes meet for a moment. A familiar face, even though the rest of him looks different. I force my eyes to keep moving, not wanting to stay focused on the one man the entire country is searching for.

My dad.

The crowd silences when David steps aside, the only sounds around are flashes and clicks of cameras. I drop my chin, steadying my breaths. Why is he here? Why would he risk his life? *For you.* My inner voice answers. *He's here to make sure you're okay.* I give myself a minute before looking back up. By the time I step up to the podium, he's gone.

But it's okay. His presence gave me a renewed sense of

strength that I can do this. He didn't raise a weak woman and I won't start being one now.

"Hi, everyone. I'm Aspen Foley," I say, leaning toward the mic. My voice travels and it reminds me of when we would use a bullhorn to get the foreigners back to the boat. "You know me as Gabriella Malone. I was kidnapped when I was one and taken to live in Tahiti. The man who kidnapped me was good to me and he raised me like his own daughter."

I blink the tears away and swallow. I was afraid that would be a slap in the face to David, but April and David both agreed if I didn't address it, there would be rumors that horrible things happened to me. As I continue talking, my voice shakes with emotion, but I stay on track so I can get this over with as quick as possible. As I speak my last words, I focus on the crowd further out and smile. "Thank you for your love and support. This is all so overwhelming…" I hold my hand over my heart, the beat slams against my palm. The crowd's cheers fill the clear open air. I turn my gaze to the reporters, "… and please bear with me while I find myself in this unfamiliar world."

As soon as they realize I'm done talking, they throw a melee of questions at me. My eyes can't focus enough on one question to hear what in the world they're asking. I frantically glance over at April. David, who is standing beside her, sends me a warm smile and steps up to my side, wrapping his arm around me.

"Listen guys, you're not helping," he says into the mic. "If you want her to stay up here and answer questions, you need to chill."

This makes the reporters chuckle. They still throw the questions at me, but in a slightly calmer manner. When I see the guy in the red tie, I point at him. He walks up to the front and someone hands him a mic.

"Hi, I'm Fred Garza with the LA Times. My question is, do you wish to be called Aspen or Gabriella?"

My shoulders relax that he's keeping to script. "Aspen."

"Aspen it is. My second question, you never mentioned the name of the man who kidnapped you and raised you."

I swallow. "Rudy Foley."

"But that's not his actual name," he adds. "Is it?"

David must feel my body freeze, so he leans over to the mic. "Fred, you had your two questions." Fred nods, still grinning, like he knows he did something wrong but doesn't care. Although, he retreats to his seat.

But if it wasn't him, it'll be the next question. Before picking the next person, I clear my throat to shut everyone up. "He was only Rudy Foley to me, other than dad. I don't know him as any other man, so I can't answer that question."

The questions come like a brick wall again, except this time, it's slightly less jarring. I find the lady in the purple dress. Her question gets a little deeper. She wants to know how I'm doing with my new family.

"To say I feel like I'm the black sheep, is an understatement," I joke. "I might look like them, but I definitely don't sound like them." The crowd laughs and my humor helps me relax a little. "Truthfully, it's going better than expected." I glance over to Beatrice and the love radiating in her eyes blankets me. She smiles through her tears and I return the sentiment. Every moment I'm with her brings us closer.

After more questions, I'm getting the hang of it. Several questions are the same, just asked differently. Until they ask the question, that has nothing to do with the family or being kidnapped.

"Are you with Ryker Dallas?"

My mouth gapes open for a quick second before I snap it shut, because I have no idea how to answer that. *You seem to know more about us than* I do is at the tip of my tongue. At least, he wouldn't be able to ignore me if they plastered it over every news channel and magazine article. A wicked grin creeps up my face and I lean forward to answer, but April lightly shoves me aside.

"We're done here. Thank you."

I narrow my eyes at her and she does a tiny shake of her head, escorting me behind the metal gates, away from the cheers and hollering.

She leans over and whispers, "It's not the time to call him out, Aspen."

"I thought it was the perfect time."

"Yeah, I could tell." She laughs. "You did great out there. You might be better at this public speaking than you think."

I laugh out loud at the ridiculousness. No way. Not happening.

WHEN A SOFT KNOCK at the door pulls my attention away from my book, I expect to see Halli walk in. Instead, Mila peeks her head inside. "Aspen, are you awake?"

"Yep, just reading. Come on in."

She walks in, shutting the door behind her. I scoot over on the bed, giving her room to sit on the full-size mattress. "You did really great today. We grew up in front of the camera because of Dad, so it's second nature to us. And now I live in front of the camera. So, I know how hard it is." Mila works on a talk show. We watched a rerun yesterday and she's amazing at her job.

"It was crazy, to say the least. People were crawling over each other to ask me a question. And then the crowd. Where'd all those people come from?"

She laughs. "You mean a lot to more than just us. People can be insane. You just watch for the ones that become fanatical. And there will be some."

"I can't wait," I respond, sarcastically.

"Have you thought about where you're going to live?"

Oh, I've thought about it. I pull my bookmark out from the last page of the book and mark my page, and place it on the dresser. "I have, but I've not decided yet."

"Would you..." she hesitates for a beat, playing with the edge of her shirt before her eyes meet mine again. "... want to live with me? In New York City?"

My eyes widen at her question. Our start was slow, but spending the last week together has helped, but this is huge. Is she doing it out of obligation or does she really want me there?

Part of me wants to leap at her offer because what are my other options? Yet, the other part doesn't want to be anywhere near Ryker. Especially if he's with someone else.

"It's okay if you don't want to, Aspen."

"No, it's not that. I'd love to get to know you better and I need a place to live, but..."

"Ryker?"

I sigh, hating that it always comes back to him. "Is it that obvious?"

She bobs her head. "A little."

I've thought about trying to start my life by myself because I have the money, but maybe the best thing to do right now is have someone helping me navigate through this mess.

"Are you asking because Beatrice asked you to? I don't want to incon—"

She puts her hand on my leg. "Neither of those. You're my little sister and I would love to get to know you more, too."

Little sister. Words I never thought I'd hear brings me to tears and I sit forward. "Really?"

"Yes. It'll be great! My bodyguard lives next door. I have enough room for you and Halli, if she doesn't prefer to live with Dean next door. Also, I've lived in the city for ten years and I've never run into Ryker."

I don't know if that's reassuring *or* disappointing. And after what he said, promising things, I deserve some answers.

"Can I ask a favor?" I've thought about this the last couple days and I'm not sure if she'll be on board with it, but if not, I can meet her there.

She lifts a brow. "Sure."

"Can we drive?"

Her eyes widen in surprise. "That's a long drive." *Yes, it is.* Six states. Eighteen hundred miles. "Oh. You're not kidding," she says.

"I was already planning on doing it." At the time I planned it though, I thought it would be Ryker in the car. But it'd be awesome if Mila came with me. "I want to drive farther than eighteen miles and not drive right into the ocean."

"You can drive to the next town for that." She laughs and points out the window, but then her expression softens. "But, I understand, so I'd love to go on a road trip with you. It's been forever since I've not flown."

We stay awake until two in the morning deciding our route and where we'll stay. One of her must-have places to stop, Nashville. But first, we're hitting Mardi Gras.

I go to bed with a smile on my face. This is the first time in two weeks that I feel my future might not be so dismal. Having something to look forward to is cleansing to my soul. And it gives me something other than Ryker's broken promise to dwell on.

CHAPTER THIRTY-EIGHT

RYKER

The news hit fast and hard.

Is Ryker Dallas' football career, dead like his love interest? Or can it be resurrected too?

Son of a bitch. My head drops after reading the headline on page six. Those fuckers have no boundaries. I'm in a contract so I'm not worried about the bullshit he spewed about my career, but the asshole who wrote this article is an insensitive piece of shit. Like Aspen needs more on top of everything else she's going through.

My phone rings in my hand, Bree's name flashing on the front. "Please tell me you have something."

"I talked to the PR person, but they're being tight-lipped on everything. I was told the family is all together, and they're only wish is for privacy. How'd the conference go?"

"It was fine. Typical," I answer to appease her, but business is the last thing I want to discuss right now. "Did you see what's on page six today?"

She groans. "Yes, I'm already working on getting that taken down. Maybe Aspen's PR rep will offer more info when she sees it too. We have to get ahead of the story, but that means we need to talk to find out where you two stand to do that."

It grates on my every last nerve that my love life has turned into a story and updates have to come through our PR people. This is ridiculous. Why hasn't she called me? A couple men in suits walk into the Admiral's Club and nod as they pass me. I force a smile in return but as soon as they pass, I sit forward, leaning on my knees and drop my chin so I don't have to make eye contact with anyone else.

"Listen, you only have three more days on the road. Focus on that and I'll do everything I can to get in touch with Aspen."

They announce the boarding for my flight so I hang up and gather my things. Thank god my gate is right outside the club. Bree might have been able to control interviews by instructing them to not bring up Aspen, but she sure as hell can't stop the random person. And they have been asking, everyone wants information on Aspen.

What they don't know, so do I.

A FUCKING ROAD TRIP?

"Where is she going?"

She was in New Orleans a couple days ago. I had no idea she was driving everywhere. It's a relief knowing she has Secret Service following her.

"I don't know. All I know is she's with Mila Malone. And she got into Nashville today," Bree says.

Watching her press release a few days ago, refueled my desire to be with her. The confident woman I've fallen in love with took hold of that stage and owned it. I've never been so proud of someone in my life. Her tan has faded, showing off her adorable freckles, natural red lips and intoxicating whiskey-colored eyes.

She's addicting, and the world feels it too. They've welcomed her with open arms and everyone wants a piece of her. But I want all of her. Her heart. Her mind. Her body.

I'd settle for her voice right now.

And then the question about me. My heart stopped beating, my eyes glued to the TV, waiting for her answer. It figures her rep cut her off. I should have seen that coming, it's what Bree would have done too. I rewound that moment a million times, trying to read her expression. It looked like she was mad. She definitely saw the picture with me and Bree. If she would just call me, I'd explain.

I glance around the room and feel like I'm trapped in a time warp. Talking to Bree inside the Admiral's Club. Might be a different airport, but it all feels the same.

At least this time, I have information.

And I'm tired of waiting for Aspen to come to me.

"Thanks, Bree. Gotta go," I say, with an idea, walking to the service desk.

"Good morning, Mr. Dallas, how can I help you?"

I flash a smile to the customer service agent. "Do you have any flights to Nashville this morning?"

CHAPTER THIRTY-NINE

ASPEN

"You expect me to get on that thing?" I point to a machine that is supposed to replicate a bull. Or part of one, surrounded by a padded floor to cushion your fall when you're inevitably thrown off.

The crowd chants my name. This is the problem with everyone knowing me. All along our trip, everyone has talked to me like they're my long-lost friends. It's weird.

"C'mon," drunk Mila says, hip bumping me. I glance behind her to Halli and Dean, sitting at a table, keeping their hawk eyes on us. Halli shrugs with a laugh. "It'll be a fun experience."

Mila has been all about new experiences for me, and it's been great, until now. Our trip, so far, has been unforgettable. But Nashville has been my favorite so far. Music and dance is an integral part of my culture. The roots are deep in this town. It might not be my type of music, but it's the drum of the melodies that sing to my soul. Making me want to dance.

"Why? Getting thrown off that thing does not sound fun?" I'm surprised Mila did it. I've had the same amount of drinks she has, and this still doesn't sound like a good idea. Does she know how many people got pictures of her with her feet spread apart in the air while her head was smashed against the padded floor? *It wasn't a pretty sight.*

"If you're looking for something to ride, I'll make it worth your while." A deep rasp whispers into my ear as a hard chest hits my back.

Ryker.

The chanting of my name morphs to girls screaming his name. I slowly rotate my body and gaze up to a wicked, crooked smile. I fight my initial reaction of wanting to jump into his arms.

"I'd rather ride that." I jab my thumb behind me at the machine that might physically hurt me, but at least it won't make me promises it can't keep.

"Oh look, Ryker Dallas is here," Mila slurs, having to tilt her head up at him too. "Wow, you really are pretty."

I drop my head as Ryker laughs. The sound shoots straight to my core, lighting a fire I don't want lit. *Stay strong, Aspen.* I roll my shoulders and attempt to stand taller. "How did you find me?"

"Hmm," he says, glancing around the room where everyone holds out their phones, making his point. "The question is, what are you doing here?"

I throw my hands out. "That's not any of your business. What do you care?"

His smile drops, and he turns his chin like he's searching for his next words. *They better be good.* I watch his Adam's apple jump when he swallows. When his eyes meet mine again, they remind me of the first night we had sex.

Raw and determined.

"I care because I love you." His voice carries above the crowd.

I must be drunker than I realized because I swear he just said he loved me. The crowd roars and I can't do anything but stand stupefied. The words freeze in my brain.

"Whoa," Mila whispers beside me.

"Did he just say…" I whisper back, leaning into her.

"Whiskey," he growls, not amused by my reaction. I extend my neck to hear him better because it's getting hard to hear over the noise, but he wraps his hand behind my waist and slams his warm lips to mine. Mint mixed with heated desire swirls in his kiss, our tongues dance and taste. His other hand spreads across my back and my breasts crush against his chest. He kisses me until I'm dazed, and my lips are swollen.

Biting my lip, he breaks our contact and stares down at me. "Whiskey, can we leave?" His voice cracks with desperation. I nod, still drunk from his kiss. "Where are your handlers?"

I tilt my head toward the table where Halli sits and the intoxicating feeling fades, reminding me I'm not here alone.

"Oh," I quip, searching for Mila. I spot her on the dance floor, a guy twirls her like a pretzel. She laughs, gripping his neck to balance her staggering. "I was about to introduce you two, but I guess that'll have to wait. But I can't leave her," I say, turning my eyes back to Ryker. With understanding, he leads me over to an empty table against the wall of the bar, situating me between his legs when he sits. I peek over my shoulder at Mila again and she catches my eyes, wagging her brows, and pointing at the guy she's dancing with. *She'll hate life tomorrow.* "She won't make it much longer."

"I give her fifteen minutes, and then we're out of here. We need to talk, and not here." His eyes dart behind me at the crowded bar and his hands tighten at my hips. "You look hot in that getup."

"Getup?" I tilt my head, confused.

He chuckles as his fingers graze my cheek, pushing my hair behind my ear. "Outfit."

I add that one to my growing list of American slang. My gaze drops to my boots. "Mila insisted that I needed to dress the part to get the full experience of Nashville. You should have seen me in New Orleans."

We wore purple and gold tutu's. Halli wasn't impressed the one time I flashed my breast to get beads. *I mean, it's a thing.* I had to experience it at least once, right?

Ryker frowns, and he wasn't even there. His jaw tics. "I saw." Well, he didn't see everything. As far as we know, people hadn't recognized us yet when I did it. But there were plenty of crazy pictures with us the next day. Nothing that was too embarrassing.

"Aww, don't be jealous." I lean in and bite his lip. "It's not like you haven't been a busy man." I meant to say it jokingly, but it comes out sarcastic.

I've yet to respond to his proclamation of love because I'm still not sure if he said it from the heart or out of necessity to get my attention.

He definitely got my attention.

He drops his head for a beat. "I haven't been with anyone since I met you, Aspen."

It's crazy how much has changed since the day I walked in on him naked. And it was only three months ago. Yet, it feels like years. I've experienced more in the last two months than I have my entire life.

And I'm just getting started.

But the one thing I want most? He's staring at me right now.

"Whew, that cowboy was hot." Mila comes to my side, wiping off a bead of sweat on her forehead. "I haven't had this much fun in forever." She beams. Mila's admitted to me she's become a recluse because of the media, which is why she's single. She doesn't trust anyone. It makes me sad for her. And worried for me. Is it possible to live a normal life being famous?

"Looked like you were having fun. What's his name?" I ask.

"Brady, and he's a fireman," she coos and holds out her hand, with a written number on it. "Don't let me wash my hand, okay?"

Ryker and I both laugh. "How about we write it down so you don't have to have gross hands." I doubt when she wakes up in the morning, she'll even want to call him. She'll probably wake up with a horrible headache and no recollection of tonight. Just pictures floating around on the web to remind her.

"Ryker, we haven't officially met. I'm Mila Malone, Aspen's sister." She holds out her right hand and spots the writing, so she quickly switches hands.

"Nice to meet you, Aspen's sister." His gaze jumps to mine and my excitement can't be contained. I want to scream, *I have a sister!*

"Where are you two headed next on your road trip?"

Oh, that's right. He doesn't know I'm moving to New York City. "I'm not sure I want to leave Nashville. I love it here. I'm thinking of staying." I lie.

Both their eyes fly open wide and they say at the same time, "You are?"

"I thought you were moving in with me," Mila pouts.

Ryker's eyes jump from Mila to me, raising a curious brow. He must already know where Mila lives. "Are you moving to the city?"

I nod excitedly. "Oh, thank fucking god." He pulls me into his chest, cradling my body. "Whiskey, I would've flown every weekend to Austin if I had to, but this is the best news ever," he says into my hair.

"Okay, you two, let's go. I'm tired and I don't want to stand here feeling awkward anymore while you two make out."

"She said it," Ryker says, guiding me so he can hop out of his chair. "Let's go." Grabbing my hand, he doesn't wait a beat to guide me to the door.

"Wait, beautiful," a guy calls out before we step foot outside. Ryker's hand tightens as I glance over my shoulder. The guy, Brady, jogs over to Mila, but Dean steps in front of her to stop him. Mila punches him in the arm and scoots around him.

I pull in a quick breath and cover my gasp with my hand when the guy pulls her into his chest and lays a hot and heavy kiss on her lips. When he breaks the kiss, her eyes gloss over and her smile is bordering on maniacal.

"Make sure you call me." He winks and walks backward into the bar.

"I will," she purrs, staring dreamily at him.

"Come on, kissing fool," Dean says, leading her out the door.

"Did you get her all tucked in," Ryker asks as I step into his room. A mixture of soap and aftershave fill the chilled room. I pull in a deep inhale, filling my senses with his smell. I've missed it.

"I did."

I spin in place when he shuts the hotel door, dropping my bag and taking two steps to him. His butt hits the door, and he stares down at me.

"What's on your mind, Whiskey?"

I bite my lip, pushing my body against his and run my palms up his bare chest. "I missed you."

His fingers grip my hair, and he tugs. He bites along my jaw, sending goose bumps down my arm. "I missed you, too. But we have to talk first."

Talk about a mood killer.

My bottom lip sticks out. Talking is not what I had in mind. He picks me up and I wrap my legs around his waist and he carries me into the room. My back hits the cool bed, but I lock my feet together so he can't get up. The white down comforter swallows me under the weight of both of us.

"I told you I loved you and not that I expect it in return, I expected a little more of a response from you."

I guess we're diving right into it.

My legs fall to the bed. "It was a little surprising, Ryker. Especially after you didn't text me back or accept any of my phone calls. And then I get to see a picture of you and Bree, looking very comfortable with each other two days after you told me you'd wait for me."

"What the hell are you talking about? I never got a text or phone call from you." His accusing voice stabs the air, piercing any buzz I had left.

Irritation builds in my chest. He can't lie when I have proof. I push him off me so I can grab my bag off the floor and dig for my phone. He watches as I search for my phone. When I have the unanswered texts on the screen, I throw it at him.

"You might think I'm at a disadvantage because I'm not tech savvy with that thing, but I know you can't say I didn't text you when it's right there."

He looks down at the phone, and his brows crease. "I didn't get these," he says, confusion in his voice as he lifts his head. He continues to look through my call log. "Or these phone calls."

I stare at him. What do I say to that? Mila said I was doing it correctly.

"Fuck," he snaps, making me jump and his face pales. He squeezes his neck as he drops his gaze to the floor. "I'm so fucking stupid."

"What? Why?"

He shakes his hand in the air with the phone. "Because I fat fingered my number."

My mind jumps to what those large fingers have done. *Stop, Aspen, this is serious.* I shake the dirty thoughts out of my head. "What does that mean, Ryker?"

He places my phone on the side table and pushes off the bed. Wincing as he steps up to me, he mutters, "It means I entered the wrong phone number."

All this time I thought he didn't want me, it was because I had the wrong number?

"I'm so sorry. This is all my fault." He squeezes the bridge of his nose. "It was a digit off."

His admission is heavy with guilt, and I hate seeing him like this. I like the playful Ryker better.

"It's okay. I'd rather hear I didn't have your correct number than you didn't answer me. But, now that we're getting everything out in the open, tell me about the picture."

He nods, grabbing my hand and walking backward to the bed. We both sit, but it's him keeping hold of me this time. "A picture doesn't tell *the* story. Anyone can take a picture and spin a story to their liking. In my world..." He pauses for a second. "Well... our world, you can't believe anything that's printed. They're all half-truths."

"Tell me, what's true about you and Bree?"

"I asked her to go with me to the gala, because *you* weren't available and she's a friend. Everyone knows she's my PR manager and we've been photographed a million times together. I thought she was safe." He shrugs.

"So, what changed? Because the photo I saw, you looked like more than friends."

He sighs. "She did. She took it upon herself to take the focus off of you and me."

My mouth gapes open. "Why?"

He shakes his head. "It doesn't matter. I fired her."

"Good."

"Buuuut... I hired her again." When I open my mouth to argue, he presses his finger across my lips to stop me. "She's good at her job and she knows she messed up." I roll my eyes. "We hire PR people to help us with our image in the public eye. Sometimes that isn't always what we think our best interest is. But she was wrong here. Did your PR person tell you that Bree called to get information to you from me?"

I do a double-take. A sudden coldness hits my core. I trusted April, and she knew I was upset over Ryker. "No. What the heck?"

"Despite being pissed, I understood. You had a lot on your plate the last couple of weeks. You didn't need relationship stuff to deal with."

"That doesn't mean she gets to make those decisions for me. What if I had written you off and found another guy?"

"After fucking three weeks? Then obviously I wouldn't have meant anything to you." His expression hardens and I regret suggesting it.

I slide my fingers up his arm. "Ryker, you mean everything to me. I couldn't have moved on from you after three weeks. It devastated me that you weren't texting or calling me."

"Sorry." He falls on the bed, brings his hands behind his head and stares up to the ceiling. "I can't believe I didn't double check the number."

I straddle him. "Well, if you hadn't been so stubborn about climbing down the ladder like you were a spy, you might have." He laughs and moves his hands up my thighs. I watch them inch up. "So, is Bree on board with this? Or is that another obstacle?"

He licks his bottom lip and raises a brow. "She found you in Nashville for me."

"Oh. She deserves a bonus." I play with the hem of my shirt, lifting it off my head and throwing it to the ground behind me.

"And a damn good one," he rasps.

CHAPTER FORTY

Why does she spring this shit on me at the last minute?

"Can't you get someone else to do it? One of your other poster boys?" I'm tired and want to see Aspen. Thanks to my overzealous PR rep trying to work me to death, I haven't seen her in three weeks. If anything, it's given her time to spend with her mom and sister.

I'm jonesing hard. I'm ready for her to move in with me. It won't be much of a change since she spends the night at my place when I'm in town.

She lets out a humorless laugh. "No. We need to do everything we can to fix your hairbrained idea to admit to something you didn't do. Maybe next time, you'll keep your mouth shut and let your teammate take the fall."

I sigh, scraping my hand across my chin. Off-season is usually fun. *Not this one.* "Fine." I relent to the public relation event, knowing when Bree sets these things up, I'm not getting out of it. "What time and where?"

"I knew you'd see it my way," she says with a little more excitement than I expected. "Eleven thirty on Friday. I'll send you the appointment."

"This Friday?" I ask, surprised she's only giving me two days' notice. She said it was soon, but I didn't expect this soon.

"Yep."

"Got it," I respond dryly and hang up. At least it's in the city. I'll still be home tomorrow night, balls deep in the woman I can't get out of my head.

"You can't be serious?"

"I'm sorry, Ryker," she says into the phone. *Don't get mad.*

"I just thought since we haven't seen each other in three weeks that you'd want to hang out with me tonight."

What is wrong with me? Why is my voice so whiney?

"I do. And it's totally my mistake. Beatrice and David are in town tonight and I had it in my head you were coming home tomorrow, so I made plans with them."

My eyes jump around the empty living room. The couch cushions sink behind my back as I slouch down further into them. "I'm sorry, Ball Boy," she whispers. "I'll make it up to you tomorrow. And the night after that."

"Oh, Island Girl, this will take at least a week to make up."

She laughs, drowning my irritation. "However long it takes," she replies.

"I guess my hand will do tonight."

"Ryker," she huffs and it's adorable. I'll never get tired of her accent. I'm sure her cheeks are bright pink. "Well, make sure your hand is tight around your cock and you slide your thumb down the vein like you love."

"Fuuuuck, Aspen. I was kidding, but now I'm hard as hell." I reach in my pants to adjust my dick. "You sure you don't want to come show me? Make sure I'm doing it, right?" She hums on the phone, the vibration shooting straight to my dick. Why am I tormenting myself?

"Okay, I'm coming," she says to someone in the room. My dick pulses in anticipation.

Not on you, asshole.

A low growl climbs out from the back of my throat. "When you say that next time, it better be my name you're screaming in front of it."

"I'll make sure the neighbors hear," she teases.

"Whiskey, you're killing me."

"You started it."

I don't want to hang up. Every time we talk, it's the same. Her voice has an anchor on my heart. But as soon as we hang up, the line breaks and leaves me feeling lonely.

The depth of my cravings for her are erratic, and I can't seem to get a hold of them. I always thought Max and Aiden were idiots, how their attraction to their wives were insane when they were dating. I get it now. But why didn't they warn me about this part?

I run my hand over my stubbled jaw. "Well, have fun with Beatrice and David." I can't get mad that she wants to spend time with her parents. It just sucks it was tonight.

As I empty the contents of my pockets on the kitchen table, I draw a deep breath in and freeze. Fuck. I'm imagining her smell now. The sugary scent fills my nostrils. The couple drinks I had must be messing with my senses. Lifting my nose more in the air, I glance around the empty condo thinking maybe Aspen brought me some cookies.

Disappointment erases my buzz. Damn, it's the whole reason I went out for a couple drinks. To drown the disappointment, not make me hallucinate her scent.

Dragging my feet into my dark bedroom, I head straight to the bathroom. Her toothbrush she keeps here sits next to mine. Hopefully soon, I'll have her other things scattered through my place. *Our place.*

With the happier thoughts, I slip into my cold bed. Tomorrow can't come soon enough. When I hit an unexpected lump in the sheets I jump out of the bed, "What the hell?"

Please, God, let that be Aspen.

CHAPTER FORTY-ONE

ASPEN

Despite three cups of coffee, I can't stop the yawn. Maybe slipping into Ryker's bed last night wasn't the best idea. Although, it was the perfect idea at the moment. I needed to see him. I suspect he was feeling the same because when he realized I was in his bed; he played me like a football game. Four quarters of constant playing, orgasmic touchdowns and *lots* of celebrating.

"Stop that," Mila says, pointing at my yawn, walking into the messy back room. Leaning against the metal sink, piled high with dirty cookie sheets and pans, I'm dreading cleaning all these. She purses her lips together. "Why are you so tired?"

"Hello, I woke up at four a.m. to be here." *And went to bed at two-thirty.*

She appraises me a little more. "You were in bed at nine last night."

I bob my head a couple times. "Not quite."

"Did you stay up talking to Ryker on the phone?"

I wrinkle my nose and wince. "Not quite."

She groans, throwing the towel she's holding at my face. "You caved and went over there, didn't you?"

I yawn again and bend over to pick up the towel. My lower regions deliciously ache. "Yes. I had to. You didn't hear the disappointment in his voice yesterday."

"You guys make me sick." She laughs, rolling her eyes. "I don't know why you just don't move in with him."

I perk up. "No. And don't mention that to him." We are in a great place right now in our relationship, I don't need someone to mention moving in or marriage to have him freaking out again. I'm not in a rush.

She shrugs. "Whatever. You're practically living there. You have a key and you spend the night almost every night."

"And we're perfect where we are."

"Mmm-hmm. Well, he won't wait too long to put a ring on that finger. You just watch." I doubt it. But I'm okay with that. I know he loves me. "Mom will be here soon. She texted me when I was on my way here."

Hearing Mila refer to Beatrice as our mom has gotten easier. But it's still awkward calling her mom. *I've tried.* And she's been so understanding. But I love being around her and this project has brought us closer together.

Mila follows me out of the kitchen through the cute black saloon doors. I glance around the space some might regard as too small, but it's perfect for me. And it's mine. A month ago, Mila and I passed by this place, the same one I saw when I was with Addison. It was still available for lease. Using some money my father left me, I decided it was time to take the next step in my new life. I deserve it.

I knot the towel in my flour coated hands. "Do you think everything looks okay?" The nerves I've been trying to bake out of my veins slam back into me as it's the first time I've had a second to think about it.

"Are you kidding? This place is a sugar fantasy. And did you notice the crowd already lining up out there?"

What?

I rush to the front of the store. The fresh nerves freeze to ice when I peek out the door and catch a glimpse of the line down the block, wrapping around to who knows where. The few people up front who notice me wave and say hi.

Oh. My. God.

I jump inside, shutting the door quickly. "Mila, what is happening?" I tug at my side braid, staring at the five cafe tables and wonder how everyone will fit in here. She leans against the counter with a smug grin. "What did you do?"

"I might have mentioned it on the morning show." Well, that explains the crowd. But now, I'm freaking out. I didn't make enough for that crowd. "Annnd, I might have mentioned that Ryker will be here."

"Mila! I didn't make enough. And we open in two hours." My voice rises to an almost panicked state. She peers at the glass cases filled to the max and then looks at me with an incredulous smirk.

"You have plenty. And if you run out, that only makes it more desirable. People will line up tomorrow if they don't get something today."

"No, they'll leave mad."

She shakes her head. "No. Your desserts are insanely delicious. People will be waiting in line every day to buy some. There are famous bakeries only open three hours a day and people will wait hours to get in."

It's my turn to give her an incredulous look. "They're famous. I'm not."

"Yes, you are lil' sister. It might not be for your cookies, yet, but you are famous. People will come here, just to see you."

"That's not what I want, though." I throw the towel on the counter and walk to the window again to check out the line. I don't want people mad at me.

"Aspen, you can't change that. You have to take advantage of it."

My stomach twists imagining the horrible things people will say about me. "That feels like I'm tricking people."

She claps her hands a couple times, pulling my attention to her. "Are your pastries horrible?"

I stand taller in defense. "Absolutely not." I might not be comfortable in my skin because I'm still learning about who I am, but I sure don't question my baking ability.

I sigh, answering my own concerns. And if they come here for me and leave disappointed, I can't help that either.

Beatrice appears from the back room, her eyes gleam with wonderment and her smile as wide as her face. She marvels at the chalkboard on the back wall displaying, in perfect print by Mila, the menu and prices. The mural behind it came out exactly as I imagined with all the flowers from Tahiti painted in pinks and turquoise and it stands out in all the white modern fixtures. The bright colors remind me of the island and where I came from. I've learned my life is more than a lie, it's my story. And the island is an enormous part of that story.

"Aspen, everything is perfect." She pulls me in for a hug. I've grown to love the nurturing touches I never had growing up. Rudy loved me but rarely was affectionate. "You two have worked so hard, I'm so proud of both of you. I even had to come in the rear door. Have you seen that line?" She points outside. We both nod. Mila's is a little more enthusiastic.

Mila glances down at her watch. "Oh! Ryker will be here in thirty minutes. We have to get moving."

My nerves knot in my belly. I hope he likes it, and he's not mad at me for doing this behind his back.

A MILLION WOMEN'S screams flood the bakery when the front door swings open. We all stop and stare as a smiling Bree strolls in, followed by Ryker. She flashes a quick thumbs up close to her chest showing he still has no clue. When Ryker steps inside, he lifts his head from his phone, plastering a fake smile on his face as if he's about to take a picture. But it drops as he takes in the bakery.

A confused expression quickly morphs to excitement when he reads the name of the bakery. Sugared Whiskey. His eyes search until they find mine.

He lifts a brow as he's still registering the surprise. "I like the name." He chuckles under his breath. "You've been busy while I've been gone."

Rounding the sleek white counter, I meet him in the middle of the room. "I figured you would." Even though I was in his bed hours ago, seeing him here makes me nervous. Everything I've ever wanted is right here. I twist my hands against my apron. "I had some help," I reply, looking over at Beatrice and Mila.

"Whiskey, this place is amazing." His fingers untangle my twisted ones, bringing one of my hands to his lips. "I'm so proud of you." His approval snaps me out of my uncertainty and I wrap my arms around his neck in excitement. His tongue darts out to his bottom lip. "I'll need you to model that sexy apron later tonight. And nothing else."

"Um, hello, Ryker," Beatrice teases from behind the cash register. "Mom, right here." She points at herself.

Ryker's cheeks flush as he puts me down. "Right. Sorry, Beatrice."

His embarrassment doesn't stop him from dragging me into his chest, his chin rests on my shoulder. "I hope you made enough for me to taste test." He stares into the square glass case filled with rows of colorful desserts. I still can't believe how beautiful the case turned out. Or the entire store. Even in my wildest dreams, my bakery never looked like this.

I shake my head wildly. "Nooo. I know you and your sugar addiction. There isn't enough here to fulfill it, so don't you dare touch the desserts. I'm already freaking out that I won't have enough for all your girlfriends out there," I tease.

He bites my shoulder and hums. "I bet they'll get me some." I tilt my head and glare up at him.

"All right you two, it's about time to open." Bree and April set up a table in a corner where Ryker and I will sign stuff and take pictures. I still don't know why they wanted me to do it. Nobody will want my autograph. Especially with Ryker sitting next to me.

Dean and Halli stand right inside the doorway. My already small shop seems cramped and we don't even have customers yet. At least, Beatrice's security has positioned themselves around the building and didn't need to be in here.

When sitting, Ryker leans over with his hand on my thigh and says, "You look beautiful." My lips quirk up and I put my cheek against his shoulder. But then he adds, "Like you've been thoroughly fucked recently." I hide my burning cheeks behind his arm.

And then the front door opens.

Ryker laughs at me as I pop up in my seat, smoothing out my apron and hair. I pucker my lips and glare at him for making me flustered. "That's for your comments yesterday." What is he talking about? "The one where you told me to grip it hard, making sure to slide my thumb down the vein."

Oh, that.

"Ryker!" I whisper-yell, turning red again, slapping him on the leg. He grabs my hand and pulls it over his bulge. *Hard bulge.* Thank goodness people can't see under the tablecloth. But as women stare at us with excitement, I'm certain they can imagine what's going on. I can sense the scarlet shade of red on my cheeks.

I snap my hand back, putting both on the table so he can't grab them again, and force a smile at the women. His laughter booms in the confined space. Ryker's having too much fun. It was different teasing him on the phone, but sitting next to him with people staring at us is wrong.

Feeling awkward sitting here, waiting for people to walk over to us and more than likely ignore me while drooling over Ryker, I fidget in my seat and arrange the Sharpies on the table by color.

"You amaze me every day, Aspen." *Aww.* I stop rolling the markers and twist in my seat. Our knees brush. "I can't believe you did this in three weeks."

Truthfully, I can't either. Had Mila and Beatrice not had as many connections as they have, it would have taken months.

"Thank you."

"I wanted to ask you something before you left this morning. But you can imagine my surprise when I woke up to an empty bed."

I wince at the memory of sneaking out. "Sorry."

"I guess I can forgive you since you did all this." He laughs, holding his arms out wide, resting one on the back of my chair. "So, I wanted to ask you—"

"Oh my gawd," a girl squeals, standing in front of our table, fanning her face. I wince at her shrill voice. Wow, that's a high pitch. She bounces on her toes, never taking her gaze off Ryker. I can't decide if I want to tell her to hold on so I can find out what he was about to ask me, or let her do whatever she wants so she can move on quicker.

"Hi there," he rasps, turning on his charismatic charm, ignoring the fact that she interrupted him. "What's your name?"

"I... I'm Sadie," she stammers and nervously bites into a Firi Firi. As if the taste catches her off guard, she stares at the Tahitian donut like it's gold. "That is..." she stops to take another bite and her eyes roll back in her head. "... ecstasy," she hums.

"Yes!" Ryker claps once, catching everyone's attention. "It's amazing, isn't it?"

"It's to die for." She glances to the cases and then the line. "I should've gotten a couple more." Her voice dips with disappointment.

"There'll be more tomorrow," Ryker pipes up.

She zones in on me and I'm afraid she's about to ask me to get her more. Excitement zips through me, I'm not sure I'd be able to tell her no. "What's it called? I'm so going to tell all my friends they have to try this."

She's already typing on her phone when I tell her. When she's done, she asks for a picture. With me. April takes the girl's phone so she can snap the picture of the two of us. I awkwardly place my hand on her shoulder, not sure what I'm supposed to do with my hands. She doesn't notice and moves on to Ryker.

Just in time for the next customer.

It takes three hours to sell out of everything and get through the crowd. My hand cramps from signing my name and my cheeks hurt from smiling so much.

I stand, excited, staring at the empty glass case. "That was amazing!" Mila and Beatrice step over to us and I embrace them both in a group hug. "We did it."

"No, you did it. We only helped. This was your dream, sweetheart," Beatrice says.

Tears fill my eyes and I find her gaze. "Thanks, Mom." Her eyes match mine almost immediately. Her hand soft and warm against my cheek.

She whispers, "Thank you."

The pieces of my life are falling in place. A few months ago, my puzzle was bleak and boring, but now it's full of color and hope. I glance over at Ryker, leaning against the table, looking gorgeous in his dark jeans and white button-down shirt. He looks as sexy as the day I found him naked.

I pull out of the hug and saunter over to him. "I heard you had a question for me."

"I do." The door swings open behind me but I ignore it, focusing on Ryker now. "Move in with me?"

"Sir, everything sold out." I barely register Mila's words because Ryker asked me to move in. This is a monumental step for him.

I bounce in his arms. "Yes!" It's the perfect ending to a perfect day. "You sure you can handle this hot mess?" I tease.

He chuckles. "I think I'm an expert at handling you." A heat wave flushes through my body thinking about last night. Yes, he is.

"Manu."

Ryker's expression hardens as he glares over my shoulder. He drops me and I slowly spin in place at the male voice I could pick up anywhere.

"Dante?"

CHAPTER FORTY-TWO

ASPEN

Ryker's hand tightens around my waist. Dante's eyes drop to where his hand sits before meeting mine again. He looks different. Bigger. More intense.

"Why is he here?" Ryker snaps, his voice deep. I shake my head, surprised as much as he is.

Dean and Halli flank Dante's sides. His brows furrow, looking between the two of them.

"He's fine," I say, quickly, holding my hands up so they don't see him as a threat and guns come out.

"I'm not sure about that," Ryker states, taking two steps to stand in front of me.

"You don't know nothing about me." Dante puffs out his chest, pointing at him. I squeeze Ryker's bicep to stop him from saying more. The tension in the room is palpable and if I don't put a stop to it, Ryker might try to make him leave himself. "Manu, can we please talk?"

I plead with Ryker with my eyes. "It'll be okay." I know Dante and I left on bad terms, but he's been my best friend for years. He won't hurt me. Ryker's jaw tics, but he gives me a sharp nod. I shouldn't have to remind him, there's also at least six Secret Service Agents within reach if he *was* to try something. They've become part of my world.

I walk past Dante out the door, and he follows close behind. The sweet smell is replaced with car exhaust and city noise. "It's good to see you," he says, shoving his hands in his jeans pockets. I've never seen him in a pair of jeans. Or something that wasn't flowers and plaids. It's weird.

"You look different." Between his short spiked haircut and muscles, he didn't used to have, I wonder where he's been and what he's been up to.

He tugs on my straight and styled hair. "I could say the same for you."

I let out a humorless laugh. "I am a different person. Literally."

"I heard."

Who hasn't?

"Where have you been, Dante? When I went back to the island Ari said you had disappeared after the fire. Did you burn my house down?" When he grips the back of his neck and paces, I know the answer. "Why, Dante? I don't understand."

He turns to me but focuses on the people walking across the street rather than me. "Your dad told me to."

I cross my arms in front of me as I do a double-take. "What? Why would you do that? Why would you listen to him?" Dante thought my dad was a loony old man, so why would he commit arson for him?

"Aspen, I've worked for your dad since I was eighteen." My breath catches in my throat and I fight to stay standing as my knees buckle. He reaches for me, but I push him away.

"What?" I whisper and then slap him in the chest as rage replaces the shock. "You were the one thing that was real on the island," I scream. He grips my hand that's slamming into him, his warmth burns me.

"My love for you has never been a lie."

I jerk my hand out of his. "Love? Love doesn't lie, Dante. Don't stand there and tell me you love me. Did you know my actual identity?" Tears burn my cheeks as I stare at him, waiting for an answer.

"No. I swear, Aspen, I didn't."

"What did you do for my dad then?"

He rubs his temples. "Watch over you."

I gasp as unexplained things make sense. My dad *always* found out about everything. Him getting sick at the exact moment I was planning a trip to the US. Or the men I had affairs with. He knew everything because Dante told him.

Rage spirals around my spine, twisting to an unbearable pang. "Is that why you thought I was yours?" His last words on the island flicker through my mind. "You had earned it? Earned me?"

I stumble backward a couple steps when he doesn't answer, regret washes over his face. I turn to walk away, stunned. How did I never see this?

"I never meant to hurt you, Manu."

I whip around. "Don't. Call. Me. That." When the door to the bakery opens, Halli walks out and leans against the wall, watching him like a hawk. Dante watches her with a scrutinizing stare. She'll kick your ass, I silently swear.

"I'll leave. I just needed to tell you everything. You might not believe me, but you were my best friend. And yes, I hoped that you would fall for me as hard as I did you."

My breath shakes at his unforgivable words. There's nothing I can say to make this better. Dante is no longer in my world. He's another man from my past who felt like they owned me. Who planned my life around what fit them best. But that's my old life. The one that is still trapped on the island. That's not me.

I'm finally free.

He looks up at the sign for my bakery. "You got your dream."

Through the window, I see Ryker watching me from inside. Worry etched in his features. I flash him a smile and nod even though he has no idea what I'm nodding about.

"I did."

All of it.

WATCHING Dante walk away that day, it was as if I was putting my past life to rest. It was a part that needed answers, or I would have always wondered. The sadness is still raw when I think about our friendship, so I try not to dwell on it. It's a coping mechanism I've had to use the last few months.

"We ready to open?" Ryker beams, walking out from the kitchen. He's been out of town for a week and returned last night. He demanded to come to work with me today so we could be together. I laugh out loud when I read his apron.

You can have the cupcake, I'll take the cook.

One thing, it's never a dull moment here with him. "Really, Ryker?"

He holds his arms out, amusement filling his face. "Hey! You should be happy I picked this one. The first draft was *You can eat the cookie, I'll eat the cook.*"

I roll my lips to not laugh. He doesn't need more encouragement. "Mr. Dallas, you're so dirty."

A salacious grin grows across his chiseled face. "Whiskey, not yet." He juts his thumb toward the back room. "But I set aside some icing for later. I plan on getting extra dirty." Heat streaks up my body.

"Eww, Ryker!" Josie freezes at the saloon doors. My new baking assistant grimaces. "I put that tube up thinking it was extra. Now, I have this picture in my head what it will be used for later."

"Hey Josie. Just make sure to clean the baking table a little extra in the morning," he teases, making her cheeks flame bright red before she disappears to the back. I whack him in the chest.

"You're going to run off my baking partner. Cut it out. I need her in my life." My voice errs on the side of desperation. I practically baked myself into the ground the last couple months. I had to hire someone. "And need I remind you what it was like when I was doing this all by myself?"

His smile drops.

One thing about being a baker. It's nonstop baking. Especially when I was the only one doing it. Which meant less time for Ryker.

"I'm kidding, Josie," he yells her direction. "We would never do that here." He turns his attention to me and wags his brows, whispering, "We are so doing it here."

Someone knocks on the door. We both turn our attention to the delivery guy holding a small box.

"I'll grab it, you get ready to open this baby up."

When he comes back, he hands me the box. Pulling out a pair of scissors to open it, I notice there's no return address. I pause, debating if I want to open it here. A tingle moves up my spine.

Ryker looks up from the box with a lifted brow. "What's wrong?"

I shake my head and continue opening it, not wanting to admit yet who sent it without confirming. Bubble wrap encases a silver frame. When I unwrap it, my breath hitches.

"What is it?"

"It's my first Franc I earned from my cookie business." I stare at the coin. I remember getting it from the hotel I worked at. They wanted a dozen cookies. I had placed the coin in a red-lined silver jewelry box and set it on my desk to remind me that everyone starts somewhere.

"Do you think Rudy sent it?"

I nod. "He's the only one who knew what this coin meant to me."

"We should tell Halli. I don't like knowing he's able to get to you."

He'll always be able to get to me.

And I'm okay with that.

"Wait, Ryker." I put my hand on Ryker's arm to stop him from grabbing Halli. "This isn't the first time."

He cocks his head to the side, confused. "Whiskey, why didn't you tell me?"

I bite my lip, embarrassed that it has brought me a little peace knowing he's out there watching over me. "Ryker, you see him as a terrible man. He's not. He's my father. One of them. I don't expect you to like him because he's not a part of my life anymore. But I have seen him a couple times and received a couple things." I hold up the frame. He looks at me like he's trying to understand. "I mean, we haven't talked. It's been in passing. From a distance."

I skip an important part though. It might weird him out. But I'm almost certain I figured out how he always knows where to find me. The necklace. The one he gave me when I was a child and told me my mom had left it for me.

We know that was a lie.

But I still wear it because he gave it to me. It was a small piece of him I couldn't part with. Not until after Dante left, did I wonder how he always knew where I was. It wasn't like Dante was still with me to report back to him. I was tempted to ask Max to scan it for me, to verify my assumption. But then people would learn the link he has to me.

Someday.

When I'm ready to let go. But not yet. For now, he makes me

smile when I receive his gifts. He loves me fiercely. I might not be his, but he saved my life.

I grab a thumbtack from the drawer and hang the picture right next to the cash register.

"It's perfect," Ryker says, pulling me into his chest.

CHAPTER FORTY-THREE

"This is the coolest place." Aspen beams. Watching new experiences through her eyes will never get old. She spins on her toes, taking in the surroundings of the small cafe under the Brooklyn Bridge. Her skin-tight purple dress shows off her petite build, but accentuates every delicious curve she has. Even after months here, she still only wears a minimal amount of makeup, showing off her natural beauty.

Twinkling lights hang overhead, the sun setting behind the city's skyline creates a warm glow as a backdrop. The air is finally warm enough for her to enjoy the nights without a sweater. I slip my fingers through hers and guide her into the restaurant. Her gaze jumps around the empty dining room, confused. "Is it closed?"

I direct my gaze toward a single table by the window set for two. The room's light dims and the candles on our table flicker. "That's our table."

She lifts a brow. "How do we have the place to ourselves?"

I lean down and whisper in her ear. "I know people." Her

cheeks redden when her laugh echoes in the empty room. As if on cue, the owner greets us.

"Bonjour, Mr. Dallas. So glad to see you." After a quick handshake, I introduce Aspen. He takes her hand in his and kisses the top of it. "Ms. Foley, it is a pleasure to meet you."

"*Merci de nous avoir invités.*"

Benny's eyes widen, and he flashes a big toothy grin at Aspen's French. He replies, "*N'importe quoi pour ce gars. Il n'a jamais été aussi heureux.*"

I twist my lip, hating I don't understand what they're saying. "Okay, enough of that. I know you're talking about me."

They both laugh and he winks at her. I slide my hand around her narrow waist and pull her into my side. A thought races through my mind about our kids talking about me in French, probably calling me names.

My body stills and Aspen looks up at me. "What's wrong?"

"Absolutely nothing," I say, my lips tug to a smile. The thought of kids has never excited me before right now. "But tell me what you guys said."

"I said '*thank you for having us*' and he replied, '*anything for you. And you've never been so happy.*'" I narrow my eyes, debating if I believe her. She laughs. "I swear that's what we said."

After ordering our drinks, a pianist plays on the tiny stage. Aspen twists in her seat to see him. Her eyes stay glued to him the entire song. She claps when he finishes and he responds with a grin and bow. When he starts another song, she turns back to me.

"He's incredible."

I nod in agreement and push my chair back and stand. "Dance with me?"

Her eyes gleam as she stands and takes my hand. "I'd love to."

Seconds into the song, someone starts to sing along with the piano. Aspen looks over her shoulder. The man sings "You Are The Reason" by Calum Scott. I hold her close to me as the words of the song wrap around us in a tight bond. There's not a slice of air between us.

"I loved that song," she whispers, her eyes glossing over. Me too. That's why I chose it. We continue to sway to the next song. My cheek rests against her forehead.

She pulls back and whiskey-colored eyes connect with mine, the same ones that made me realize there was something missing in my life. Made me realize that my love for football was only skin deep, yet my love for her is so deep inside me that it makes my entire being shift every time I'm with her.

"What's on your mind, Ball Boy?" Her smile lights up the dim room.

"Just thinking how important you are to me." Her expression softens, and she slips her hand behind my head. Nails scrape against my scalp and I hum at the glorious feeling. "I never thought I needed a woman to complete me. I mean, I'm pretty awesome alone." She rolls her eyes and chuckles. "But when I'm with you, you stimulate these feelings I never knew I had, and everything I thought was perfect is lacking. You've filled a void in me I can't hide from. *You are the reason.*"

I drop to one knee and she gasps, holding a shaky hand over her mouth. Reaching into my suit pocket, I pull out a Tiffany Blue Box. "Aspen Foley, will you destroy my bachelor status and be my wife? My forever?"

She stares at the ring in shock.

"Oh, and be my forever sugar dealer?"

She laughs, still in shock. "You don't need a wife for that." I blink several times, waiting. Why isn't she answering? A bead of sweat runs down my back, but I stay on bended knee, staring up at her.

Please catch my last Hail Mary.

What feels like an eternity later, but was actually only a

minute, she nods her head excitedly. "Yes, I will be your forever. If you'll be my forever taste tester."

"This contract is leaning in my favor."

I blow out a ragged sigh of relief and loosen my tie as the heat radiating off me becomes uncomfortable.

She holds her hand out for me to slip the diamond ring on her finger. The caveman instinct in me rages as I mark my woman as mine forever. I stand back up and lift her in my arms, kissing her for a solid two minutes. We will conquer this world together.

I knew she wouldn't want me to ask her to marry her in front of a crowd, but I want to share with everyone that she's mine. And I'm never one to say no to a party. At eight, after we've eaten, all our friends and Aspen's family file into the empty restaurant until we've filled the entire place.

As Aspen is making the rounds showing off her ring, my best buddies surround me. I look around the circle of guys that I've spent the last twelve years with and I get choked up. We've been through a lot since college.

"We didn't think it'd ever happen," Aiden starts.

"This playboy is hanging up his single life," I joke.

Max glances over at Aspen and slaps me on the back. "You found a good one."

"It's more like she found me."

All our women glance at us and we lift our beers to them. Seeing Aspen with all their wives, laughing and enjoying her new friendships, rocks my world. They say everyone has a soul mate. I never believed the bullshit that one person was made for another. Until Aspen. She's my person.

"Thank you guys for being here. It means a lot to me." I glance at Aiden, Max, Jaxon and Ryan. I lift my beer in the air. "To years of friendship and marriage." We all clink bottles.

As if the place wasn't packed enough, the sound of a freight train, or rather my football team finally shows up.

"Sorry Dallas, we got held up at the event." Donnie comes over and we shake hands with a shoulder bump. "So, did Mo tell you no way?"

The sweet sound of laughter comes up from behind me. "No, I did not. Someone has to keep this guy in line." Aspen laughs, snuggling up to my side, adjusting my tie.

"Damn straight, Mo. Welcome to the family." He pulls her in for a teddy bear hug and she loves it.

When he lets her go, she steps to my side. "Hey, can we go talk to my dad?" I've stopped having the knee-jerk reaction that she's talking about Rudy. It's a little confusing that she now refers to both as dad, but I'm learning if we're seeing one, it'll be David.

I slip my hand in hers and we head over to their table. David stands, giving both of us a hug.

"Congratulations you two."

"Dad, I wanted to ask you…" She pauses, her emotions getting ahead of her. She blinks back the tears pooling in her eyes. "Will you walk me down the aisle?"

A throaty rasp escapes his lips. He clears his throat and wraps his arms around Aspen, hiding his face. His emotions vibrate through his body and I even tear up at their special moment.

"Yes. Yes, I will," he murmurs.

They share a long embrace and Beatrice wipes away her tears, sidling up to my side. "Thank you for finding her," she whispers. "Bringing her home to us."

We were two stars from different hemispheres, destined to meet. Her life might have been a wild distortion, but she made mine as clear as the water on the island.

She just didn't know her place in the universe yet.

She found it.

With me.

EPILOGUE
RYKER

Five years later

"Whiskey, I'm home."

I shake the déjà vu from my head, looking around the empty condo. Tanner, the most rambunctious three-year-old ever, comes running out of his room in his typical attire. Undies and a red superhero cape. It doesn't matter that it's ten degrees outside and we're in the middle of one of the worst snowstorms New York City has seen in years. Thank god for the subway or I would have never gotten home from practice.

"Daddy!" I shoot him up in the air, giggles fill the room.

I walk into the kitchen with him on my hip. "Where's your mom?"

"She's having a baby," he deadpans.

I jerk my head back. "What?"

The sound of a moan comes from our bedroom and panic clogs my throat. I lower Tanner to the ground and dart to the bedroom.

"I wouldn't go in there, Daddy." Tanner's eyes are wide with fear. "Mommy doesn't feel good."

"She'll be okay, buddy. Just stay out here."

Swinging the door open, I wasn't ready for what I saw. Aspen on all fours, swaying back and forth on the bed. She moans again as she drops her head between her shoulders. Her hands fist the comforter.

"Whiskey, are you okay?" It's a dumb question because obviously, she's not. But she's only thirty-five weeks. She can't be in labor.

Her head shoots to the side, sending a demonic level stare my way. "My water broke," she sneers, returning to her swaying. "I've tried to call everyone, but my fucking phone won't work." The signals are horrible right now from the storms. "I don't want to have her in the back of an ambulance. And she's coming. Soon."

My eyes widen and I run back and forth like a chicken with its head cut off, not knowing what in the hell I should be doing. "Soon? Like how soon?" My voice raises a few octaves in panic mode.

She roars out a moan and I have the foresight to at least check my watch so I'll be able to time the contractions. "Ryker," she screams, "they're two minutes apart. You don't think I'm already checking?"

Fuck! "What do I do, Aspen?"

"You might have to catch her," she jokes through her pain.

My heart stops beating for a moment. Panic floods through every extremity, making it impossible to move. I break out in a sweat at the image and take a quick step backward. Finally, I reply, "I don't catch, I throw!"

She drops her head in hysterics. Her body convulses. "Don't make me laugh! She might pop out."

"Oh! I have an idea! I'll run down and ask the front desk if any doctor's live here. Just squeeze your legs shut till I get back."

She throws a pillow at me. "You're an idiot. But that's a good idea. Hurry."

I dash out the door and grab Tanner, hoping the neighbors are home so I can hand him off. He's been traumatized enough.

"Is Mommy going to die?" he whispers as we wait for the elevator. I blow out the panic in my body. I can't reassure him that Aspen will be okay if I look like I'm about to explode.

"No, buddy. She's going to be okay. You're going to be a big brother soon."

He looks me dead in the eyes. "She's already trouble."

ASPEN

Two years later

"I CAN'T BELIEVE it's been two years since you were having her in a bathtub in your own home," Mila says, dusting sprinkles over the cupcakes after I finish icing them.

I laugh at the memory like it was yesterday. "Hey, at least there was an obstetrician living in the condo so he didn't have to deliver her. That might have put a damper on our sexy times. It's bad enough he can't look at the bathtub without a shiver running up his back."

"What are sexy times?" Tanner asks, walking into the back room, surprising me. He's not supposed to be here yet. I watch the doorway and sure enough Ryker appears with a smiling crazy girl attached to his hip, with her curly blond locks as wild as she is. Amber-colored eyes light up when she sees the cupcakes.

"For me?" She stretches out her chubby arms.

"Hold on, Lady Bug, I want to hear Mom's answer to Tanner's question."

I twist my lips at the spiteful ass. "No 'old on. My cake." She wiggles to get out of his arms until he puts her down. Fuzzy-lined boots pitter patter across the floor. She runs over and I hand her a cupcake. "Happy Birthday, sweet girl." She takes off running to the front of the bakery.

She has a sweet tooth like her daddy.

Ryker comes over and sticks my icing-covered finger in his mouth, licking it clean. "Is that sexy time?" Tanner asks, watching us with an eagle eye.

I burst out laughing, wiping my finger off on a rag. "It is for your daddy."

He hums in my ear. "Sugared whiskey is definitely sexy time."

Pushing him away, I point to the door. "Go check on Leighton. Who knows what she's doing with that cupcake. I have to finish these before all her friends get here."

THE BIRTHDAY PARTY was an easy distraction, but now my focus is on our trip. Depending on the minute, I'm having a panic attack that we're leaving the kids, or don't care what's happening around me because tomorrow, I'll be on a beach. Not any beach, *my beach*.

For our seven-year anniversary, Ryker surprised me with a trip to Bora Bora. I haven't been back since I found my home in ashes and I'm nervous. It's a different world, like a dream I woke up from years ago. But I've hinted that I'd like to go back someday.

Someday is today. We leave tonight.

"You sure are packing a lot," Ryker says, staring at the largest bag I could find. Then he turns his head to his medium-sized suitcase. "I mean, if I remember correctly, you only wear string bikinis there."

"Well, my swimsuits are a little *more* than string these days." Even though I've worked hard to maintain my weight after two kids, I'm still not the same as I was when I was in my early twenties. And I am perfectly okay with that. I love my new body.

"Who are we kidding, you'll be naked most of the time."

Ryker can't hide his excitement to get me alone. He hasn't stopped talking about all the *sexy time* we'll be getting in. He doesn't know about all the relaxation I plan on doing. Two weeks on a beach, away from kids and work. Now I understand why everyone thought the island was paradise. It is. It was when I was there, I couldn't see past my reality.

"Is that who I think it is?" Mama Doe screeches from the dock before we pull up. I wave at the woman dressed in a bright yellow and red dress, excitedly. Somehow, word got out we were coming. "Come here, girl." Before I can get both feet on the dock, she's pulling me into a tight embrace. She pulls back, her gaze sweeps over me. "You've grown into a beautiful woman."

"It's so good to see you." I wrap my arms around her again. The feeling of home envelops me in her arms. The taste of salt and the sound of the ocean. It brings me back full tilt.

"Where are those babies?" She looks past me to the boat, searching. My brows furrow, surprised she knows I even have kids.

"We kept them at home this time," Ryker answers, helping pull our bags out. He leans over and gives her a hug.

"Don't stare at me like that, girl, I know how to use them internets. I've been following you." She crosses her thick arms in disappointment.

"We'll bring them next time, I promise. We didn't think

Leighton would make the thirteen-hour trip. At least not enjoy-able, that is." Instead, I pull out my phone and show her pictures.

"They are beautiful," she gleams, taking in picture after picture. She can't stay long, so before she leaves, we make plans to meet her for dinner later this week.

Our footsteps are the only sound down the long winding freshly painted walkway. The place feels deserted until we pass a woman rushing by us. I bite back the word *Orana* at the tip of my tongue. *Where the hell did that come from?* I broke that habit years ago. As we continue our stroll, I give Ryker the side-eye.

"Did you get the same hut?"

"Of course. It's where I fell in love with the island girl."

The nickname makes me smile. He hasn't called me that in years. I haven't felt like her in years. The craving to have salty water on my skin faded with my memories. *And my tan.* "Well, you might get lucky again and see her, Ball Boy."

He flashes a wicked grin, the one that will always give me butterflies in my lower belly. "Maybe if I get naked and act like I'm passed out on the bed, she'll show up." He wags his brows and I drop my head. I would say it wasn't one of the brightest moments of my life, but that would be a lie. *It was the best.*

I run a hand up his chest with my back against the door as I swipe the key with my other hand. "That's a fantastic idea." I twist the knob, pushing on the door with my butt.

"That sounds like a horrible idea," a male voice rasps.

I yelp, stumbling back into Ryker's chest, staring at the man in our living room. My lips quirk up and I jump forward into his arms.

"Dad."

His frame is larger than the last time I saw him. I guess when you're not pretending to be sick, you don't have to watch your diet.

"Hi, hun."

I don't have any regrets, I'm welcoming him with open arms. Whether he was right or wrong keeping me, he was a wonderful dad. My real parents' understanding of my feelings helped me get over the anxiety I was having. They might not welcome him to family reunions, but they accept him for what he was to me and not what he is to the world—a monster.

"Rudy," Ryker says, extending a hand. An offering of peace. I know how hard this is for Ryker. My dad is a murderer. A wanted man. And I've never asked Ryker for acceptance.

My dad takes his hand in his. "Thank you for taking care of her."

"Thank you for not killing me," Ryker says, half-jokingly. I slap my hand against my forehead. Is this what their relationship boils down to? Relief?

Rudy's laugh echoes against the wall. "I won't say I didn't think about it."

Ryker's eyes widen at his admission. I jerk my gaze in his direction, surprised too.

"I'm kidding. Geez." He holds his hands up in the air. "I saw how much you loved my daughter. But don't think I'll ever stop watching." His voice is heavy, leaving no question that it's not a joke.

Out of the corner of my eye, I notice Ryker shove his hands in his pockets.

"Where are you hiding out these days?" I scramble to change the subject.

"I'm around." He winks but then wrings his hands together. "Do you think…" He pauses for a beat. "Maybe you guys can go on a sunset sail with me this week sometime?" He gestures to his boat, docked against the deck.

I glance at Ryker before answering. He nods with a subtle smile. I silently promise to do whatever he wants me to do this vacation. "Yes, we'd love to."

"It's a date. I'll let you get back to settling in. It's great to see you, Aspen." My heart squeezes at the emotion in his voice. He mock salutes and turns on his heels, exiting the back door. Before stepping into his boat, he casts a quick glance over his shoulder. "Don't worry, I won't be dropping by out of the blue again."

"Thank god," Ryker mumbles into my shoulder. We watch his boat drift away and as soon as he's out of the shallow water, it disappears around the island. "How the hell does he know everything? Like how we were staying here?"

"He knows people," I tease, making him chuckle. I twist my body, wrapping my arms around his neck. "Thank you. I know how awk—"

He puts his finger against my lips, stopping me. "He's your dad. I get it. Seeing you happy is everything I've ever wanted for you."

"How did I ever find you?"

His tongue wets his bottom lip as he pulls his shirt off in one swoop. "It seems you need a reminder." He walks inside, dropping his shorts and underwear on the way to the bedroom. "Make sure to sing and swing those hips as you're walking in."

While he gets situated on the bed, I strip, shaking my hair out of the bun. When I round the corner, singing off tune, I stop and stare at the gorgeous man. I had no idea eight years ago that he would change my life. That I would *find* my life.

Thank god I took another peek.

"Whiskey, you going to join me?"

This time, I'm not running.

THE END

BLINDING ECHO PREVIEW
PROLOGUE

Love stories typically begin with boy meets girl. *Ours did*. Yet, our story is anything but typical.

I had always thought the heart led us to 'the one.' But, I've learned the heart doesn't have a memory. Its beat is steady until our brain triggers an emotion, making the beat so unmistakable it takes your breath away. It's blinding, life-altering and sometimes earth-shattering. The feeling of true love. We grow up with the grand illusion there is only one person made for us—our soul-mate. But what if your memories are stripped from you? Your soul-mate forgotten. The unmistakable heartbeat gone. The love that completely filled your heart, now an empty space.

That was my heart. Vacant.

He was a stranger, determined to make me fall in love with him. He made it easy. Even though I didn't know him, he felt familiar. The scars that riddled my body, illustrating my past, he made them feel invisible. Made me feel like I deserved to be cherished and loved.

He was also lying.

Doctors told me my memories were locked in my brain. Eighteen years of my life was under lock and key inside my head somewhere. It was Pandora's box.

I wish I had never found the key.

Our love story began with boy meets girl. Now…

I love two men.

He loves two women.

One click to continue reading!
Blinding Echo

ALSO BY TINA SAXON

TWIST OF FATE Trilogy

Aiden and Addison

Fate Hates

Fate Heals

Fate Loves

Twisted Wings

Max and Sydney

Blinding Echo

Kase and Ellie

Wild Distortion

Ryker and Aspen

Engaging Chaos

(Coming soon!)

Brooks and Reece

Join my reader group to get to know me and get early access to what I'm working on! Saxon's Sirens on Facebook

FOLLOW ME!

Facebook

Instagram

Website

ACKNOWLEDGMENTS

THANK YOU for being here with me! Readers, bloggers, and friends will always be the reason I'm here, so from the bottom of my heart, THANK YOU for all your support!! I truly hope you enjoyed Wild Distortion.

I can't forget to thank the people who helped bring my story to life. Hang, you gave me the most gorgeous cover and I still can't stop looking at it!! You hit it out of the park on this one!! Home-fucking-run! Ellie, you and your crew always polish my words and I definitely couldn't do this without you. Tiffany, Lori and Melissa for calming my inner demons doubting myself and helping improve the story! Your input is invaluable to me as is your friendship!

If you want to know what's next... Brooks is coming up. He's a sexy, single dad, marketing executive and when he meets his match will he be able to engage her long enough to catch her? Find out soon! Engaging Chaos is coming later this year.

Made in the USA
Coppell, TX
05 October 2020